MudCat Moon

MudCat Moon

A Jake Eliam ChickenBone Mystery

CLIFF YEARGIN

ISBN-13: 9780692960080
ISBN-10: 0692960082
REV2

Praise for the first two books in the ChickenBone Mystery Series

■   ■   ■

RABBIT SHINE

Expertly captures the soul of Atlanta with all its eccentricities, quirky characters and distinctive sense of humor. With characters as strong and intriguing as the story they move through, it was easy to read cover to cover without coming up for air. I'm looking forward to see what is in store for the next installment in this of uncommonly clever series.

Bob Koenig
Baltimore, Maryland

Great plot line and characters I look forward to following in future installments! I can't wait for the next one!

Janet Pamfilis
Asheville, North Carolina

Loved this book! Can't wait for the next one!

Anne Pitts
Hartwell, Georgia

Rabbit Shine is a fun, breezy yarn utilizing excellent character development and good old-fashioned southern storytelling. Baseball fans will especially enjoy the author's insights into the lead character's association with America's Pastime. Look forward to the next Jake Eliam adventure!

David Steele
Orlando, Florida

Great Story!
LOVED, LOVED, LOVED IT! Move over Sue Grafton. Loved Jake, Chance, Catfish and Toot was My hero.

Linda Fox
Fallston, Maryland

HOOCHY KOOCHY

■　■　■

I love the language, the dialogue thick with southern twang, and the eccentricities of each and every person in this series. Super fun read. love it!

Mommy 28
New Hampshire

Reminded me of James Lee Burke. Yeargin is a true son of the south.

Jeff Duckett
Atlanta, Georgia

This book feels alive. Every page seems to breathe with life and atmosphere. The inside of Jake's head is a wonderful place to be. He's smart but knows he's a working class stiff. He's old fashioned, but adaptable. Most of the time, he is looking for a beer and something to eat and something to listen to. Even if you are not from the deep South, anyone who enjoys the simple life will find a kindred spirit in the characters of this book.

There is an old saying: Step onto the road and there is no telling where you might be swept off to. If there was any book that could teach this saying it is this one. Jake lives his life in a fairly routine manner. He likes routine. When he steps off of that beaten path, the places he goes are as exotic as if he had hopped a plane to another continent.

The BookWorm Speaks
The Cultureworm blog

Cliff Yeargin has become one of my favorite writers. I trust that there will be other volumes in the Chickenbone Mystery Series. Fast read that holds my attention. The Soul of the south!!

Billy T. Lowe
Cherryville, NC

HOOCHY KOOCHY
Silver Medal Finalist in the Mystery/Detective Category

■ ■ ■

Judges Comments

With a taste of noir in the storytelling, Hoochy Koochy *grabbed me from the beginning with voice and action. Dialogue runs this story, which is a special interest of mine when it comes to reading a new author. Clipped one-liners. Snappy retorts. Guys who accept their lots in life and roll with the punches. Loved the fact this protagonist had so many flaws yet I found myself loving him still. It's terse, quick writing, my favorite type of prose. Minimalist with no wasted words. Yet the words used were spot on in keeping me engaged. Loved it. Really did.*

C. Hope Clark
*Author of the Edisto Island
& Carolina Slade Mysteries*

ChickenBone
Train Yard
Atlanta
3 Pigs
BBQ
June Bug
Tires
John Bell Hood Avenue
Jake's Work
Shop
Alex's
Studio
& Western Railroad
Mason Dixon Plumbing Factory
Bug Slinger Road
Follow Jake & The Series
@cliffyeargin.com

1

M Y NAME IS Jake Eliam and I am a creature of habit. I am comfortable in my routine. I do not like change and I am not much interested in the new. When I need something, I resort to the familiar. Then I wait around until my routine circles back around and bites me in the butt.

"You need new tires," June Bug said as he strolled bowlegged around my old truck.

"I need the clutch fixed," I said.

He didn't answer me. He just rubbed his bony fingers across the worn tread. He wiped his hands on his greasy overalls. They were rolled and hiked up a good six inches above a pair of red floppy socks. He stopped and bent down to look at my front left tire.

"Yep, you need new tires," he repeated.

"The clutch is bad."

"Yep, clutch is bad, too," he ran a hand across the white stubs of hair on his head. "But you need new tires."

June Bug was one my routines. There had to be at least five other mechanics within a few miles and maybe a dozen places nearby to get tires without an argument. Yet here I was fighting with a stubborn old man next to his dirty blue concrete building on the south end of John Bell Hood Avenue. I knew why.

A decade ago I was an unemployed minor league baseball coach on my way to Florida to look for a new job. A busted water pump sent me off the interstate at the edge of downtown Atlanta. Through a mist of steam my headlights landed on June Bug as he sat on an upside down grease bucket eating fried chicken. He sold tires but agreed to fix my water pump while I waited. His dinner advice that night sent me north, up the street a mile to the brightly lit *3 Pigs BBQ*. An untimely incident that night involving my 34-inch baseball bat and the left knee of a would-be robber led to a sit down with the owner, a man everybody just called Catfish. In that moment, my life took a sharp left turn and ground to a slow halt in this hidden but oddly likeable place called ChickenBone.

"You a ball man, right?" June Bug stared up at me.

"I am, I suppose."

"How long you been doing that, big man?"

"Most of my adult life, I guess."

"How old you think June Bug is?"

"I have no idea."

"Eight-tee-four," he stretched out the word. "Eighty four years old, last month."

I waited.

"Been doing this since I was fifteen years old."

I waited some more. It wasn't the first time I had heard this from June Bug and sometimes the numbers drifted on him.

"I can't do no math without my pad and pencil, but tell me big man, how many years that add up to?"

"About seventy years or so, I guess," I replied.

"Seveen-ee-tee dang years," he drug it out again.

I didn't say anything.

"And what is painted up there on that wall?" He pointed up to the faded red and white sign above the service door.

"June Bug Tires," I answered him.

"That's right," he said. "And you gonna stand there with your hands in your pocket and tell me you know more about tires than ol' June Bug?"

"I didn't say that," I protested. "I just said I need my clutch fixed first."

"So, you just gonna drive around all willy-nilly on these here bald as a butt tires, till you run yourself into some light pole?"

I sighed. Thought I would try one more time.

"How much if you just fix the clutch today and the tires later?" I asked.

"Done told you, can't do no math without my pad and pencil," he patted his overalls like he was looking for it.

Make a note: Never try and win an argument with a man who has been selling used tires out of the same building for more than seventy years. He is more a creature of routine than you will ever be.

We both just stood there for a minute. I glanced at my watch. He paced around and ran his hand across another one of the tires.

"Nobody listen to June Bug no more," he mumbled under his breath. "Everybody think they know better."

I gave in.

"Okay, stop your grumbling. So how much is it going to cost me to get my clutch fixed and you go ahead and put some used tires on today?" I asked.

He straightened up, shoved his hands in the pockets of his overalls.

"Four tires and fix that clutch," he said as he jingled the coins is his pocket. "Do it all by closing time for two hundred fifty dollars cash and a bottle of good whiskey."

"I thought you just told me you couldn't do math without your pad and pencil?"

"It comes back to me every now and then," June Bug smiled.

2

I HAVE FOUND THAT when I do not drink before I fall asleep that I wake up at the same time every morning. 5:22 AM. Not 5:20, not 5:25, 5:22 on the nose. Not sure what that says about drinking or sleeping but I just find it odd, especially since I spent the majority of my life awake into the wee hours of the morning. Many of those long nights were spent trying to wrap my 6-4 inch frame around a creaky old bus seat as we bounced down some dark highway. Now at 5:22 my eyes pop open, and I can't go back to sleep.

I lay awake on the old sofa where I sleep most nights and watched the clock drift to 5:30. I realized I felt cold. I looked down and on the floor my dog Chance was deep asleep with his hind feet in the air, his mouth open and wrapped warmly in my blanket. The place I lived was one big open room and the factory style windows I had left open now carried a steady cool breeze throughout.

I sat up, pulled on my socks, walked over to the window. Yesterday it was cloudy and humid but a front had rolled through turning the air clean, crisp and pretty dang cold. October in the south. I stood there for a bit and enjoyed the cool air. It was still dark but the train yard was coming to life. My place is over one hundred years old. A two-story brick building in the heart of a working train yard on the top end of ChickenBone. They tell me the name comes from an old poultry processing plant that once flourished here and left the streets covered in chicken bones. Not real sure if that is true, or not, but it does make for a good story, and it tends to keep most other folks away, including condo developers.

I lived above my work place that used to be a machine shop for Carolina & Western Railroad. Upstairs was sparse. A kitchen, a TV, some old wooden bookcases filled with my baseball leftovers, a bed in one corner and two saw-horses that held an old door that served as my desk. I went over and fired up the coffee pot and woke up Chance. He protested with a grunt when I took the blanket.

The World Series was going on and my plan was to get work done early then relax and enjoy Game 3 later tonight. I took my mug of coffee and stepped out onto the metal stairs facing the train tracks. A single engine churned along looking for cars to pull, his lights bounced off the side of my building. The sun was just thinking about rising above the tree line to the east. I was headed downstairs but changed my mind and took the old steps upward and onto the roof. I kept a couple of old metal lawn chairs up there to enjoy the sunsets over the skyline but today it felt so fresh and cool I decided to enjoy the sunrise from up top.

I took a seat in one of the chairs and watched as the light made a slow creep and soon turned the slick buildings on the distant city skyline into a golden glow of steel and glass. Chance joined me and quickly drifted off again with a soft snore. He was a good dog who had found me beside a creek on another forgotten quest in another forgotten town a while back. Loyal, but stubborn. His background and breeding were a mystery. He stirred as something woke him. He lifted his head. He had one ear that stood and one that flopped. A beat later the second ear stood up and he took off to the edge and looked over the roof, his curled tail began to shake. I knew what was going on.

He sped off at full speed and headed down the stairs. He had spotted my neighbor, my only neighbor, Alex. I made it down and crossed over to where Alex parked her jeep. Chance turned in circles and waited for more treats. When it came to Alex I questioned his loyalty, but didn't question why.

Alex Trippi was maybe thirty-five, tall, athletic, dark brown hair always in a ponytail, blessed with classic good looks and a quick wit. She lived, and ran her photography studio, on the third floor of an old plumbing factory across the way from my place and we were the only two residents of the aged buildings owned by Catfish on this side of the tracks. I admired her independent streak, cringed at her choice in boyfriends, butted heads over her failure to listen, grew tired of her chastising me for my lack of tech skills, yet somehow, we had become close friends and so had Chance.

"Give me a hand with this silk," she said as I approached. She pointed toward a long black nylon bag about six feet long. I had no idea what it was but I helped her boost it to the top of the Jeep where she quickly strapped it down.

"Headed out early for a shoot?" I asked.

She gave me a look. "And they call you a detective."

"Just trying to be neighborly," I said.

"You mind getting your dog out of my front seat, neighbor?"

Chance was upright in the front passenger seat, convinced he was going with her. I ignored her and Chance and took another sip of my coffee.

"So, what time does the clown show start?" She asked.

"What?"

She pointed at what I was wearing.

"I don't want to miss the part where the tiny clown car comes out," she said with a straight face.

I had on an old pair of bright red sweatpants with the logo of the Tupelo Red Raiders on one thigh, a bleached out green sweatshirt stained with a faded Rawlings logo and a blue Cubs hat with white sweat circles on the brim.

"I was planning on putting on work overalls in a bit," I said in my defense.

"What? And disappoint the other circus clowns?"

I decided not to engage her. I was guilty. My closet was filled with mostly old clothes left over from my baseball days. I often dressed in the dark.

"So where are you headed?"

"North, two hours in traffic toward the mountains."

I noted that she was dressed nicely in jeans, a fleece and hiking boots.

"Some sort of outdoor shoot, whitewater again?" I asked.

"I wish," she said and continued to pack a multitude of bags in the rear.

She was a really good photographer. Her studio was filled with some impressive work and a lot of outdoor photos, such as kayaking. But we both worked for ourselves and jobs were hard to come by. Some were not of our choice, or to our liking.

"What are you doing today this early?"

"Nobody likes a nosy neighbor," she said.

I waited, handed her the last of the bags and she shut the tailgate. Chance was still sitting in the front seat ready to go.

"It's an agricultural economic shoot," she said finally.

"What the hell is that?" I asked.

She smiled.

"I am driving two hours to shoot pictures of a Black Angus bull named Clyde so his owner can put him in a cow magazine and sell him for stud."

"Like a girlie magazine for lonely farmers?"

"Why are you up so early?" She changed the subject.

"Work to do," I said. "And the weather is nice."

"Football weather," she said.

"Baseball weather," I replied. "Game 3 tonight."

"Did Chance wake you up?"

"No, I just woke up on my own."

"Didn't drink last night, did you?"

"Nobody likes a nosy neighbor," I said as she got in and pushed Chance out.

3

THE OLD GARAGE style door to my workshop rattled and clanged as I pulled it open by the chain and the cool breeze slipped in. Bits of sawdust kicked up in the morning light and bounced around like tiny diamonds. I went from one old machine to the next to click on switches and bring up the steady hum of productivity.

Decades ago, this space was occupied by a group of strong men with calloused hands, that crafted metal parts to keep trains on the tracks. Today it was just me, Chance and a somewhat sideways idea of crafting custom baseball bats to be used by young professional ballplayers. Chance rarely helped with the work and today was no different. He was highly disappointed that Alex did not take him to see Clyde the bull and had sulked his way over to his old chair and curled up for another nap.

I set the guides on the old lathe that turned my bats. The lathe had been around a long time. The old machine, like most of the gear in my shop, was handed down to me by a man who had taken me in as a lost teenager and taught me the craft. It bore a faded metal plate that told me R.D. Fergenson & Sons had manufactured it in Aliquippa, Pennsylvania, in 1928. Every now and then I looked at that plate and wondered if the Fergenson family had any idea something they had made by hand was still hard at work. I also wondered if the sons were still around, and if they still made anything at all by hand.

Today I was working on an order for an Instructional League. I made each bat by hand, one at a time. It was not a good business plan. Catfish reminded me of that daily, and it was the reason I often took work of another variety which did not bring me as much satisfaction but did contribute a good bit more toward the rent. I had no marketing skills, no website, could barely work a computer enough to do my invoices but I did have a guiding principal. I wanted to make a baseball bat good enough to not let down the player in a time of need. I knew what it was like to search for a good bat. The top players got hundreds from the large companies, even a top draft choice could count on Louisville Slugger to send him boxes of good bats. But the rest of us? Sometimes it felt like we had to poke around a scrap pile looking for a piece of wood that would deliver. My business was based on old friends and contacts in the Minor Leagues, and most of those guys had been down the same road I had traveled and they knew my bats were a good bet and made with a dash of hope.

I made my bats with ash. I know maple is the rage right now and I am told that every single day. Maple bats are harder and lighter. But I feel a well-turned bat made with ash has a better sweet spot and is more likely not to shatter into a toothpick when you get busted in on the hands with a nasty slider. It all starts with the wood. A fellow named Buddy Lee Bowman, a third generation lumber man from Sautee Nacoochee, a small town in the hills of North Georgia, supplies my wood. Other than a five year stint in the Marines, he had spent his whole life on the 5000 acre spread that is the family lumber mill and he knew every step of all 5000 acres. He handpicked the lumber for all my billets.

I loaded one of his billets in the lathe and started the process for another bat. It is a slow process. Once you mark the center and round out the billet it takes long strokes with a spindle gouge to shape the wood. Smoothed out with a nose scraper, brushed with light sandpaper and then rubbed down to a soft finish with beeswax. I add clear varnish, then a coat of lacquer by hand. The warmth of your hands turns the lacquer tacky and it seeps slowly into the grain of the wood. When a bat is dry, I head to the stamp press and burn in my logo on the barrel. *CAROLINA & WESTERNNN* is the name I took from the front of this old building. On the end of the barrel I add a model number and underneath in smaller letters, *Made in ChickenBone*. One at a time, maybe twelve hours per bat. Did I mention that it was not a very efficient business plan?

On the wall near the garage door I have an old black phone mounted with a bare light bulb that flashes when it rings due to the noise. If you aren't looking you can miss it. I glanced up and saw the bulb flashing but had no idea when it had started. I wiped the lacquer on my overalls and picked up the phone.

"Goodness gravy and biscuits. Dang if you don't take your own sweet time picking up the phone, son."

It was Catfish.

"Some of us don't sit around on our butt all day waiting for the phone to ring," I answered.

"Some of us know how to make a good bit of money sitting around on our butt all day talking on the phone," Catfish shot back.

"Talking on the phone is eating into my profits," I said. "What's up?"

"I need to talk to you about the big game," he said.

"Well, I plan to finish up here today and watch it tonight."

"Tonight?"

"Game 3 of the World Series."

"That ain't the big game."

"It's not?"

"No it ain't," he said. "Georgia-Alabama. Saturday over in Athens. Heard 'bout that one?"

"Think I saw a little something about it in the paper."

"Bet my big sweet potato butt. Biggest in years and a damn bit bigger than your big game."

"So why do you need to talk to me about this big game?" I asked.

"Because it would behoove you to," he said.

"Behoove me? That's a pretty big word for you to be using this early in the day."

"Dressing up my vocabulary for television."

"What?"

"Never mind, I'll explain later. What you need to know is that I once again have come up with gainful employment for you."

"Gainful employment? For me? At a football game?"

"You do remember the type of gainful employment that actually makes a profit?"

"Is this the same type of gainful employment you arranged last time that ended up with me getting shot at? Several times I might add."

"How does playing bodyguard to a beautiful young lady who wears really short skirts sound?"

"Sounds better than getting shot at," I said.

"Then be over here at ten tomorrow morning and bring Alex with you."

"Why Alex?"

"Because I have also come up with cash business for her at the game, as well," he said proudly.

"Gainful employment for the both of us?"

"It would behoove me to have my tenants be able to actually pay their rent," using the word again just to irritate me or impress me. Maybe both.

"Have you seen her?" He asked. "Been trying to call her."

"She is spending the day with Clyde," I told him.

"Clyde? Another boyfriend?"

"Something like that."

"Tell her to call me if you see her," he said.

"When you talk to her, make sure you ask her about Clyde."

"Why would I want to do that?"

"It would behoove you to do so," I said and hung up.

4

MY VERSION OF the big game got underway a little before nine, twilight out in San Francisco. The aerial shots of the stadium were amazing. Somebody had somehow figured out how to take a tiny sliver of land that jutted out into the bay and plop down a baseball stadium. Water was all around, boats drifted near the outfield and if you had a seat in the upper deck on the right field side you could watch the sunset over the Bay Bridge. Not to mention, you could watch baseball and a really good team.

The San Francisco Giants had run away with the National League this year and were heavy favorites against the Detroit Tigers. The Tigers had stumbled in September, lost a four-game lead and backed into the playoffs.

Detroit was already short on outfielders and in the first round they lost their leading hitter when Johnny Burkes went down with a knee injury. They won the divisional round without him but his replacement hit .129 and struck out three times with runners in scoring position.

Without a lot of options, they added a 27-year-old rookie who had never seen the Majors and hoped for the best. They got better than best. They got Curly Cossaboom. His real name. He had played for four different organizations, been hurt a few times, bounced between AA and AAA but never had a shot on a big club and now he was asked to play left field and hit against the best pitchers in baseball during the playoffs. He should have melted like ice cream on a hot August night, but he did not. He hit everything they threw at him. He hit the fastball. He adjusted to the curve and the slider. He played flawless defense, stole a few bases and did it all with a huge grin on his face.

I was watching the night he made his debut. Batting left-handed, he went down and scooped a 98 mile per hour fastball off the plate and looped it into right field for his first big league hit. Baseball players are taught to remain cool and stuff emotion in their back pocket with the batting gloves. Curly hadn't gotten that memo. He bounced up and down at first base like a little kid, the smile on his face spread from corner to corner. The pitcher glared at him for nearly thirty seconds and took another ball. The first base coach had to tap him hard on his helmet to get him back in the game.

The series was tied at one game each. The Tigers won the opener in Detroit. Curly hit one out against the Giant's ace, the likely Cy Young winner. Then San Francisco evened it up before heading home. After a long bit of pre-game hoopla, the game moved along at a steady clip. It was the sort of game the TV Networks don't care for and for that matter neither do most of the fans. No big pile of long home runs, no long streaks of guys flailing at some unhittable fast ball, no fights or umpire dust ups and no time to do the wave. It was just good fundamental baseball. Sharp, well called pitches. Solid, calculated base running. Good defense that sparkled but wouldn't make the highlights and a flurry of back and forth signs from the dugout. In a world filled with text, tweets and instant whatever, it is a joy for me to watch grown men yank on their ear, touch their nose and wipe their hand across a jersey to send signals that control a baseball game and most fans had no idea it was going on.

It was 2-2 in the sixth inning and San Francisco had the go ahead run at 2nd base when the camera landed on a father and son in the stands. The kid was maybe ten and wore a baseball cap. Both the kid and his dad were face down in their cell phones. Good seats at the World Series and still not paying attention. I yelled at the TV so loud it woke up Chance.

Baseball is losing kids in droves. You just don't see kids playing pick-up baseball these days. Dads who only care about winning and turning their kid into the next Bryce Harper coach little League teams today. At eight years of age you should not be yelled at for missing a ground ball. You should not care one bit about a trophy.

The fat kid shouldn't be put at first, the skinny fast kid at shortstop and the big kid at catcher. At that age you should rotate to a new position every inning. First base, then second base and on to all nine positions. How are you going to learn which one you like or if you are good at a certain position if some lawyer dad dressed in full uniform decides you should pitch just because you look like a pitcher.

Why should a kid get rockets hit off an aluminum bat at him on a bad bumpy infield? He is going to get one that bounces off his lip and then quit baseball. Why not roll it to him? Why not show him how to get down to catch it or teach him a simple cross step to catch it backhanded. You do that first and you can cut back on the fear.

Baseball is a tough game and fear is a big part of it. It does hurt to get hit by the ball, no matter what the dad tells his kid. When young kids do watch the big league players it is hard for them to see the fear but believe me, fear is a huge part of the game at the Major League level. Fear is present in the field, on the mound and most of all at the plate. And tonight's game was a good example because of the pitcher on the mound for the Tigers.

Mac Snyder was a tall left handed pitcher, over six foot six, with long flowing blonde hair and a devastating 12-6 curveball that exploded from behind unseen, with his nearly full body turn. For the left handed hitter, the pitch could look like it was coming right at your head before it took a sharp break over the plate. They liked to call a pitch like that a *Yellow Hammer.*

The game was still tied at 2 in the bottom of the 7th and the Giants had Snyder on the ropes. His pitch count was up and runners were at second and third with only one out. The hitter was a veteran. Bobby Kisco had played in three World Series, won one of them and was hitting around .280 this season with maybe 15 home runs. He was a good hitter with a slow methodical pace at the plate. He fought off nine pitches from Snyder, working the count full. The crowd rose and Snyder unleashed the hammer. It was a good one, came in high toward the head and broke very late. Kisco flinched. His knees bounced. It was called strike three and the crowd groaned.

I watched as the camera followed Kisco back to the dugout. He talked to himself, shook his head and tapped his helmet with the butt of his bat. Striking out in that spot was tough, but it happens. That was not what he was muttering about. He was upset with himself for giving in to the fear. He knew the curveball might be coming. He knew how big a break it could take and he knew how to time it but he could not overcome the fear. He flinched, and that will make you mutter to yourself late into the night.

The next hitter didn't even take a chance on seeing that pitch. He swung at the first fastball and blooped a ball down the left field line. Curly Coosaboom got a great jump and ran under it easily and the Tigers got out of the jam. Fear had left the game tied.

In the top of the ninth Detroit took the lead with a single, a nice bunt by Coosaboom, a passed ball and a sacrifice fly to make it 3-2 and then closed it out 1-2-3 in the bottom half to take a two to one lead in the series. The large crowd left disappointed and I am sure somewhere later that night Bobby Kisco would spend a long sleepless night thinking about that last pitch. Awake all night, thinking, howling at the moon, muttering in the dark about why he flinched and how fear had snuck up again and beaten him.

5

I DID NOT WAKE up at 5:22 today. Four beers during a game will do that. I woke up once and thought I heard rain but thought it was a dream. It wasn't. When I finally came around it was after nine in the morning and it was indeed raining, hard. Yesterday cool and clear, today low fog and rain. I had to meet Catfish in less than an hour so I pulled myself up and fired up the coffee pot. I woke up Chance and let him out. He was back in less than two minutes, soaking wet and I'm not sure about this, but I think he growled at me as he shook off the rain and headed back to the couch. He did not like rain. I didn't like rain much myself. Baseball is the only game that is played without a clock. It can be played in heat, in cold, in wind and a game can go on endlessly in theory, 300 innings if needed. The one and only thing that can shut down a game is rain, and I never enjoyed those long tedious rain delays. Especially, when you knew there was a bus outside gassed up for a long, overnight drive to Oklahoma.

I don't own a raincoat. I just have an old nylon pullover with a hood from my coaching days. It would have to do since I was running late. I headed outside into a steady downpour. The fog hung low over the train yard. You couldn't see the trains, but you could hear them as they eased through the soup with the mournful blast of a horn. I noticed that Alex was still at home so at least I was going to get there before her. I crawled into my old truck and hit the key. It growled, turned over once, then twice, then it just clicked. Nothing. I tried again. That awful sound when the key clicks and stutters but nothing happens.

I banged my fist against the seat and stepped out into the rain. I grabbed some pliers, a screwdriver and an old wooden yardstick from behind the seat and pried open the hood. I had to use the yardstick to prop the hood open, the springs long since broken. I poked at the battery. I had no idea what I was doing so I just kept banging on things. My truck is old. A Ford born in Detroit the same year a man of the same name was in the White House and Al Kaline was hanging on in Detroit to get his 3000th hit. I plunked a couple of other things with the screwdriver. Nothing.

There was a sudden and loud blast from the horn. It scared the hell out of me. I jerked upward, hit my head on the hood, it lifted up and back down, and snapped the yardstick into two pieces and the hood slammed shut. I tried to grab it on the way down and it took a slice out of my thumb. I jumped backward out of the way and looked around, expecting trouble. Instead I found laughter. Alex.

"Sorry," she said as she laughed out loud. "I had no idea the whole thing would fall."

"What the hell was that all about?" I shook my hand, blood pouring from my thumb.

"Seemed like a good idea at the time."

"Really?"

"I'm sorry, are you okay?"

"No, I'm not okay, I'm bleeding."

"Well that's what you get."

"Get for what, trying to fix my truck?"

"For telling Catfish to ask me about Clyde," she said. Her smile turned to a glare.

"Oh, he asked you about Clyde, did he?"

"He did."

"And what did you tell him?"

"I told him Clyde was a bull."

"And what did he say to that?"

"Nothing. He laughed for nearly a full minute then hung up on me."

"Yeah, that sounds about right."

"Then why did you tell him to do that?"

"Seemed like a good idea at the time," I said.

She was dressed in nice rain gear. A waterproof parka, rain pants and duck boots. She bent over and picked up the pieces of the broken yardstick and held them together. She read out loud what was written on the yardstick.

"Get a measured deal on a new Pontiac from Dixon Motors."

She gave me a look. It was not a good look.

"What?"

"They don't even make Pontiacs now."

"They used to make a pretty good yardstick up until about a minute ago," I said.

She banged the pieces on the hood.

"So, what's up with your truck?"

"The battery has gone bad, I guess."

"Sounded more like the solenoid," she said. "Open up the hood and hold it up for me."

"Really? You're serious?"

She gave the same look again. I opened the hood with the hand that wasn't bleeding. She flipped her pony-tail back and stuck her nose deep into the engine. I wasn't sure if she was messing with me or not.

"You do know what you are doing?" I asked.

"I do."

I didn't say anything. Blood dripped from my thumb. She poked around some more.

"Looks like maybe corrosion," she said. "Can't tell if it is around the battery cables, the starter or maybe the solenoid. When it stops raining I can get a scrub brush, some baking soda and clean them all, just need to be careful not to crack the plastic casing on the solenoid. We can jump it afterward and test it."

My thumb throbbed and I rubbed some blood off on my pants. She was full of surprises.

"You know cars?"

"My dad taught me."

"You never told me this."

"You never asked."

I shrugged.

"You told me your dad was an Army man, not a mechanic."

"Spent his career in the Army but he also worked on all his own cars."

"What did he do in the Army?"

"He was with the Green Berets," she answered.

"Well, that explains a lot," I said.

She stood up and shut the hood.

"And what do you mean by that?" She asked.

I didn't answer. I just stood there in the rain and stared at my bloody thumb.

6

As WE PULLED into the parking lot the rain picked up. The fog blended with the smoke from the barbecue pit and hung low over the neon *3 Pigs BBQ* sign. Catfish didn't open until 11:00am but he left the big neon lit up twenty-four hours a day. It had become a bit of an icon in a city that didn't have many. There was a big chicken north of town, The Varsity Drive-In, the neon art deco Majestic Diner, and the legendary Clermont Lounge strip joint but that was about it. So, tourists would sometimes wander into the edge of ChickenBone to take photos of the red, green and blue smiling neon pigs dancing with fingers pointed upward. When he pulled that broken sign out of a junkyard in south Georgia years ago I don't think he had any idea it would become such a tourist attraction.

This morning you could barely see the pigs through the fog. They created a mist filled blur of color that softly blinked in the morning rain. Since the pigs stayed up all night, a large green neon OPEN sign had been placed in the front window. It was turned off. We ran through the rain and tapped on the front door and waited. A minute later Slick made his way toward the front. Slick was the manager, head cook, bouncer and just about any other title you wanted to add. He had been with Catfish since the start and ran it with a no knuckleheads policy. He had sixty years plus in his rearview mirror and was just a few inches above five feet tall yet I had seen him toss a much bigger man out on his rear without breaking a sweat.

"Round the back," he shouted at us.

"What?" I shouted back through the glass and rain.

"You two drowned rats ain't coming in here and mucking up my floor I just mopped," he said. "Get your rear end around to the back door."

I knocked on the door again. He walked away shaking his head and muttering. I couldn't hear him but I could imagine what he was saying. We looked at each other and headed around to the rear.

A rusted metal shed covered the outdoor cooking space, and ran from a steel double back door all the way to a metal fence that backed up against the train yard. Four burnt brick barbecue pits topped with heavy metal lids sat in a long row. An open fire fed by solid hickory wood crackled beneath each one and the smoke spilled out of the lids and drifted up and over the metal roof. The man who worked out back every day with Slick was a fellow named Marvin. I only knew that because I had heard Slick call him that. Marvin never said a word, just showed up in the middle of the night and spent his time feeding the fire and pulling the meat off the racks. He glanced up at the two of us as we came under the shed but didn't speak, and didn't stop his work.

Slick met us at the back door with two large dishrags and a glare.

"Clean up good before you come through this here kitchen," he said.

He looked down and spotted the blood-soaked rag around my thumb. He mumbled under his breath and turned away. Alex shook off her high-quality rain gear and duck boots and went in totally dry. Slick came back and handed me a first aid kit as I wiped more blood on my pants.

"You bleed on my floor, big man, I'll toss your butt out of here before you can say jump."

I removed my soaked pullover, dumped water out of my shoes and went to work on trying to bandage up my thumb. I did a terrible job and it looked a lot like a white popsicle. I held my hand up to show Marvin. He paused for maybe two seconds, gave me a quick stare, chucked another piece of wood on the fire and ignored me.

Make a note: Never bother a man when he is deep in concentration with a slab of pork.

I slipped past Slick in the kitchen and went behind the front counter to find some coffee. Polly, one of the long-time employees, was behind the counter putting the finishing touch on another plate of her homemade biscuits.

"Hey sugar," she said and handed me a small towel. "Your hair is still soaked. Don't let Slick see you like that."

I took the towel and ran it through my hair as she handed me a hot mug of coffee. I took it with my good hand and took a sip. She spotted the wad of bandages on my thumb.

"You hurt yourself again with something silly Catfish got you doing?"

"No," I answered. "I did this to myself."

"Lord have mercy, you a mess." She made a clucking noise and went back to her biscuits.

I took my coffee and headed over to the back booth where Catfish and Alex sat. They were both laughing but stopped when I got near.

"Hear you had trouble with your truck," Catfish said.

"No, I had trouble with my neighbor," I said and held up my thumb.

"Don't worry 'bout it," he said. "I'm sure I can round you up a new yardstick somewhere."

Catfish was working his way through a huge slice of apple pie. You don't get to be his size eating kale for breakfast. He wore the same thing nearly everyday since I had met him. A blue denim shirt and khaki pants. His large hands smothered the fork as it poked at the pie.

"I'm beginning to rethink my job offer for you two," he said between bites.

"Why?" Alex asked.

"Well, Gomer here can't close the hood on his truck without cutting his hand off and now you out taking pictures of cows. That don't breed a lot of confidence for prospective clients."

"Clyde is a bull, not a cow," Alex said.

"Fine by me," I said. "I wanted to watch baseball this weekend anyhow."

"Not me," Alex protested. "I don't want to keep doing cow shoots."

"Bulls," I corrected.

"Go ahead be a smartass," she said. "I don't know about you but I need the work and from the looks of your truck, so do you."

Catfish finished off his pie and pointed his fork at me as he spoke.

"So, Jake, what do you think?"

I looked at my thumb. "I think I may need stitches."

7

I<small>N THE SPRING</small> of 1973, so goes the story as it was told to me, a legendary coach with a country drawl offered a big pimpled-faced kid from Pearl Falls, Georgia a full scholarship to play football at the University of Georgia. Bobby Wilson told everyone who would listen to just call him *Catfish*. Nobody listened.

When he arrived on campus Bobby Wilson was told about two simple rules. If you were not a starter you do not talk and you do not get a nickname. So, the big kid kept his mouth shut but kept on knocking people on their butts in practice.

In the ninth game of his sophomore year Bobby Wilson was still on the bench and still not allowed to talk. His uniform was as clean at the end of the game as it was at the start. The Bulldogs were not having a great season and the opponent that day was none other than Bear Bryant and the fourth ranked Alabama Crimson Tide. Georgia held a two point lead late in the fourth quarter, on the verge of a huge upset, when the starting left tackle went down with a twisted ankle. Bobby Wilson heard the line coach call his name.

Three plays into his college career the defensive end slipped by Wilson and forced a duck of a throw from the quarterback that fluttered toward the ten-yard line. Alabama safety Dickie Blake, a member of the Playboy Magazine All American Team, snatched it out of the air with one hand and headed up the sideline with nothing but green grass in front of him. But near midfield, right in front of the Georgia bench, he was met head on by all 260 pounds of Bobby Wilson at full speed and screaming at the top of his lungs. The hit sounded like a gunshot and echoed off the metal seats of Sanford Stadium. The ball flew forward and Blake flew backward, end over end. He stopped only when he tumbled into the rear bench. A running back recovered the ball for Georgia but Bobby Wilson kept after Blake and grabbed him by his facemask.

"You ain't at no damn Playboy mansion now pretty boy!" He yelled into his face.

The refs yanked him off as Blake rolled over and threw up.

"Drag his pretty ass back to 'Bama," Wilson continued to taunt him.

His teammates pounded his helmet so hard it rattled his teeth. The offensive line coach jumped on his back and barked in his ear. The fumble gave the ball back to Georgia and they ran out the clock to finish off the upset of Alabama and secure a bowl trip later that year.

The next Monday at practice everybody began to call Bobby Wilson *Catfish* and he was finally allowed to talk. He hasn't stopped since.

"Ala-damn-bama," Catfish drew out the words in disgust and leaned back in his old wooden chair. It groaned from his weight. We had moved from the booth back to his cluttered office as the lunch crowd strolled in. He was wound up about the game this weekend.

"I hate them. I really truly do hate the bastards."

"Why?" I asked just to egg him on.

"They are a bunch of loud mouth, arrogant, cocky..."

"Winners," I injected.

"That's why they are so damn cocky," he spat it out. "And why I hate the..." He glanced at Alex and didn't finish his sentence. Alex was standing up and looking through some of the old pictures on the wall. It was the first time she had been in the tiny back office.

"Is this you?" She asked and pointed at a photograph of two bigger players with a smaller player up on their shoulders.

"Yeah, on the right, number 77," he answered. "That was my senior year when we beat Georgia Tech on a field goal as time ran out."

"Looks like a good time," Alex said.

"Was, but I would give up every time we beat Tech, plus my two big toes and maybe some other body part if we could beat Alabama this weekend."

"It's just a game," she said.

I cringed. Catfish leaned forward and plopped his huge hands on the desk with a thud. His face turned a bit red and the veins in the rolls of fat around his neck bulged out a little.

"College football is not just a game down here."

"It's not just a game?" Alex asked. "Then what is it?"

"Hell, no," Catfish got a bit louder. "In the south, college football is more like a religion."

Alex was not one to back down in an argument and this was quickly turning into one.

"A religion?" She turned toward him. "Really? God has time to care about a football game?"

"God cares very deeply about Georgia-Alabama," Catfish stated firmly.

"And just how does God decide which team to pull for?" She asked with a grin.

"I do believe he weighs the power of prayer of each team," Catfish came back.

I joined in. "I have always found that God seems to answer the prayers of the team that has the better players."

Catfish shot me a look.

"So, do people really get worked up about college football around here that it is bigger than religion?" Alex asked.

"Think 'bout it," Catfish said and relaxed a bit. "Every weekend the stadiums are packed down here, right. Damn near hundred thousand at each one. Add 'em all up and that's more than a half million or more at the games, tons more watching on TV. Come Sunday morning, if you could get even a smidgen of them to show up at a church, you would end up turning out enough preachers that you could stack them end on end like cord wood from here to Texas."

"So, what you end up with is a lot more football players than preachers," I noted.

"We pay them a lot better," Catfish smiled.

"Do people really care that much if they win or lose?" Alex asked.

Catfish looked at me and then pointed toward Alex. I shrugged. He shook his head.

"When you lose the sky turns dull, even on a sunny day," Catfish said. "The color is just sucked right out of everything. Red bricks turn brown, green grass looks dead, you got no appetite and your head hurts."

"Could be the liquor," I added.

"Could be, but then how do explain how all that changes when you win?"

"What changes?" Alex asked.

"When you win everything changes," Catfish leaned back again and wrapped his hands around the back of his head. "When you win, fat guys get skinny, bald guys grow hair, short men get tall, ugly girls become pretty, the whiskey goes down slow and smooth and there ain't no hangover."

8

"**S**o, THREE HUNDRED dollars a day for two days?" Alex said to confirm. "And all I got to do is follow this lady around and take pictures of her?"

"That's right," Catfish said. "And maybe a few posed shots which shouldn't be too hard, since she used to be a model."

"What did she model?" Alex asked.

"Underwear."

"I assume she wears a bit more now?"

"Not much more," Catfish smiled.

Alex had sat down now in a hard chair across from the desk. She had both of her legs curled up under in a yoga position. If I tried that they would have to make a call to the paramedics. I propped my shoeless feet and wet socks up on a Coke crate.

"So, how did you get involved with these folks?" I asked.

"Because I am a fully invested member of the Athletic Association Alumni Advisory Council," Catfish leaned back and made a grand gesture with his hands.

"What kind of advising do you do?" I asked.

"We do exactly enough advising to keep getting four season tickets to every home game and a free RV on site to tailgate."

"Sounds a little bit like being in Congress."

"Sounds like my advising got jobs for you two."

Catfish got up, grabbed the coffee pot and poured himself another cup. He held it up to offer us more and we both declined.

"The group is just a bunch of ex-players. Most of the time we just talk about projects, maybe coaches, but this new sports network wanted to meet with us. Said they wanted to get a flavor of UGA and some stuff for background for a pre-game show they now do live on campus each week."

"Is this like ESPN?" Alex asked.

"They can only wish," Catfish said and sat back down. "BTSN is the name. Stands for Big Time Sports Network and they ain't big time."

"I thought you told me SEC football was big time, especially on TV," I said.

"It is, but BTSN ain't."

"So how did they get involved with televising the games?"

"Billy Ray Kincaid."

"Who is that?"

"Billy Ray Kincaid is an arrogant rich guy with a big mouth and bigger bank account. Got this motto he likes to spout...*If you ready to play...Billy Ray is ready to pay.*"

"Good grief, that's stupid," Alex said. "What does he do to make all this money?"

"He is officially known as a professional turnaround specialist."

"And that means what?" I asked.

"He fires people. Lays off people. Lots of them," Catfish answered.

"How?" Alex asked.

"Works mostly in the south. Buys up small plants and factories that need capital. Then slices and dices the place with widespread cost cuts, layoffs, strips it down to the bare bones and then sells off the scraps for profit to some big cats or overseas guys."

"What happens to the places?" Alex asked.

"Some stay alive with less workers and much lower wages," Catfish said. "Most just end up a pile of bricks and metal and the workers just left out of luck."

"What kind of plants?" I wondered.

"All kinds. Most are in small towns. Textile, linen, potato chips, timber, peanuts, candy and such. They don't have unions, don't have anywhere else to go or to work, so they take what they can get and it is pretty good work until somebody like Billy Ray comes along and leaves them with the dust scattered along the back roads. He's wrecked a lot of lives."

"Sounds like a real sweet guy," Alex said.

Catfish made a face and shrugged. "His nickname among the workers is Killer Kincaid."

"So how does a sports network play into all this?" I asked.

"BTSN was started a few years back but couldn't get a good line up and was about to go under when Billy Ray came up with a plan to buy it. The fellows who owned it had lost their shirts and he got the whole thing at a bargain basement price. Then he set out with his plan to steal part of the SEC contract from ESPN to get the big game of the week."

"How was he going to pull that off?" I said.

"Boat loads of cash, cash and more cash."

"But ESPN has the same kind of cash or more don't they?"

"They do. But what they don't have is Kincaid's connections."

"Like what?"

"Like donating over two million a year to the football program at Alabama. Like providing cars and girls to the recruits while flying them around in his own helicopter all painted up in Alabama colors."

"Doesn't a lot of that go on everywhere?" Alex interrupted.

"I ain't done," Catfish said. "He hangs out at the ballgames with all the other rich guys who give money to whatever school they support. He parties with these guys, cuts them in on deals every now and then as well. These fat cats are the ones who pull the strings on contracts and conference deals like TV."

"And they are big enough to influence a deal like that?" Alex asked.

"Like the only rooster in a packed hen house," he said.

"So, the contract goes to BTSN and they all end up rolling around happy in a big pile of money," I said.

"Only if people tune in and watch and the advertisers plop down their money."

"That's not happening?" Alex said.

"Billy Ray set out to run the damn network the same way he would a pork rind factory. Slashing cost and firing people left and right. Let go the two top play-by-play guys that the fans loved. Cheaped out on the TV trucks and cameras and other stuff. Cut the rates he paid people and thought nobody would notice."

"They noticed?" I asked.

"They noticed. The fans noticed. Advertisers started dropping like flies and revenue projections began to look more like volleyball than football."

"His rich friends turn on him?"

"Rich hogs get fat. Greedy pigs get sent to the slaughter house," Catfish said.

"What?" Alex asked.

"They turned on him. The conference pushed back. He had to upgrade the production team. Invest in all the same toys ESPN uses and now they are trying to add more on campus shows, more local flavor, doing shows right there at the school all day long on Friday and Saturday.

"So, that's a good thing, right?" Alex noted.
"Good for everybody but Billy Ray. If they don't grow the audience over the rest of the season he's going to lose his butt and the contract. But he did make one smooth move when he hired this Cissy lady to be his sideline and feature reporter."

"Cissy, that's her real name?" Alex asked with more than a touch of disdain in her voice.

"Ain't sure, but she just goes by the one name, Cissy. No last name."

"You're kidding?" Alex said.

"Like Cher," I added. Alex looked over at me and rolled her eyes.

"They're trying to make her the big dog of the whole show," Catfish continued. "Got her on all the things, all the promotion, out with the tailgate crowd and then they put her on camera a lot during the games doing little spots and talking with the coaches, stuff like that."

"She good at what she does?" I asked.

"Well, when it comes to Cissy I got good news, bad news and worse news for you," Catfish said with a grin.

"Start with the good," I replied.

"Good news is she's got glowing blue eyes that would freeze a rattlesnake, legs longer than the Mississippi River and none of her skirts have ever come close to knowing her knees."

"The bad news?"

"Word is that off camera she is one mean, conniving, manipulative, hard ass of a woman."

"And that's not the worse news?" I said.

"No it ain't, the worst news is that when it comes to football she ain't got no more idea than a snake has fleas."

"That's a bad thing, right?" Alex looked at me with a grin. Catfish smiled and pointed a big finger at her.

9

"So, I can understand why the network might want Alex to take pictures of this Cissy but why do they think they need to hire me to play bodyguard?"

"Don't," he said. "They got their own security guys. The idea to hire you came from Jay Clark, one of the ex-players on the advisory thing. He's now with the UGA Campus Police and he remembered I used to own that security company, and he asked me to find somebody. Said they were stretched too thin with all the campus drunks and what not during a football weekend and he didn't trust the other guys anyhow. Wanted to make sure nothing happened to her while she was in Athens, so they're footing the bill for you."

"And why does this Cissy with just one name need protection of any sort?"

"Anybody like her on TV always gets weird messages and e-mails and such and then a couple of weeks ago her security boys had to tackle some gooberhead who tried to kiss her on the air."

"That doesn't sound like much. Sounds like college kids."

"Last week it got a bit more serious."

"What happened?" Alex asked.

"They were down at Ole Miss for the game with LSU and while everybody was out doing the game somebody got into her hotel room in Oxford and tore up the place, messed with stuff."

"Police catch anybody?" I asked.

"Nope. Nobody. No cameras in this hotel. No forced entry of the door. Left valuable jewelry, took what they took and left."

"What did they take?"

"Underwear. Every pair she had in the room."

I laughed out loud.

"Just how many pair of underwear did she have?" Alex asked.

"How the hell would I know?" Catfish shrugged. "Just know that's what they took. Then they turned the TV on to BTSN and wrote across the screen with a marker. It said, *Next Time I Will Take You.*"

"Now that's pretty creepy," Alex said.

"Most likely scared her out of her underpants, if she woulda had any left," Catfish said with a smile.

"So exactly what I am supposed to do down there?"

"Just stay close, stick around, keep your eyes open, your mouth shut and earn five hundred bucks each day for going to a college football game."

"I think I can miss a baseball game for that," I said.

"Wait a minute," Alex said and unfolded her legs and plopped her feet hard on the floor. "Did you just say he was getting five hundred a day?"

"One thousand bucks to watch a football game. Not bad, right?" Catfish answered.

"But six hundred bucks to do actual work?"

"I do actual work," I added.

"Yeah, right," she said. "I load up a ton of gear, I lug it around for two days, I work my butt off taking pictures of this Cissy person and they pay me three hundred dollars each day and the campus cops are going to pay him five hundred a day just to stand around and watch her?"

"There is work involved," I protested.

"Work? What work? Following some underwear model around a football game?"

"That's work," I said. "Or least it could be."

"Not worth two hundred dollars more a day than I get," she said, her eyes flared a bit.

I looked over toward Catfish and asked. "How many people in this stadium?"

"Place holds over 90,000 folks," he answered.

"What's that got to do with anything?" Her ponytail bounced with agitation.

"You taking pictures of just one person, right?"

She didn't answer but gave me a hard stare.

"While you're doing that, I have to keep an eye on that one person and meanwhile keep an eye on 90,000 other people trying to spot the one person in that big crowd that just might be an underwear thief," I said. "Surely that should be worth an extra couple hundred bucks a day."

Catfish laughed. Alex did not.

10

I'M NOT SURE what it was that woke me up. Could have been Chance barking or the pounding on my metal door. I rolled off the couch and pushed myself up. The TV was still set to the channel that carried the World Series game that ended late last night. The Giants had come back from being down to win the last two games. They came from behind to win 5-4 in 11 innings and take a 3-2 lead in the series. The teams had Friday off and then games 6 & 7 were back in Detroit over the weekend. The game had ended long past midnight.

The door bounced again with the sound of a pounding fist. Chance was at the door. His tail wagged as he sniffed the bottom of it. Alex.

"You were supposed to meet me downstairs thirty minutes ago," she said, as Chance followed her in. "We're running late."

"Give me ten and I'll be with you," I said and headed off to shower up.

"I'll get the stuff ready for Chance," she said.

Chance usually stayed with her when I had to go out of town, but since we were both taking this trip for two days Catfish had said he could come along and hang out at the RV. He did say that Chance might be outfitted with a Georgia Bulldog pet sweater by the tailgaters. I had not mentioned this to Chance. I knew he would think it was a really bad idea.

"You ready?" Alex asked.

"Ready," I said. I had on a pair of cargo pants, low-cut work boots, a white oxford shirt and a pullover blue fleece with the Louisville Slugger logo on the left chest. I had a small duffel bag with the rest of my stuff.

"That all you taking?"

"I'm good."

She had my TV remote in her hand, pointed it toward the screen and turned it off.

"Did you know that the timer on your DVR was set to a date in June three years ago?"

"Really?" I had no idea what she was talking about.

"So how do you set the time to record shows you want to watch later?"

I didn't answer her. I took my pistol out of my holster, checked the safety, put it and extra clips into my bag. Never know when you might have to wing an underwear thief.

"You don't know how to use a DVR, do you?"

"The shows I watch, other than baseball, will come back on sooner or later if I miss them."

"You're hopeless," she said. "You probably think Bush is still in the White House."

"Which one?" I asked.

She tossed the remote on the couch and picked up the bag she had packed for Chance.

"Let's go," I said. "You're making us late."

Make A Note: When I get back figure out what all those buttons on the remote actually do and just what a DVR really is.

Just over an hour and a half to the east later we rolled into Athens, Georgia, and the University campus. Alex steered the jeep down the narrow streets. She glanced at her cell phone mounted to the dash. It beeped and clicked and she poked at it for directions. I just enjoyed the view. We had turned down an avenue lined with very old, very stately homes except they all had huge Greek letters attached to them. I had no idea how to read them but knew enough to determine it was fraternity and sorority row. Plus, every house had bed sheets hanging from the windows that said 'Beat 'Bama' and a few other more colorful phrases.

We made a few other twists and turns and slowed as traffic backed up on the main part of campus. It was early afternoon and the streets were lined with students loaded down with heavy backpacks. Most of them had their heads down locked into a cell phone, fingers texting while they walked. If they had even bothered to look up they would have seen a beautiful fall day spread out around a nice well groomed college campus. The trees were a mix of gold and red and the low fall light made them glow. Small patches of white clouds hung over the dorms and classrooms and the air felt clean and crisp. Chance squeezed his head out my window between the headrest and the front door to get a better view. I had to assume this was his first time at a college football game. I knew it was mine.

"Can't believe you have never been to a college football game," Alex said at the next light.

"One of the many things in my life I have missed out on."

"But you spent your whole life in sports," she said. "And you were a professional athlete."

"Baseball not football."

"But that was just in the summer."

"Not for a minor leaguer," I said. "Winter ball was year round most of the time."

"Winter ball? Where did you play that?"

"Mostly the Dominican Republic for me. Mexico a few times, even Venezuela one year."

"Every winter?"

"No, but if it wasn't that, it was instructional league, fall league or some really bad job to pay the bills."

"What kind of jobs?"

"I did a lot of carpentry work. Worked on a shrimp boat once in Louisiana. Built cabins in the snow in Montana. Once I started coaching it was baseball all year. So, I only saw college football on TV."

"And you've never been to a tailgate party?"

"No."

"Then you are in for a treat," she said as she poked at the beeping cell phone. "Catfish calls them a food orgy. A barbecue dream."

"Catfish always dreams of barbecue," I noted.

Two or three more pokes of the phone and two turns later we pulled into a parking lot barricaded by a long metal gate. A sign hung from the barrier that noted it was VIP PARKING. Another first for me. A young man checked the paperwork Catfish had printed out for us and gave us two large envelopes with credentials and such. Apparently, VIP parking was still a mile from the stadium and we were told to gather up our bags and gear to wait for a golf cart to take us over there. Guess it wasn't that VIP after all.

Alex opened the rear of the Jeep and began going through a host of bags pulling out her gear one piece at a time. She reached over and pulled out a black vest of sorts with more pockets than I could count.

"What is that thing?" I asked.

"A vest, what do you think it is," she said, and hung it off the rear open tailgate door.

"Looks like a life jacket to me."

"It is for me," Alex answered. "I can load most everything I need for a full day of work in this one vest. Keeps me from having to carry the big bags around all the time if I don't need to."

"Looks like it would be heavy?"

"It is. Fifteen pounds or more loaded up. Another reason I should be making the extra two hundred dollars a day," she said without looking up.

I reached for my one bag and clipped my lightweight pistol on my belt. Even Chance had a bag that weighed more than mine.

Alex stuck one thing after another in the many pockets and compartments of the vest. A tiny flashlight, a small toolkit, a pocketknife, several little plastic things, and then a can of mace.

"Mace? What's that for?"

"I can tell you've never been to a college football game," she said but didn't really answer me.

She went around and took the cell phone off the front dash and placed it in an upper front nylon pocket. I noticed she had what seemed like another phone in the back pocket of her jeans.

"Wait a minute," I said. "You have two phones?"

She put the vest on and pulled it around her. "Yeah, two phones."

"Why would anybody possibly need two phones?"

"One for business," she tapped the big one in the vest pocket and then pulled a slim phone out of her back pocket. It was bright purple. "And one for personal use."

I had nothing to say. I reached down and touched the tiny flip phone that I carried in my pants pocket. She reached inside and handed me another heavy nylon bag with still more pockets.

"What's this?"

"My laptop, my drives, back up media, cables, card readers, batteries, chargers, a run bag and everything else that I can leave in the RV in case I need it."

I felt very inadequate and unprepared.

"You good to go?" Alex asked.

"Got everything I need," I shrugged.

"Five hundred dollars a day," she said. "Unbelievable."

11

THE YOUNG COED that picked us up in the golf cart didn't even flinch when I crawled in the back seat with Chance. Guess she had seen a lot stranger things at the VIP lot. We crossed the campus taking streets and sidewalks and headed down a hill into a large parking lot filled with a circle of RVs all painted up in identical red and black colors and each with a huge picture of a bulldog on the side. A large red and black tent was spread out in the middle of the circle. The Alumni Advisory Compound. Nice perk.

We got out and took in the scene. Under the tent was a large buffet line that stretched from one end to the other. Huge stainless steel grills puffed out smoke at the edge of the tent. I counted at least five 50-gallon trash barrels packed with ice and beer. A row of leather lounge chairs sat in a circle around a TV screen bigger than a highway billboard. Three guys stood near the TV smoking huge cigars and were sharing a laugh. No sign of Catfish.

"Look at this," Alex said and pointed down the lane where a golf cart was approaching. "Check out this big mamma-jamma driving up."

I turned to look. The cart squeaked to a stop and Catfish was behind the wheel. At least I think it was Catfish. He certainly didn't look like Catfish. He had on a bright red sweater with a big 'G" on the chest. A white silk dress shirt was topped off with a red and black bow tie. Three huge rings were scattered out across different fingers and he wore a large gold watch. His normal ruffled hair was pressed down and combed back flat. I think he may have been wearing some sort of makeup.

"What the..." Alex started to speak but Catfish stopped her.

"Don't say it," he said. "Damn time, you two got here. Hop in and I'll take you over to the setup. I'm on in less than ten minutes."

"On what?" I asked.

"TV, what else?" He said. "Why else would I be dressed up like a member of the dang marching band? Now get in."

"What about Chance?"

"Bring him."

We climbed aboard as he hit the pedal and took off. The cart struggled to make it up the hill.

"This why you were practicing fancy words the other day?" I asked from the rear.

"It would behoove you to hold on tight and keep your trap shut," he said.

We went down two more streets, cut across a sidewalk between dorms and then headed down a steep hill toward the football stadium that I could now see looming in the distance.

"Nice bow tie," Alex said without looking at him.

"You don't get a free RV for free," Catfish said as he steered the cart up on the sidewalk and around a corner. "BTSN is doing all these campus shows as I told you and they got to fill up a lot of time. So, part of the deal is that we go on the show and yap about football and tell stories and such. I got a bit coming up in a few minutes."

"And the outfit?" I asked.

"Some lady from the network did it all. Think she got it all at the bookstore. Even put some grease in my hair. Whatcha think?"

"I think you need a hat."

We parked behind a large brick building that Catfish told us was the Tate Student Center and made our way through a parking lot filled with vans and rental trucks packed in tight. Up against the building two large 18-wheelers were squeezed together end to end. Lift doors were open and hundreds of cables of all sizes, shapes and colors snaked out and headed off somewhere under yellow covers. Stairs led to doors every few feet and people popped in and out in a rush. A huge generator truck hummed nearby spewing out diesel fumes. Up against the generator stood a trailer with a large satellite dish mounted on it.

"Takes a lot of stuff to televise a football game," I noted.

"If it was up to Billy Ray he would be doing it out of the back of a pick-up truck," Catfish said as we stopped at the edge of long set of temporary aluminum stairs that seemed to lead all the way to the roof of the building.

"You ain't seen nothing yet," he said. "Come on up here."

We climbed the long stairs that opened out onto the roof. On the far side of the roof at the edge of the building was a huge maze of scaffolding that rose about thirty feet or more off the roof and must have been more than a hundred feet wide and fifty feet long. TV lights hung from more steel grids up top and blazed bright white in the sunlight. A long anchor desk sat facing a row of cameras and two more cameras moved gently while mounted on long metal arms. From up there they would have an amazing view that peered right across a long bridge and into the massive football stadium.

"Big damn set up, ain't it?" Catfish said.

"Bet this thing cost a few bucks."

"It's what they have to do to keep the contract and match what ESPN does. Word is Kincaid is losing his ass, but the league is putting a lot of pressure on him to get the numbers up by the end of the season."

"Looks like a great view from up there," I said.

"It is and just think about what it will look like tomorrow when the place is packed to the gills. They say it took them a full week to build the dang thing and get all the stuff up there."

A young woman wearing a headset and holding a clipboard waved from top of the stairs and motioned for Catfish to hurry up.

"Showtime," he said and grinned. "Wait here, I'll be finished in a bit. You guys grab a drink over there and you can watch me on one of the TVs."

He adjusted his bow tie. "So, how do I look?"

"You look spiffy," Alex said with a smile and gave him a thumbs up.

"He looks like Porky Pig," she said after he got out of range. "I can't believe he is going to be on national TV. How do you think he'll do?"

"I think Catfish could juggle chickens and chainsaws without a bobble."

12

U NDER A SMALL tent sat a table with leftovers from lunch and a big TV on a stand. Alex fiddled around with the TV to get the sound to work. I spotted a plate that someone had left behind with a half-eaten hamburger, potato chips, and several cookies. I took it and sat it down for Chance. He started in on the chips first.

"They have speakers but I can't get sound," she said.

There were a few people scattered around but everybody was locked into their cell phones. I spotted one fellow, an older guy with a scruffy beard, long hair and three walkie-talkie type radios hanging off his belt. A pair of faded work gloves stuffed in his back pocket and he was eating a hot dog with dirty hands. Bet he knew how to get the sound on. I went over to ask him if he could help.

"They cut the program audio feed while up live, to avoid ambient feedback," he said between bites.

I thanked him and moved back to where Alex stood waiting.

"What did he say?"

"They cut the program audio feed because of ambient feedback," I said with confidence.

"What's that mean?"

"It won't work," I said.

We watched without sound. A few minutes later the camera swooped down from above the set and there he was, Catfish in his bright red sweater and greased hair, live on national TV. He talked, laughed, pounded his hands on the desk, threw his arms up in the air several times and the cameras moved in while all the hosts joined in with big laughs. They put up a title thing on the screen that said, *Bobby 'Catfish' Wilson, Former All-SEC Lineman Georgia Bulldogs.* He would never say it, but I know he loved every minute of it.

"The things you never thought you would see in your life," I said.

"Think he is getting paid for this?" Alex asked, still thinking about our fees.

After a bit, they tossed things over to Cissy, with one name. She wasn't behind a desk but standing in front of a monitor where they could get a full shot of her. Catfish was right. She was a nice looking young woman, and certainly had the figure to model underwear or anything else. She had long blonde hair that twirled down across her bare shoulders. A gold necklace fell deep into the low cut bright blue dress she wore and if the dress had been a few inches shorter we may have gotten a sample of some of the evidence from the underwear theft last week at Ole

Miss. It was easy to see why adding her to the broadcast had boosted the ratings. I doubt most guys gave a damn whether she knew a football from a cantaloupe.

"Excuse me," a voice popped up from behind us. We turned to see.

"What is that dog doing up here?"

I looked down at Chance. "Eating a hamburger."

"Get him out of here."

"Who are you?" I asked.

"I'm Boo Dickman, Executive Senior Producer of Programing and Production for BTSN Network Sports," he introduced himself like a business card.

He looked like he was at most twenty-five and had the real hipster look going on. Nice haircut made to look like it wasn't cut nice, a slick finished blazer, plaid shirt, tight skinny jeans and beige loafers with no socks. A tiny headset with a microphone hung around his neck and he held what appeared to be a tiny laptop computer open in one hand.

"Is your name really Boo?" I asked.

He ignored me and looked over at Alex and noticed her vest full of photo gear.

"You my promo photographer for Cissy?"

"Alex Trippi," she said and stuck out her hand.

"I don't need your name. Just make sure you get some good shots. Make them sexy. Show off her body and keep the fans and coaches out of them."

"Got it," she said and glanced at me.

"I'm just making real sure we get what we paid good money for."

"Not that much money," she muttered under her breath.

"What's that?"

"Nothing," she said.

"After this segment, she will go do the tailgate feature. Meet her outside the Green Room. Her field producer will brief you on everything you need to know. After the hotel thing last week, a lot of other paparazzi shooters are following her around. That's a good thing, so don't get in the way of those dudes. We're getting great publicity all across the nation. So, do your job and stay out of the way. We good?"

Alex did not reply. She gave him her death stare but he missed it while looking down at his little laptop.

He looked up at me. "And you, whoever you are, get that damn dog off my roof."

"Sure thing," I said. "Right after he finishes his burger, Boo."

13

A FEW PEOPLE DRIFTED down the staircase from the set. We spotted Catfish as he walked next to a tall man in a dark blue police uniform. They made their way over to us.

"So, how do you think I did?" He asked us.

"You sounded great," Alex said and smiled at me.

"This is Jay Clark, best damn Tight End the Dogs ever had and now the top Major for the UGA Police Department."

We all shook hands. I'm a big guy but Clark had another inch on me and still looked like he could block a college linebacker with ease. He sported a Marine buzz cut and his uniform fit him like a tailored suit.

"I appreciate you taking on the job for us, Jake," his voice matched the buzz of his haircut.

"Thank Catfish. He set it all up."

"He says you're pretty good."

"He tends to exaggerate for effect every now and then," I said.

"Yeah, he does," Clark said. "And I just witnessed some of that."

"I'm still not sure what exactly it is I'm supposed to do, since I hear they have their own security guys, right?"

"That's a long story," Clark said.

"Run down the short version."

"Short version is that he owns the security company and treats it just like some bug spray factory he owns."

"Sounds a little like I've heard this before," Catfish added.

"Original company, called MPS, was formed up in North Carolina near Fort Bragg. Paid good money, hired on real solid military guys when they finished their tours. Had some big contracts both here and overseas, but fell on hard times when the founder of the firm got caught stealing funds from his partner and the business went into bankruptcy."

"And in stepped Billy Ray, I bet," Catfish said.

"Like a dog on a pork chop," Clark said. "Made a deal to buy the firm, slashed the staff down to nearly nothing, cut the wages and ran off all the good veterans that worked for it."

"So, what does it look like now?" I asked.

"Not much," he said. "Calls it *Hot LZ Security.* Bunch of puffed up guys in black uniforms with a lot of pistols and rifles. They mostly work at shopping malls, car lots and sometimes at his plants when he needs a show of force when firing workers. Guess that's why he wanted to buy the company."

"So, how does he get these former military men to work for him?"

"All bad cases. He picks the guys the Army kicks out for drugs or other stuff. Most all of them have a dishonorable discharge so they take the work for ten bucks an hour because nobody else is going to hire them to even bag groceries. Just a bunch of dumbass rejects."

"Dumbass rejects with guns," Catfish noted.

"So, you're taking the security measure in your own hands," I said.

"No, sir," he said. "I'm putting it in your hands."

Catfish looked over at me and patted me on the back.

"I talked to my counterpart at Ole Miss and they still don't know what happened last week. Could have been a prank but I want them in and out of Athens, with no muss and no fuss. The media is making a big deal out of this underwear story and that can bring out all kinds of knuckleheads. I do not need any more knuckleheads. I got my usual ninety thousand to worry about."

"So, my marching orders are?" I asked.

"Eyes open and stay close. You see, hear or smell anything hinky, get her out of there and call in the Calvary. We will take it from that point. The whole television crew is staying outside town at a motel, but she's got her own room at a fancy little place downtown. We booked you in a room, three doors down. After they wrap up today you'll go with her and stay with her until she is locked down for the night. Then back here in the morning early and we'll all go over the plan for the game day coverage at that time."

"She onboard for all this?" I asked.

"After meeting her, I highly doubt it," he said. "Seems to me to be a real hard ass."

Alex looked up at me and grinned.

"Well, I never went to college like you three," I said. "But I do have a PhD in hard asses."

14

We made our way down the long stairs and back into the street. Dodged our way around all the cables and stopped in front of a red canopy outside the two double doors to the student center. Catfish was going to take Chance and head back to the RV and we had been told to wait inside for the field producer. The double doors burst open and laughter spilled out along with a big group of people. The bulk of the group hung back and trailed a tall man as he made his way forward. It was always easy to spot the big dog in a pack.

The fellow stood about 6-3, more round than strong, and a good thirty pounds overweight. The extra weight showed on his face. It was wide, a strong chin dropped into his neck and his tight collar pushed small rolls of fat up toward his cheeks. The cheeks were spotted red from either the sun or afternoon drinks. He was old enough to have gray hair, thin and combed back toward the crown but the hair was a light blond and groomed with a touch of gel. Not drug store dye but an expensive salon job.

He wore a nice fitting dark suit with subtle pinstripes. Cuffed pants with a sharp crease hung perfectly at the edge of high glossed wingtips. His starched shirt was light blue with a solid white collar and was topped off by a bright gold silk tie with a perfect knot. He stopped for a moment and the whole pack stopped behind him. He reached into his suit pocket, pulled out a huge cigar nearly eight inches long and slowly fired it up, pausing to let the first long puff of smoke twirl upward around his chubby face. He motioned to his group to stay put and made his way over to where we stood.

"Bobby Wilson, Bobby Wilson, you old dog...Roll Tide," he said as he came over and stuck out his arm for a handshake. Silver cufflinks slipped out from under his suit coat and flickered in the sunlight. They shook hands but it was not a cordial greeting. In all the years I had seen Catfish greet people, I had never seen him not grin, slap a back or make some sort of sharp retort. I looked over at Alex. She had noticed as well.

"Just saw you on the tube, Bobby. I thought maybe it was TV that was putting on the extra pounds but I do believe you have been packing on the weight, son."

"Honest work and too much barbecue," Catfish said flatly.

Catfish turned to the three of us and introduced us by name. He skipped over Chance, which might have hurt his feelings, but he didn't say so.

"This is Billy Ray Kincaid, the owner of the network."

"Just call me Billy Ray or just Ray-Ray," he said.

Nobody did.

"So, you're the girl that's going to take pictures of Cissy, this weekend?" He spoke to Alex.

"Yes, I'm the girl," sarcasm dripped as she emphasized the word girl. He didn't notice.

"Boo tell you what we wanted? I don't want serious. Sexy is what we're going for."

"Sexy," Alex repeated. I prepared myself to grab her if she started to punch him.

"We got all sort of idiots crawling around here taking photos of her after last week but we need more posed pictures and crap like that. The marketing folks are draining my damn wallet ready to churn out a ton of promotion."

"Speaking of which," Jay Clark spoke up. "Mr. Eliam will be working with our force this weekend to help provide security for your young lady reporter."

I was impressed that he pronounced my name correctly with the hard E. Few get that right.

"He will be providing Cissy with 24-hour security while she is here for the game."

I nodded toward Kincaid.

"What the hell does Cissy need with extra security?" He stuck the big cigar in his mouth, rolled it around a bit, took it out and spat on the sidewalk.

"Your reporter has created a media storm. There are significant threats online and in light of the incident last week at Ole Miss, my department feels when a crime takes place, measures have to be taken."

"Crime?" He waved the big cigar in the air. "Stealing underwear is a crime? Hell, I must have stolen dozens of pairs of underwear from sorority houses when I was in college. That's a damn prank, not a crime."

"Not in my world," Clark said.

"Well, in my world I will tell you what it is. It is publicity. Damn good publicity. Three weeks ago, there were only four camera crews and two writers at our weekly press lunch. This week we had over thirty camera crews and so many writers we ran out of sandwiches in about five minutes. And the more we talk it about it, the more that show up."

"The more you talk about it, the worse you make it," Clark told him.

"Well, you can bet your sweet ass I ain't going to stop talking about it," he scratched his nose, dug a pinky finger in one side, picked something out and flicked it away. A long nose hair dangled from his nostril.

"I could buy spots on every damn TV network in the nation and not come close to getting the free publicity we've got from some idiot stealing her underwear," his voice began to rise a bit, and his face turned a bright red. "Hell, right now we're working on an idea to sell a brand of *CISSY* underwear online."

"That would be a really bad move," Clark said.

"Things people call bad moves have made me a lot of money," Billy Ray said.

"With all due respect, sir. Bad idea or good idea, while she is here in my town, her security is not your call."

"Well, I don't need any help from your school crossing guards."

Clark reset his weight. All the leather and gear around his waist creaked with the motion.

"My department has over one hundred officers. We have nearly 40,000 students, 10,000 more staff here everyday and this campus becomes one of the largest cities in the state on football Saturdays."

"With all due respect, chief," he said getting his title wrong. "I have my own security team."

"I know all about your security team," Clark replied. "*HOT LZ*. Mall cops on steroids."

"Big guys with big muscles and big guns," Kincaid said. "Cost me a pretty penny."

"So, where are they?"

"I bring them in here on Saturday."

"Today's Friday," Clark said, and shifted his leather gun belt again.

"No way I'm paying for any of this so called 24-hour crap," he said.

"Not asking you to pay."

"Well, I don't like it. I don't like it one bit," he said.

"Not asking you to like it."

Billy Ray looked at Clark. They locked eyes for a beat before Kincaid flinched. He dropped his big cigar on the sidewalk and smeared it out with his expensive shoe.

A young man in a much cheaper suit came up behind him and said something in his ear and Billy Ray glanced down at what was on the screen of a cell phone the kid held up to him. He looked up at Catfish.

"Been too long, Bobby," he said. "When was the last time we saw each other? At the SEC Championship game in Atlanta?"

"Nope, didn't run into you then."

"So, when did we last see each other?"

"Been a while," Catfish said. "Town Council meeting eight years ago in my hometown of Pearl Falls. A week before Christmas when you announced you were closing down the old shirt factory and moving it to Taiwan."

"I don't remember that," he said.

"The two hundred folks you fired that night sure remember it. Most likely they still do," Catfish said.

Jay Clark let a tiny smile slip out. Kincaid reached into his suit pocket and took out another huge cigar. He rolled it around in his fingers and smiled at Catfish.

"Roll Damn Tide," he said as he turned and walked away with his group.

We all stood there in silence.

"Now what?" I said out loud.

"I'm headed back to the office," Jay Clark said. "You're on your own with Cissy."

"Can't wait."

"And this girl," Alex said with a bitter grin. "Has sexy pictures to take."

"How about you, Catfish?" I asked.

"I'm gonna go back to the RV, change clothes, wash this crap out of my hair, get a big ol' bottle of whiskey and drink 'till I forget just how much I hate it when some fool says Roll Tide."

15

ALEX SAT ON the floor with her legs crossed and toyed with one of her cameras. I leaned against the wall in the corner and tried to look professional. I was getting paid a lot to do so. We waited at the end of a hallway outside a door with a white paper sign that said *CISSY*. We had been waiting thirty minutes and it would soon be dark.

The door opened and we both looked up. A young athletic looking woman in a blue BTSN sweatshirt stepped out and closed the door behind her and leaned against it with her eyes shut. Her short brown hair dropped near her neck and fell a bit over one eye. She wore faded jeans and a pink pair of running shoes. She muttered softly and repeatedly hit her head with a clipboard. This went on for maybe a full minute until she opened her eyes and saw us smiling at her. Her face turned a flush red.

Alex uncurled and stood as the young woman came over to us. She bounced back quickly and introduced herself.

"Sam DeNelli," she said. "I'm Cissy's producer. Sorry, I didn't see you. Sorry you had to see that."

I told her my name and introduced Alex.

"You're the security the campus police ordered?" She asked.

"Expert in underwear theft of all sorts," I said.

She laughed and looked at Alex and all her camera gear.

"I assume you're the promo shooter for Cissy?"

"That would be me," Alex said.

"I guess Boo already filled you in on what he wants?"

"Boo says he wants sexy," Alex told her.

She rolled her eyes. "A Journalism degree from Northwestern, 4.0 grade point average, four years with ESPN and now my life has come to this."

"Working with Cissy hard?" I asked.

"No, working with Cissy is impossible," she said and shook her head. "It's like teaching a rabbit to dance."

"That hard?" I laughed.

"Just wait," she said. "The only thing she hates more than producers are security guys like you."

"Is Sam short for Samantha?" I asked.

"Short for Sammy."

"Sammy?"

"Sammy Sosa," she smiled. "From Chicago and my dad was a huge Cubs fan. So, Sammy it is."

"Could have been worse," I said.

"Yeah?"

"He could have been a huge Andre Dawson fan."

She giggled. "Yeah, being named Hawk could have been worse, I guess."

Make A Note: A young woman that knows baseball and her Cubs history is a woman worth keeping an eye on.

The outside door burst open and a lanky fellow loaded down with camera gear rolled through it in a flurry of arms and legs as he kicked at the door.

"Time to get it on and get down," his loud baritone boomed against the concrete walls. "Get the Princess outta of her castle and let's do the boogie woogie."

He was tall, maybe 6-5, had skin the color of mahogany and a red driver's cap was pushed back around close cropped hair that showed a touch of gray around the edges. A toothpick rolled around in his teeth. He had a huge camera with a small light on top slung from his right shoulder, a huge backpack hung from his left arm and he wore a large dark blue industrial size fanny pack turned around toward the front. He seemed to carry it all without effort as he strolled up with ease.

He looked at Sam. "You good to roll?"

"Guys, this is Terrence Thibbadaeu, the best sports camera guy around."

"Thank you, little lady," he said as he shifted the heavy backpack off to her. "Everybody just calls me Shaky."

"Shaky?" I said. "Isn't that a bit of a bad name for someone who does camera work?"

"They tell me it's a term of endearment," he said with a deep laugh and a wide smile.

When he smiled the toothpick bounced and exposed a row of bright white teeth bordered by two gold ones on the right side.

"We waiting on the queen bee?" He asked Sam.

"We are."

"Not for long."

He walked over to the dressing room door and banged on it hard with the butt of his left hand.

"Shake that tail feather, Miss Cissy," his huge voice boomed. "Get your skinny butt on out here, now."

A moment later the door jerked open and Cissy popped out. She glared hard at him and turned her attention toward Sam. He grinned over her shoulder.

"I can not believe we have to go talk to these morons, every week," she said.

"They call them football fans and you work for a football show," Sam said flatly.

"They're all stupid rednecks."

I knew why we had waited so long. It must have taken her hours to squeeze herself into the white jeans she was wearing. There wasn't a stitch between them and her skin. Her purple top was low cut and crept up enough to show off her belly button. The matching purple shoes had pointy toes and six-inch heels.

She looked up at us and back at Sam.

"I told you I don't have any more time for the press today."

"They aren't with the media," Sam said and pointed to Alex.

"This is Alex Trippi," Sam said. "She is the photographer Boo hired for publicity shots."

Alex started to lift her hand to offer it to her.

"Are you any good?" Cissy asked.

Alex drew her hand back and rolled it into a fist.

"What kind of question is that?"

"The last one they hired made my ass look big."

"It's always been my policy to avoid the big butt shots, whenever possible," Alex replied. "Matter of fact I tend to not show butts at all."

I looked over at Alex. With the heels Cissy had a slight height advantage but my money was on Alex because I doubted Cissy could fight in those tight pants.

"You have done this before?" Cissy pressed.

"The last pictures I took resulted in sales of over three thousand dollars," Alex answered.

Cissy had no reply to that. I had no idea what she was talking about either. Sam jumped into the silence to change the subject to me.

"This is Jake Eliam," Sam said. "He has been hired for extra security while we are here in Athens."

"That's ridiculous," she said. "Billy Ray already has his soldier goons all around me and the last thing I need is a babysitter."

"That's a good thing then," I said.

"Why?"

"Because I am not a babysitter."

"Why not?"

"Because babysitters don't carry a gun," I said and lifted my fleece.

Shaky let out a small laugh and Cissy turned and gave him a hard look. He didn't flinch.

"Well, you sure as hell aren't hanging around me all weekend."

"Not your choice," I said.

"It damn sure is. All I have to do is call Boo and tell him to fire you."

"I would never work for anybody named Boo."

"Then who the hell do you work for?"

"He works for the University," Sam said.

"We gonna talk or we gonna work?" Shaky said loudly.

She paused for a beat. We all just stared at her.

"Just stay out my way," Cissy pointed a long purple fingernail at me as she turned and blasted out the door on her six-inch heels.

"Well, Sammy," I said. "Maybe we should name her The Hawk."

She shook her head and grabbed the heavy backpack as she and Shaky headed outside. Alex stuffed all her gear back in her bag. I could tell she was still pissed off.

"What was all that stuff about your last photo bringing in three thousand bucks?" I asked. "What picture was that?"

"Clyde, the bull," she said. "That's what they were selling him for. I wasn't lying."

"Hopefully she will never find that out," I said.

"Why?"

"Because I got a feeling Clyde's big butt was showing in those pictures."

16

TEN MINUTES LATER, we were pushing our way through a crowded maze of football fans in two golf carts. Darkness was closing in and a breeze had picked up as the sky had turned from clear to cloudy while we were waiting. Sam drove the first cart with Cissy up front beside her. Cissy held her huge phone tilted out and away from her mouth and shouted into the device. She seemed agitated. Maybe that was a semi-permanent state for her. Alex was in the rear seat that faced backward toward us. She pointed her camera and checked out shots as we went along. She was squeezed to the left side of the seat by a bright red plastic toolbox strapped down by a bungee cord. It was huge and took up most of the seat. I drove the second cart with Shaky in the passenger seat, his camera in his lap. My stint as driver had bumped some poor intern out of his job for the night.

"You been doing this long?" I asked Shaky as we bumped along at a crawl.

"Too damn long," he said. "But beats the hell out of my other options when I was a kid."

"Like what?"

"First summer out of school I worked with my pops doing utility work for the city."

"Where?"

"Charlotte."

"Doing what?"

"He fixed things down inside manholes. Pipes and such. I worked side by side with him that whole damn summer and swear I never saw daylight. In that hole before dawn, dark when we come out."

"Tough job."

"Tough man."

"So, how did you get to doing this?"

"Got a fifty dollar gig holding the camera cable at a basketball game. The guy hurt his wrist in the first quarter and I took over. Didn't ask, just did it. Never looked back."

"Beats crawling down manholes."

"Damn straight," he twirled his toothpick and smiled. "Never saw a pretty cheerleader down in one of them holes."

We inched along through the edge of another parking lot and dodged a group of drunken kids who yelled *'Put Us On TV!'* when they spotted the camera. Another guy wandered right in front and held up his hand for me to stop. The cart lurched as I hit the brake. He asked if I had any tickets for sale. Shaky cursed him and waved for him to get out of the way. I punched the pedal flat but I was having a hard time keeping up with Sam.

"So, you were working for ESPN when they did the games?" I asked.

"Fifteen years doing the games for them as a free-lancer. Things getting better every year and then Kincaid comes along and wrecks it all in a few months."

"Why did you stay on instead of leaving like the other guys did?"

"I like the games and I didn't want to travel out west for work," he answered. "But there is this one other thing."

"What thing?"

"This business attracts fools like bees to honey. I have worked with some of the biggest dang fools you can think of and my long time motto is a simple one."

"Your motto?"

"Plain and simple. Go ahead and do your fool thing but my ass will be here one day longer than your ass," he smiled wide when he said it.

"Good motto," I said.

"Plus, I keep one of these things nearby just in case," he said and pulled a tiny device out of his shirt pocket.

"What is that?"

"Voice activated digital recorder," he said. "This will record anything within range for two days."

"It's recording what we're saying, now?"

"Bet your ass it is."

"Why do you keep it?"

"Job security," he said. "You can't imagine what folks say when they think certain people ain't listening."

"Like Cissy?"

"Her especially," Shaky said. "Got tons of her yapping that I might need down the road. That fool Boo, also."

He stuck the little device back in his pocket and rolled the toothpick in a circle.

"What has Cissy got going for her in this business?"

"Incredibly large boobs," he said with a grin.

"That's it?"

"Wasn't for those two, she would be serving up burgers and fries at some fast food joint in Jersey."

"Not long for being on camera?"

"Oh, she'll be on camera, just not at a game. She ain't got any sights on being a sports reporter at all. She just wants to be famous."

"Famous for what?"

"Just famous will do for her," he said.

"How about Sam? She seems bright."

"Sammy is a keeper. Knows her stuff and she's good people."

I turned the cart down another lane and dropped off a curb I didn't see with a thud. I sped up and soon caught up with Alex and Sam. Cissy was still talking or yelling at her phone.

"How did you end up with this job?" Shaky asked me.

"Favor for my friend, Catfish."

"Catfish? The big guy they had on the show today telling stories?"

"That would be Catfish."

"That dude is a natural. He on TV around here?"

"No, played football at Georgia. Owns barbecue joints now."

"Good business."

"I would starve without him."

"And he got you into this?"

"It's a sideline of sorts. Catfish has got his fingers in a lot of stuff. He got me doing this sort of stuff for him some years ago."

"Make a living at it?"

"Not even close."

"So, what else you do?"

"I got a little thing going where I make baseball bats by hand."

"Baseball bats?" He let out a chuckle and pushed his cap back on his balding head a bit. "Make a living at that?"

"Not even close," I said.

It seemed Sam had found the people she was looking for. We had turned down a row of RVs all decked out in Crimson Alabama colors and logos. Flags with large elephants flapped in the breeze and fire flickered from grills of all sizes. The smell of smoke mixed in with the strong odor of beer. The strains of the song *Sweet Home Alabama* could be heard somewhere down the way. Sam nosed her cart up against a large SUV next to a tent.

Maybe a dozen people sat around a metal fire pit drinking beer. I inched up behind her. Alex snapped off a shot of us as we parked.

"What is that huge red toolbox for?" I asked Shaky.

"First aid kit."

"First aid kit?"

"You'll see," he twirled the toothpick and stopped it next to one of his gold teeth.

17

SAM AND SHAKY went to work right away. I stood back out of the way and sat on the rear bumper of the second golf cart. Alex got all her gear ready to go but she had nothing to do since Cissy was still in the cart talking on the phone. She joined me and leaned against the cart.

"Who has she been on the phone with?"

"Her wardrobe person apparently," she answered.

"Really?"

"She just told her she needs some more pop to her tops. Whatever that means."

Sam dove into the work fast. We watched as Shaky put a small microphone on the fans one by one and she asked them questions from off to the side of the camera. She prodded them with ease and they responded with laughs, made faces at the camera and of course shouted out Roll Tide at every chance. The beer most likely helped but she was at ease getting them to react and she made easy small talk as they moved from one person to the next.

When they finished the interviews Shaky set up his tripod and backed off twenty feet or so and leaned in over his camera. Sam came over to where we were and put a few things back into a small case.

"When Shaky finishes up the B-Roll I will get Cissy to do her bit and you can get some shots," she said to Alex.

"B-Roll?" I asked.

"Video of the people we just talked with. We need some shots of them just sitting around the fire and such. Shots when they are not looking at the camera. We have to make a three minute piece out of this tonight for a sponsored feature they call *TD Tailgate*."

"The sponsor a beer company?" Alex asked.

"How did you ever guess?" Sam said with a smile.

She shouted over to Cissy to get her attention and motioned for her to get ready by circling her index finger in the air. Cissy made a face but closed out her call. She slid out of the cart and unhooked the big red toolbox. She opened it up and pulled out multiple layers of drawers topped off with a small mirror. She turned on a tiny light around the mirror as she reached into the toolbox and pulled out a small makeup brush. With her other hand, she grabbed a small jar and spun the top off with ease. She flicked the brush across her cheeks and forehead in a fast blur. *The First Aid Kit.*

Shaky ambled back over to the cart and sat the camera down in the seat. He caught my eye as I watched Cissy working away at the toolbox. He winked at me. Cissy approached us and without a word turned her back and pulled up the back of her blouse. Shaky clipped a little box onto her tight pants and handed her a cable with a microphone attached to it. She ran it up under her blouse and clipped the microphone to her bra. Sam held another tiny device. Cissy turned to her with her hand out.

"You got my ear?"

"Here you go," Sam said and handed her a tiny earpiece. Cissy stuck it in her right ear and they all headed off to the circle of fans. Alex clicked a few buttons on her camera and followed them over. Shaky flipped the camera up on his right shoulder in one smooth motion.

"Showtime, big man. Time for Miss Cissy to wade in among the evil doers."

"To serve and protect," I said but kept my distance as they went to work. Chances of an underwear thief among this crowd seemed pretty slim to me. Sam gathered up the fans and placed them next to Cissy. Shaky reached up and flipped on the little light on top of his camera and on cue Cissy lit up like a moth to a flame. The smile grew wide. Her eyes sparkled a bit in the bright light. She appeared engaged and involved in the interviews. It was a bit unsettling to watch the sudden transformation. Off to the side of the camera Sam watched every move, her chin tilted down toward her neckline. It looked as if she was talking to herself. I had no clue what she was doing. Meanwhile, Alex circled the group from front to rear and fired off shots quietly from a distance. The whole thing was over in a minute or so at most. Cissy ended up by tossing it back to somebody she called Ted and held her smile for a beat.

Shaky cut the light off and she bolted out of the crowd before it went fully dim.

"Idiots," she said to no one in particular as she brushed past me and reached for her phone again.

Alex backed out and walked over to me while she clicked at the back of her camera to check her shots.

"What do you think?" She showed me a photo.

I looked at the shot. It was a close-up from the side of Cissy with her face tilted back and toward the camera in a big smile. Her hair seemed to glow in the camera light. Her face was rimmed by the soft image of a fire from a grill in the background. An Alabama football flag was frozen in action at the corner. On the other side, you could just see the very edge of a camera. It was a great promotional shot of Cissy.

"I can't see her butt," I said.

Sam thanked the fans one by one and went over to Cissy and pulled the little thing out of her ear and took off her microphone. She joined us and Shaky began to pack up the rest of the gear.

"What is that thing you just took out of her ear?" I asked Sam.

"It's an Ear-Prompter," she held it up. "Audio version of the Tel-e-Prompter you see the anchors use to read copy off a screen easily."

"How does it work?"

"I speak into this mic," she pointed down at a micro- phone mounted just inside her sweatshirt. "And Cissy fol- lows along repeating it."

"So that's what you were doing over there? Feeding her lines to say?" I asked.

"One by one. Every single word."

"Every word?" I repeated.

"Every damn word," Shaky added.

I could only shake my head at that. This was a very odd business.

"Wait a minute," Alex looked up from her camera as she tuned in to what Sam had just said. "Did I just hear you right? You plan all this, set all this up, do all the inter- views and then she comes in for minute or so and you still have to tell her what to say?"

"And don't forget hanging around past midnight to edit it all together," Sam said.

"And just how much does BTSN pay her for this over- whelming contribution?" Alex asked.

"Oh, here we go," Shaky took a step back and grinned.

"They won't tell us," she said as her face flushed a bit. "But what we have been able to learn from the media websites is that she just got a boost and now makes about ten thousand dollars."

"Ten thousand?" I said. "Ten grand a year seems pretty cheap to me."

"Ten thousand dollars a game," she said and raised her voice a notch. "Ten thousand dollars every single week."

"Ten thousand dollars a week," Alex got louder also. "That's criminal."

"I agree," Sam said. "Plus, she gets a wardrobe allowance, upgraded hotel and her personal car service."

Alex stared back down at the image of Cissy on her camera. She looked up and opened her mouth to say something but stopped.

"And you were complaining about my fee," I said to her.

18

IT HAD BEEN over an hour since we returned to the compound of network trucks next to the stadium. The others, including Alex, had headed off to another one of the 18-wheelers to put together the segment on the tailgaters. I was left in the hands of a young intern as once again I waited for Cissy. The kid told me she was trying on different outfits with her wardrobe consultant. That could go on for a while. Sam had told me I could wait in the main production truck and watch a part of a live show that was coming up. The intern promised to alert me when Cissy was ready to leave.

I had seen these trucks before at baseball stadiums. The sides rolled out with expansion units and cables that snaked everywhere but I had never been inside. There are two things that hit you when you enter one of these trucks. First, just how many video monitors you are blasted with from wall to wall and just how dang cold it is inside. It must have been below sixty degrees despite the fact that it was packed with people.

There were small lights buried in the ceiling of the room but most of the ambient light came from the glow of the massive row of monitors that ran completely across the front wall. Too many to count but I would hedge it was upwards of fifty or more. Three rows of console type desks rose toward the rear and each one of those had small monitors buried in the front. About a dozen people sat shoulder to shoulder across all three rows with computers and other devices in front of them. Four people in the front row perched on top of large layouts with row after row of tiny buttons lit up in red, blue, green and white. Another huge console held a maze of round buttons and sliding bars. Lights and meters flickered and blinked in every direction. A multi-colored dance of electronics, none of which made any sense to me.

A number of the monitors had narrow white strips of adhesive tape stuck along the bottom with abbreviations and names written in black marker. *Cam-9 Billy, VTR-4-Dan, Elvis 6-Dana, Jib2-Buddy, Gfx-A-Gina.* It was nearly the top of the hour and I didn't notice any sense of urgency or energy in the room. Everybody seemed to be head down into their own work. On the main monitor two anchors up on the big set outside the stadium chatted with each other and every now and then spoke out with a *1-2-3-4* when asked.

"Stand by," a young lady in the second row shouted out. I jumped a bit when her voice broke the low chatter and hum of the air conditioner. "We go in thirty," she shouted again.

"Here we go," an older man next to her said in a low and calm voice. "Stand by with your move Buddy and sweep in high."

"Ten," the young lady shouted.

"Stand by to track Elvis," the man spoke into his headset. "Ready on jib 2, open their mics and go with layover G then B to C."

Music boomed from the speakers and filled the room. The BTSN logo flew across the big monitor in the center of the wall.

"Cue them and fly it out high, Buddy," he said as the two guys welcomed everybody to Athens and the University of Georgia. Behind them the football stadium showed up on the screen as the camera floated high above the set and drifted out toward the bridge and the huge scoreboard.

"Stand by 6, go with it and dissolve to 6 and slow it in. Ready 3, take 3. Cross to 4, ready 4, take 4 and go VTR B and take it full. Gina with G next. Slide in crossover G-11 on the bottom, hold it, and… get it out."

I stood silent and watched in awe as the chatter continued. This was just a couple of guys in chairs talking to each other and I couldn't imagine what this room might sound like when there was a live football game going on. Ten minutes of watching this and I was more than ready to get back to my little workshop and spend the whole day with a piece of wood and some sandpaper.

The show rolled on for a bit more before the intern opened the door and motioned to me that Cissy was ready to go. I grabbed my bag and followed the kid down to where a dark black town car sat waiting for her. I introduced myself to the driver and leaned against the rear fender as we waited for another ten minutes. The intern returned with some bags and put them into the trunk of the car.

Cissy came down the steps to the parking lot trailed by a scruffy group of guys with cameras and phones pointed at her. One camera with a microphone on a boom pushed in close and a young woman shouted questions. She stopped about fifty feet from where the car was parked. She just stood there on the curb. I looked over at the driver and he looked back with a shrug of his shoulders. He got in the car and I joined him in the front seat. We eased up the short few feet to where she stood and stopped again. She waited for the driver to get out and come around and open the door. The cameras surged at the window as we pulled away. Things were getting stranger by the minute.

We eased our way out of the campus crowds and onto the city streets of downtown Athens. We quickly hit gridlock on the streets as fans of all ages packed the bars and stores on a Friday night before a huge game. We moved one car length at a time through each traffic light.

"Driver, excuse me, driver," Cissy broke the silence from the rear seat.

"Yes," the driver answered. "My name is Dave. Do you need something?"

"I do," she said. "I need to ask you if there is any way humanly possible that you could drive any damn slower?"

"Sorry, miss," Dave said. "We're just stuck here. The hotel is only two blocks away so I'll have you at the front door in a few minutes."

"Just wonderful," she said.

We sat through the same red light two more times before Dave eased the car up tight against another car to cross the intersection.

"You don't like me, do you?" Cissy asked from her seat.

"Excuse me?" The driver asked. His voice sounded nervous.

"I think that question was meant for me, Dave," I said.

We sat in silence for a moment.

"Well?" She insisted.

"Well, what?" I asked.

"You don't like me, do you?"

"I don't know you," I said.

"But you do have an opinion."

"I do."

"So?"

"You seemed a little two faced around those fans tonight."

"So, what's wrong with that? Putting on a show is part of my job," she said.

"When people are two faced, I figure that you can't trust either one of them," I replied.

"Oh, that is really cute," she said harshly. "Who said that?"

"Somebody a long time ago," I said. "Been so long, I've begun to take credit for it myself."

In the muted reflection of streetlights in the front windshield I could see Dave smile. He turned the car onto the next street and told us the hotel was just up the way on the right.

"Are you going to be hanging around all day tomorrow?" She asked.

"I am."

"How much are they paying you to do this ridiculous job?"

"Not nearly enough," I said. Dave smiled again in the reflection.

19

THE HOTEL HAD a small sliver of a driveway to allow cars to pull up under a canopy. Dave pulled the car up behind a BMW. We were next in line. The hotel was a three-story blonde brick building and looked as though it was old construction upgraded to an upscale expensive place. A thin strip of red neon ran up the right side of the building. Green neon matched it on the other. A white strip of neon glowed bright and ran from left to right across the front and intersected with a polished steel sign rimmed with blue neon. *The Dogwood* it read.

The car in front pulled away and Dave eased up and stopped at the front door. A young college kid in black slacks, a crisp white shirt and red bow tie bounced toward the rear as the trunk popped open. Dave went around to open the door for Cissy who kept her head buried in her phone as she brushed past him and headed toward the front door. The young man was right behind her with all her bags in tow. I reached out and touched her on the shoulder. She turned and glared.

"Wait for me before going up to the room," I said.

She didn't bother to answer and disappeared inside. I reached into my bag and took out the envelope that Major Clark had given me with my room card. We were on the third floor. Dave closed the door and looked back at the other cars in line. I dug into my pants pocket and pulled out my cash. I had a ten and a five. I gave the ten to him. He nodded a thank you.

"Good luck with that one," he said. "I think you're going to need it."

"You're a good judge of character, Dave," I said and smiled.

I entered the lobby and walked past rows of leather chairs and brass lamps. A young woman was at work behind the mahogany and gold front desk. I did not see Cissy. I moved down a hallway in search of the elevator. I passed the hotel bar as the sounds of live jazz led by a trumpet player poured out the door. The elevator was around the corner and a small group waited for it to arrive. Cissy had gone up without me. I decided to bypass it and take the stairs. I entered the third floor hallway and spotted the kid with the bags in front of an open door. The door closed in his face.

"That is the lady from TV, right?" He asked with a goofy grin on his face.

"It is," I said.

"You think I could get her autograph?"

"Maybe. But be careful."

"You her boyfriend?"

"Gratefully, no," I answered. "Did she take care of you?"

"What?"

"No tip?"

"Nope, but I don't care. She's really pretty."

I reached into my pocket and pulled out the five dollars I had left. I handed it to him.

"Cool Dude," he said as he headed back to the elevator.

She makes ten thousand dollars a game and I was already down fifteen bucks. I knocked hard on the door and waited. A moment later the door cracked opened a few inches. The security chain was already in place.

"What do you want now?" Cissy said from behind the chain.

"Thanks for waiting on me, like I asked."

"I never planned on waiting for you."

"Let me in," I said.

"Why would I do that?"

"I need to do a check of the room."

"For what?"

"Just a routine check. That is what they are paying me for."

"There is no way in hell you are coming into my room," her voice was tinged with anger.

"It will only take a minute."

"Screw you," she said and started to shut the door.

I stuck my foot in the door and blocked her from closing it. I gave up on the idea of a room check.

"Are you going out again tonight?" I asked.

"Maybe. Maybe not," she said and looked down at my
foot in the door.

"I need to know if you are going to leave the room
again."

"Then you better plan on sleeping in the hall because
I'm not going to tell you or anybody else when or where I
go or what I do," her voice was getting loud.

A couple came down the hall and stopped to look. I
removed my foot.

"See you in the morning," I said.

"I can't wait," she said and slammed the door shut
hard.

I looked over at the couple. "I just wanted her autograph," I said and smiled at them.

I went down the hall and found my own room. It took
me nearly a full minute to get the key card to work and
beep my way inside. I really miss hotel room keys. The
room was huge and laid out like a suite. A large bathroom
was off to the left of the door and in deeper was a small
living room area with a nice couch, a chair, a desk and a
television. Two large closets framed a short hallway into
a bedroom with a king sized bed and another television
mounted above a nice dresser with two gold lamps. In the
corner of the room was a stainless steel mini-bar stocked
with snacks, soft drinks and even beer. Nice place and I'm

sure a lot better place than the motel out on the highway where the rest of the crew had Minor League rooms with a view of the parking lot and a vending machine at the end of the hall.

I tossed my bag on the bed and emptied stuff out of my pants. I had twenty two cents in my right pocket and my old cell phone in my left. I took the gun off my belt and placed it on the dresser. I turned on the big TV and lay back on the end of the bed with my feet on the floor. A sports show was on the channel that popped up. I muted the sound and rubbed my eyes. I could feel the edge of a headache. I needed to come up with a plan for the night. Plan A was to do what Cissy had suggested. Take a couple of pillows and hang out in the hall near her room to make sure she didn't go anywhere or to keep an eye out if someone else showed up. That would be the prudent move and the safe one. It was also the one they were paying me to do but it was not my first choice. I had another plan. Plan B was to break open the mini-bar, drink a couple of cold beers and watch TV.

I thought it through for a minute and voted unanimously to execute plan B. After being around her tonight I wasn't in the mood to be overly concerned about an underwear thief. Besides from looking at her outfits I'm not sure she even had on any underwear. I pulled myself up and took a cold beer from the mini-bar. I flipped the top off and took a long slow drag. The first swallow went down smooth and sweet. I slumped down in the deep leather chair in the middle room and took a deep breath. It felt nice to relax after what had been a really long day. I took another hit of the cold beer. I closed my eyes and rested my head on the back of the soft chair. That's when the screaming started.

20

THE SCREAMS WERE loud and shrill. Horror movie screams that ran out long and stretched past what seemed even natural. It was the screams of a woman beyond panic. I bounced out the door and into the hallway. The screams were even louder as I ran down the hall. I saw a couple of heads pop out of doors to see what was going on and one man in a red bathrobe stood barefoot outside his door but did not move. The screams stopped for a second and then started back up like a loop on a tape. The door to Cissy's room flung open and banged hard twice against the wall. Feet first and in high heels she was being car-ried kicking and screaming out into the hallway. Her legs pumped like she was on a bike. A man dressed all in black and wearing a ski mask had his arms around her waist and was struggling to get out the door as she grabbed for the door jam.

"Shut the hell up, bitch!" He shouted and pried her hand off the door.

She let out another wail that would get you fired if you were auditioning for a movie. I never slowed down and the man in black never saw me coming as he struggled to get Cissy to let go of the door. I lowered my shoulder and ran hard into the two of them. The force of the impact pushed all three of us back inside the room and we landed in a pile on the floor. The door slammed shut behind us. The room was dark except for the glow of the TV. Cissy continued to scream and kick. I grabbed her by the legs and half pulled, half rolled her into the bathroom and slammed the door. She screamed some more. I felt like telling her to shut the hell up, myself.

The guy in black kicked me hard in the chest from his position on the floor. It surprised me more than it hurt. I rolled up to my knees as he stood and kicked again. This time he missed. I gathered myself and stood to face him in the dark. He did a full spin and kicked again, his leg high and quick, it hit me near my left shoulder and knocked me back into the door. He made a couple of martial arts type motions with his hands and came after me again. I hate that kind of fighting. I especially hate somebody who is good at it. His right leg flew out and just missed my head. Another spin and his left foot came at my chest. I grabbed it with both hands and slowed the force as it bounced off. He wore a pair of combat boots with the toes rimmed by a rounded steel plate. Not very stylish but real nice if you plan on kicking somebody in the head.

I spun him around on one leg but he broke free, reached and grabbed me around the chest and flung me across the desk. Glass bottles, a tall makeup mirror and lamps crashed to the floor as I slid across the top of the desk and knocked over a chair as I hit the floor. I tried to get up but he hit me hard with a gloved fist on the left side of the head and I fell back to the floor. He began another spin but I was tired of being kicked with a steel-toed boot so I reached for the glass makeup mirror and rolled to one side. His kick caught me in the ribs and stung like hell but my roll left him a little off balance. I came up fast and hit him hard as I could over the head with the mirror. It shattered into pieces. The noise he made reminded me of an agitated crow call. At last, a good use of a makeup mirror. I grabbed him by the top of his shoulders and rammed him head first into the TV set on the wall. The TV blinked and shattered with a pop and an electrical spark shot out near his ears. He fell flat and hard on the desk below. His head bounced twice and he hit the floor. I bent over at the waist and clutched my ribs. Housecleaning was not going to be happy with me.

I thought I was done. I was wrong. A huge right arm came out of nowhere and circled itself around my throat. It clamped down on my windpipe like a pipe wrench. There were two guys. I never saw or heard the second one. He clamped his left arm over his right and pushed down hard. I could feel my breath shorten.

"You should have just stayed out of this," he grunted into my ear. "The lady ain't worth it."

At the moment, I had to agree with him but I couldn't speak to let him know. I reached up. He had arms the size of an anaconda. I tried again. Nothing.

The cable attached to the smashed TV gave way and it fell to the desk. It tumbled over and sparks popped out of the broken glass. The noise caused him to glance left and shift his weight. It was my only opening. I shifted with him and raised my right boot and aimed for his foot. I know nothing about fighting techniques but I do know what it feels like to get hit with a fastball on the top of your foot. It hurts like hell and it hurts worse than a fastball to any other part of the body. I slammed my foot down on top of his. It hit the sweet spot. He yelped, cursed, jumped and let go of me. I reached around to grab him. He was a big man. Tall and wide as a bulldozer. I grabbed him around the neck at his ski mask and bent him over. I wrapped both my arms around him and held on like a cowboy trying to wrangle a steer. He bucked, grunted and tried to pull my feet out from under me with his strong hands. There are moments in your life when you wonder just how in the world you ended up where you were and this was certainly one of them. Two big guys doing a death dance in the dark room of a fancy hotel. Where are the TV cameras when you need them?

Cissy burst out of the bathroom door with a scream and one of her six-inch heels in her hand. She began to pound on both of us with a shoe but most of her swings landed on my head and back.

"Stop that and get out of here," I choked out. I could barely speak as we both pulled and tugged at each other. I was losing my grip on the anaconda.

"Go," I grunted as loudly as I could.

The pepper spray hit me square in the face. I let go and fell to the floor. The anaconda kicked me hard as he stepped over me and ran from the room. My eyes were on fire. It felt like I had stuck my head in an open blaze. I coughed hard and stumbled toward the bathroom.

"Why did you do that?" I yelled at her as I splashed water in my eyes.

"I was trying to hit him," her voice high and nervous.

"Well you missed."

"He's getting away!" She screamed.

"Well what would you like me to do about it? You just blinded me."

"Do something!" She shouted at me even louder.

Now she wants me to do something. I wet a towel and rubbed my eyes. That made it worse. I threw more water in my face. I opened my eyes. Everything seemed a blur and the light in the bathroom fuzzy. That is some nasty stuff. I opened a bottle of water from the sink and threw more at my eyes. The big guy had left the door open when he left. I grabbed her by the arm and pulled her out in the hall. I yanked the little thing of pepper spray out of her hand and threw it back in the room. Heads poked out everywhere. The man in the bathrobe had not moved. I could hear sirens in the distance. I stood just outside the door of the room. The kid from earlier with the bags came down the hall at a jog. I motioned for him to come over.

"Stay here with her. Do not let her move, do not let her go, you hear me," I said to him. "The cops will be here in a minute."

He took her by the arm and grinned. I did not have a lot of faith he could handle her.

I pointed a finger at Cissy. "When they get here tell them everything from start to finish and don't leave out the part about nearly blinding me."

I opened the bottle and poured water in my eyes. They still burned. I forgot about my eyes when the legs of the desk chair from the room hit me across the shoulders. I went down in a lump, pain shot all the way to my waist. I heard a gasp from the people in the hall. Cissy screamed again.

"Oh, that dude got you bad, man," the kid said. "You hurt?"

I rolled over and stumbled to my feet. Yeah, I was hurt. Getting hit by a chair will do that to you.

"Where did he go?" I asked the kid.

"He's gone man, down the stairs. That dude's head was bleeding like crazy."

My eyes hurt, my shoulder hurt, my neck hurt, my face hurt, my ribs hurt, and I was really pissed off.

Make A Note: When you recover, plan on having a serious long talk with Catfish about the quality of his offers for gainful employment.

21

THE LIGHTS IN the hallway looked fuzzy and blurred as I stumbled toward the stairs. It was hard to see with my eyes on fire. I banged my shoulder hard on the side of the door as I started downstairs. I wasn't really sure where I was headed or what I was going to do when I got there. I couldn't see. I didn't have a weapon. I had no idea where the two guys had gone. Maybe I just wanted to get away from Cissy.

The emergency exit door at the bottom of the stairs had been breached. The sound of the alarm blasted against the concrete stairwell and made my head hurt even more. I slipped out the door and into the parking lot at the rear of the hotel. Red and blue lights swirled in a pattern down the driveway toward the lot and bounced off the cars. At the head of the drive a police car with an open passenger door blocked the lane. In the rear of the lot I spotted a blur of white lights and thought for a moment it might be the guys from inside. I wasn't sure because right now I couldn't tell Fred Astaire from Fred Flintstone with my eyes this screwed up. I strained to focus and saw flash-lights being held up high by one hand and moved about the way cops would do it. I decided to leave them to it as I could hear more sirens on the way.

I spotted a gate that led through a high wooden fence around the parking lot. I eased through it and emerged into an alley behind the row of bars and restaurants that fronted the busy street we had driven earlier. Had to guess this was the only route out for them. I started down the alley to see where it led. I rubbed my eyes with my sleeve to stop the burning. It only made it worse. I finished off the last bit of water in the bottle but it didn't help much.

I stopped short when I heard the sound of metal on metal. I squinted to see a figure working under a bare bulb that hung off a wooden porch. A skinny fellow stood just beyond the back door of what I guessed might be a bar. He wore a long white apron and had a water hose aimed at the inside of a beer keg. It rattled with noise as he rammed the hose down inside. His long gray hair was pulled back into a ponytail and a cigarette jumped and bounced in the right side of his mouth. He looked up without expression when I approached him.

"Can I borrow that hose for second?" I asked.

He released the handle and handed it to me. I bent over at the waist and began to drench my head with the cold water. I let it run slowly down over my eyes. I twisted the knob to make it a soft spray and turned it up and directly into my face, holding it there for a good sixty seconds. It was cold and I drenched my clothes but for the first time the pain eased up and my eyes began to clear a bit.

The fellow handed me a dirty dishtowel and I wiped my hair and head with it, careful not to rub the eyes again.

"Thanks," I said. "I just needed some relief."

"Don't we all," he said, in a voice that thumped deep like a bass guitar. "Need a hit?"

The cigarette was a joint and he flipped it around in his hand and offered it to me. I waved him off.

"You been out here long?" I asked him.

"Nope."

"You see anything odd back here in the last few minutes?"

"Like a guy with red fish eyes hosing himself down?" He smiled and showed off several broken teeth.

"Well, there is that," I said.

He took the hose and stuck it back down inside the beer keg.

"You didn't happen to see two guys dressed in black come down this way, did you?"

"Nope."

I had guessed wrong. They must have headed off in another direction. At least I had found some water to help my eyes.

"Just the one," his voice plunked out.

"One what?"

"You said two. There was just one guy dressed in black that just come by here."

"You saw a guy like that come by here? When?"

"Right before you showed up."

"Did you get a good look at his face?"

"Hard to tell."

"Why?"

"His head was covered in blood."

"And you didn't think that was odd?"

"On a football weekend in this town?" He coughed out a laugh. "That ain't even close to what I would call odd."

"Where does this alley go?"

"Dead ends into another alley but that one comes out on the street down there a bit," he pointed about a hundred yards past where we stood.

"Thanks, that helps."

"This fellow a friend of yours?" He asked.

"No."

"He the one who messed up your face?"

"No, some lady did that."

"And you ain't looking for her?"

"No, just the two guys in black that I mentioned."

"Now, that my friend is what I would call a bit odd," his voice rumbled as he went back to his work.

I headed in the direction he noted. Nobody was in sight. I could hear music and laughter inside some of the places but the alley was dark and empty. I hit the spot where it dead-ended into the side of a brick wall. To the right I could see where the tiny sliver of an alley intersected with the street as cars crawled up a hill in traffic. To the left the alley ran into complete darkness and appeared to end at maybe a fence. I couldn't tell. A dirty trash dumpster with the lid open partially blocked the view so I headed further up the dark alley to get a look. It was so dark that I had to take my time as I moved step by step toward the end of the alley. No street lights back here. I was beginning to think I had run into an actual dead end and lost them for sure.

I froze in my tracks when I thought I saw some sort of movement ahead of me. I couldn't be sure if my eyes were still playing tricks on me. It was just a sense of movement, a reflection, a small flash and then it was gone. I stood still and listened. Nothing. Music way in the distance. I thought maybe it was just a flicker of light from some-where else. I strained my eyes to see what was ahead of me. Nothing. I released my breath and took a few more steps forward.

The lights hit hard and blinded me in a flash. The sound of a car engine followed and the roar bounced off the narrow walls and swallowed me up. With a heavy clunk and rumble the lights came at me. I turned and ran, pain shooting through my legs as I tried to make it back to the corner. The car shifted and picked up speed. A power-ful engine, a muscle car and it closed fast. No way I was going to outrun it. In times of panic you are taught to react with training. The only training, I ever had was as a professional athlete, and one of the things they teach you in professional sports is that during the heat of the game you don't think, you just react to the moment and let your instincts take over. I was two feet away from the trash dumpster and the car was ten feet behind me and closing in. Instincts took over. I grabbed at the edge of the dumpster with one hand, then the other and flipped myself in the air and landed with a plop in the bags of trash. The sound of metal scraped across the dumpster. My bones shook with the harsh metallic sound. The car banged hard into the side and shoved the heavy dumpster into a wall with a thud. The impact tossed me across the loose trash and my left knee hit the side hard. I might have screamed but I wasn't sure.

The car bounced beyond it, stopped hard and skidded. I tried to gather myself in the mess expecting them to come after me. I heard somebody yelling. I thought it was coming from the car but I realized it was coming from behind me. Somebody was yelling, 'My car. That's my car.' The pop of a small caliber pistol to my left. Then one more. Then a burst of reply from an automatic weapon from the opposite direction. Six, seven shots maybe more. 'Sonaofbitch!' The voice in the dark yelled. Another burst of shots rang out, a couple of them hit the dumpster and sparks kicked up above me in the dark. I flattened out into the trash head down. Tires spun on the pavement, a door slammed and the engine roared to life. Seconds later I heard another huge crash, then another. Horns blasted. The engine roared again and then moved away. The voice moved away toward the street cussing all the way. I heard more horns up the hill, maybe another scrape of metal, then the car was gone.

I eased up to the top of the trash dumpster, my hand slipped in a box of left over pizza. I peered over the edge and saw people in the street along with two damaged cars. I could see a big guy in a tight T-shirt with a small gun in his hand. He was pointing up the hill and waving his other hand in the air. The police would be here quick and there was no reason being around when they came up the alley or for that matter when the guy whose car was just stolen came back. I crawled to the rear of the dumpster and rolled myself out. I had to assume the guys in the car were the two from the hotel but I had no proof. It didn't really matter now. They were long gone and that was fine with me, at the moment.

I headed back up the first alley. My pants were torn in two places, my clothes were wet, I was covered in old pizza sauce and it had started to rain. I limped from the pain in my left knee that had banged the side of the dumpster. The good news was the pain in the knee made me forget the pain in my ribs for the moment. I passed the open back door of a bar and from inside came a football battle cry as the crowd yelled, *Gooooooooooo...DAWGS!* And then they barked loudly. More people came back with the retort, *Rooooooooool TIDE!* A bell sounded and laughter poured out into the alley.

I limped along. I knew very little and understood less. About fifteen minutes earlier I was in a comfortable chair in a nice hotel sipping on a cold beer. At this point I had no idea what the hell was going on. I didn't know much but I was absolutely sure of one thing. This was my first time ever at a college football weekend. I was damn sure it would be my last.

22

I T WAS NEARLY eleven o'clock, three hours after we left the stadium. I sat under a small blue tent that was attached to the rear of an Athens Police van. A soft light rain fell and played a steady tune on top of the tent. The van was parked on the sidewalk across from *The Dogwood* now surrounded by a haphazard ring of patrol cars, a K-9 unit, an ambulance and even a fire engine rumbled nearby. No more sirens, just the crackle of radio traffic and a slow circular dance of red, blue and white lights.

Down the hill a row of TV news trucks lined up and stuck their tall poles in the air. Behind yellow crime scene tape the reporters stood in front of bright lights and waited their turn to tell everybody about the latest news on Cissy.

A young paramedic had checked me out. He washed my eyes out good with a solution. He got a few cold packs and helped me wrap them where needed most. He offered up five small packets of pain medication. His instructions were to take only one packet now and space the rest out over the next 24 hours. Right. I opened and swallowed three of the packets as soon as he left. Now if I only had a beer to wash them down.

Major Jay Clark was at the hotel when I returned. He made sure the media didn't know who I was and moved me over to where I sat now. I told him all I knew.

I had almost nodded off in an upright position when I heard a familiar voice. A familiar laugh. Just down the way I spotted him. Catfish. He had his arm around the shoulder of an older cop and they were posing while a young female cop took a picture with her phone. Catfish is one of the few people known well enough around Athens to be recognized at a crime scene. He had changed back to his regular outfit. Blue denim shirt, khakis, boat shoes and no socks topped off tonight with a red rain parka. Over his right shoulder he had a square nylon bag of some sort with a Georgia Bulldog logo. He rolled his way up the hill with his normal limp and plopped down the bag.

"The rumors of your demise have been greatly exaggerated," he said.

"But not by much," I answered.

"You good?"

"I will be."

I held up the packets of pain meds the kid had given me. He took one, looked at it and handed it back.

"Ain't sure 'bout them eyes though, son," he leaned in to look. "You look like a raccoon that got in a fight with a bobcat and lost."

"What exactly are you doing here, Catfish?"

"I got a 911 text from Clark," he said. "Told me the fellow I hired to keep an eye on Cissy was blind as a preacher at a strip joint and I should get my butt over here and check on him."

"My eyes will be fine. You want the details of why I was blind?"

"Already know."

"Course you do. Not going to ask how you know."

"I am, if nothing else, always well informed."

"That you are."

"Your little adventure did however interrupt me at the worst possible time."

"It did?"

"I was smack dab in the middle of the story 'bout the time in college when the whole offensive line decided to get naked and streak right through a women's swim meet when I got the text."

"Good story," I noted, having heard it a few times before.

"Damn good story."

"Then you got the text."

"Ruined my story."

"Ruined my night."

"Where's Clark?"

"Across the street," I pointed. "Told me to stay here and wait to talk to the guy in charge."

"Where's Cissy?"

"I have no idea."

"So, let's summarize all this mess," Catfish said as he pulled off his rain parka. "I get you a cushy job watching this Cissy lady and in less than a half day you manage to get yourself beat up, blinded by the person you supposed to be protecting and then you let the two guys who beat you up get away. I got it all summed up 'bout, right?"

"Left out the part where I nearly got run over and shot."

"Yeah, I forgot that. Let's add that in."

"The key word in all of that is two. As in two guys against one."

"Hell, that ain't nothing," Catfish barked out. "When I was playing, I took on two guys every day at practice and twice on Saturday. One guy blocking two guys is the key. Can't have a running game without it. I had to handle two big guys damn near all the time."

"How much you had to drink tonight?" I asked.

"How many of them little pills you done took?"

He grinned and reached over to open the square nylon bag next to him. He pulled out a bag of chips and two large round items wrapped in tinfoil. He handed one to me. I opened it. It was a huge cheeseburger. It was still hot.

"Hot on one side, ice on the other," he said and stuck his big hand down inside the Bulldog bag. I heard the stir of ice and the clink of glass. He pulled out a tall longneck beer in a bottle, wet and cold. I could have kissed him on the lips.

"Ain't it dangerous to mix all them pills with alcohol?" He asked me as I took a huge gulp.

"That's what they tell me," I said and dug into the cheeseburger.

He tore open the bag of chips and we each grabbed a handful.

"But not nearly as dangerous as being run over in an alley," I added.

"To danger," he said and held up his bottle.

"To Cissy," I replied and clinked bottles with him.

"To cold beer."

"To cheeseburgers and well placed trash dumpsters."

"To blocking two guys at one time."

"To a good running game."

"Go Dogs," he said with his mouth full.

23

MAJOR CLARK HAD to duck his head to come under the tent. The short fellow with him made it under with an open umbrella and room to spare. Clark nodded at Catfish. He expected him to be here. The short man did not and eyed him warily. The short man shook the rain off his umbrella and ran both hands through his dark crew cut. He unbuttoned his suit jacket to reveal a shoulder holster and a badge on his belt. He did it to let me know he was the man in charge.

"Feeling better?" Clark asked as he looked down at the empty beer bottles.

"Just putting out fires," I said.

"Looks more like getting drunk before talking to the lead investigator," the short man said.

Clark shot him a look and then swallowed it. I could see him take a deep breath and glance at Catfish.

"This is Detective Stacy Lumpkin of the Athens Police Department. He needs to ask Jake some questions about tonight."

"They name you after your mama?" Catfish asked. He was more than a little bit toasted by now.

"Who are you?" Stacy asked.

"Name is Catfish, which is a damn sight better name than Stacy."

"You know this man?" The detective asked me.

"He's my legal advisor," I answered.

"Legal advisor?"

"Or spiritual advisor, I forget which one."

The detective rubbed the back of his neck with one hand and pulled a small notebook out of his inside coat pocket with the other.

"This is Bobby 'Catfish' Wilson," Clark said to Detective Lumpkin. "He's here at my request."

"Why?" Lumpkin asked.

"Because I asked him to come," Clark said. "How long have you been working in Athens?"

"Just under six months," he replied.

"That explains it," Clark said. "Take some time and ask around about Mr. Wilson. You might be surprised what you find."

"I don't care who he is. I need to question Mr. Eliam about his activities tonight and I need to do it in private."

"I'm not going anywhere," Clark said. "Mr. Eliam works for me."

"A spiritual advisor never leaves his flock in a time of need," Catfish said.

We all were silent for a moment. The rain picked up a bit and trickled down the side of the tent.

"Ask away," I said. "You got about another half hour before these pain pills turn me into Forest Gump."

He scribbled notes and only lifted his head every now and then as I ran through it all once again. This time I started back at the tailgate shoot to fill in some background on Cissy. I picked it up on the ride over here and mentioned the fifteen bucks in tips I laid out. I thought it might make me look a little better to him. It didn't. I ran down the fight with the two guys, the alley chase and ended up with the dumpster story. He wrote it all down in his little notebook.

"Why do you think she hit you in the face with the spray and not the intruder?" He asked me.

Catfish laughed and ducked his head. Detective Stacy Lumpkin glared at him.

"That is a damn good question detective," I said. "Did you ask her?"

"I did."

"And?"

"She said she was doing everything she could in the confusion to help because you were getting your ass kicked."

"She did?"

"She did. She also said you didn't check her room on arrival. Said you weren't at your post outside her door and she also said you told her on the ride over that you didn't like her very much. That all true?"

"The last part about not liking her very much," I said. "I confess to that. Write that down."

Clark's phone rang and he stepped away to answer it. Stacy glared at me.

"Interview is over," Clark said to Lumpkin as he clicked off his phone.

"Not till I say so," Lumpkin replied.

"Not your call, anymore. That was my boss on the phone. This is now a state case. A state case with UGA as the secondary. Give your notes to my officer, take your pretty little umbrella and get your ass out of here. Clear out your men while you're at it."

"Politics, right? The big bad university pulling rank on the local cops?"

"Could be. Could be they just wanted smarter cops running the show."

"Or taller ones," Catfish added.

"You're going to regret this."

"No, I'm not," Clark said.

Detective Stacy Lumpkin took his umbrella and walked out into the rain.

"Say hey to your wife Marvin for us," Catfish yelled after him.

"Thanks, thanks a lot," I said to Major Clark.

"Careful what you thank me for. From what the boss said the GBI is not real happy to be dealing with this mess."

"Sorry I let this turn into such a mess," I said to him. "I thought I had the last guy for sure and that would have made things a lot simpler if we could have talked with him."

"Well, it was two guys," Clark said.

"According to Catfish I should be able to take on two guys with no problem."

"Yeah? He said that?" He looked over at Catfish. "Well, if telling tall tales was a job he would be the richest man in the state of Georgia."

"It's getting damn late," Catfish said. "Big game tomorrow. I need some sleep."

"Speaking of sleep," I said. "Can I go back to my room now and get some as well?"

"Afraid not," Clark said. "Your room is booked."

"Booked?"

"Cissy is in your room."

"What?"

"While you were getting your ass kicked you tore down the door to her room. It's also a crime scene and the hotel is full, so you're out of luck."

"So, what do I do?"

"My guys will keep an eye on Cissy for the night. You can bunk at our building, clean up there. We got a good overnight locker room and beds."

"Sounds great," Catfish said. "Breakfast is on me. I'm gonna take you to a little hidden joint nobody knows 'bout but the locals. Run by a lady named Maybellene. Good eating and I want you to meet a friend of mine from my playing days."

"What about following Cissy around tomorrow?" I asked both of them.

"I'll figure that out and talk to you then. I'll have a car take you back over to our place."

He took a little radio off his belt and spoke into it. He motioned for a young UGA officer to join us.

"I almost forgot," he said.

The young man handed him my duffel and a large plastic yellow bag with *Evidence* written in black in large letters. He handed it to me.

"From the room you did have," Clark said. "Your gun, your wallet and twenty two cents in change. Wouldn't want you to lose all your cash."

"Thanks," I said.

"You owe the hotel mini-bar nine dollars for the beer."

24

IT WAS JUST before seven in the morning. A long hot shower, three bags of ice, two more packets of pain pills, three hours sleep and I felt like a new man. At least that was the lie I told myself. Major Clark checked in on me before he headed to the stadium. I don't think he had slept at all but he still looked spit-shined and polished. He told me one of his officers would take me over to meet Catfish for breakfast.

The officer was in uniform but was headed home after the overnight shift. Her nameplate said Corporal Breedlove. She asked that I call her Sally as we crawled into her truck.

"The Major says you're going to meet Bobby Wilson for breakfast," she said as we pulled out of the parking lot.

"You know him?"

"Catfish? Can't live long in this town without knowing him or knowing about him."

"I'm learning that."

"Did you play football here at Georgia?"

"No, first time here."

"Today is going to be really crazy with Alabama in town."

"I'm learning that too," I said.

She shifted gears and turned out onto a main road. She was tall and slender and when she reached for the gearshift I could see the edge of a tattoo that ran under her uniform sleeve and up her right arm.

"Where are you meeting him?"

"I should call him to check. All he told me was that it is a place where the locals eat and it was run by a lady named Maybellene."

She let out a small laugh. "Got it."

"You know the place he is talking about?"

"It's called *The Rising Sun* but you won't find it on any Google map."

"Is that why he said only the locals know about this place?"

"One of the reasons."

"Ever been there?" I asked her.

"Few times when I was working for the Sheriffs' department."

"So, cops hang out there?"

"On occasion," she said. She smiled and it turned into a small laugh.

"I say something funny?"

"Think about it cowboy," she said. "Off the map, no signs, tucked away where only locals go. Rising Sun, as in *The House of The Rising Sun*."

I looked at her with a blank stare. She raised her eyebrows back at me with a question mark.

"The place used to be a whorehouse?"

"Not used to be," she said. "Still is."

"Catfish is taking me to a whorehouse for breakfast?"

"Maybellene takes care of business at night and biscuits in the morning."

"So, it's both?"

"Hooking and cooking," she said with a grin.

She left the main road and turned back into a neighborhood filled with old homes and scattered small buildings. A few more turns and she stopped in front of a two-story red wood house. It had a four-column front porch and a large front yard. The yard was neat and anchored by a tall magnolia tree. A dirt driveway ran down the right side of the lot and a dozen or so cars and trucks were parked on the grass. I couldn't see any people and no sign that it was anything but an old house.

"This is the place?" I asked.

"You expecting the House of Pancakes?"

I opened the door and got out with my bag in hand.

"Just go through the front door and they'll lead you back. They serve breakfast on the screen porch in the rear. Don't worry. Upstairs closes down long before breakfast." She waved and pulled away.

I opened the front door and was surprised to find a large front room decorated with antique furniture and ornate paintings on the wall. I told a young lady seated behind a large wooden desk my name and that I was meeting some people for breakfast. She led me down a hallway and out to the large screened porch. It had smaller tables around the edge and one long table in the middle. Over in the right corner I spotted Catfish and Alex. A large woman in high heels and a bright purple dress was next to him with her hand on his shoulder. I walked over to join them.

The lady in high heels stopped in mid-sentence when I approached the table.

"Goodness gracious, sugar pie," her voice dripped like honey from a spoon. "What in the blue blazes happened to your face?"

Alex nearly snorted. Catfish pushed his chair back and stood up.

"You should have seen him last night, Maybellene," he said. "Hell, he looks like George Clooney now compared to a few hours ago."

"So, you the poor fellow they been telling me about?" She said. "Have a seat, baby, and we'll fix you right up. I'll have you percolating like a hot pot in no time."

I was a little afraid of what that might really mean. I took a seat next to Alex. Catfish looked ready to roll. Dressed the same as always and not a red eye to be found. The man could drink like a fish and bounce back like a shark. Alex took her hand and turned my face toward her.

"You look like hell," she said with a smile. "Good to see you earning some of that money."

"Can I please get some coffee," I said to nobody in particular.

"I filled Alex in on what happened last night with Cissy," Catfish said.

"I'm sure you did."

"Twice," Alex said.

"Twice?"

"I made him tell me twice," she said. "I was laughing too hard the first time."

I wanted to change the subject. "Can I ask you a question?" I said to Catfish.

"Shoot," he said.

"Why are we having breakfast in a whorehouse?"

"Ain't a whorehouse right now. It's Maybellene's breakfast place."

"*The Rising Sun,*" I said.

"That is correct."

"Get the pancakes," Alex said as she looked at the hand written menu. "She says they are huge."

"This place is a local legend. Maybellene's aunt used to run the place when I was in school. We would come over here all the time."

"To eat breakfast?" I asked.

"To eat and then the other times we tried, but failed."

"Failed?"

"Coach knew we would try so he paid this fellow that worked here to run us off. Name was Moody and he'd chase us off with a broom or a pickaxe."

"A pickaxe?"

"Coach paid him well."

"Breakfast in a cathouse."

"Good food, good people and look around, not a dang Alabama fan nowhere in sight."

"When is your friend getting here?" Alex asked. "I'm hungry."

"Dumptruck will be here soon. Tends to stay out late drinking the night before the game."

"His name is Dumptruck?" I said.

"Well his driver's license might say different but as far as everybody else knows, just Dumptruck."

Our attention was diverted when a loud booming voice broke through the breakfast talk like fireworks.

"Let the big dog eat!" The voice boomed as heads turned to see what was going on.

"Let the big dog eat!" Catfish boomed back as he jumped from his chair and rushed to meet the voice face to face and then chest to chest with a thud.

The booming voice belonged to a man who could pass for a human fireplug. He was just under six feet tall but rounded off on all sides. Had a barrel chest, thick thighs, thin waist, arms that bulged from a tight shirt and a head that was slick as a bowling ball. His face wore the deep wrinkles of someone who had spent years in the sun and was framed down the chin by a thin gray beard and a light goatee. His large nose tilted off to the right and his eyes were white around the edges most likely from wearing the sunglasses that hung around his neck.

Catfish and the man both began to pound on their chest with open palms. The beat and noise grew faster and faster. They started in a low growl, *'Goooooooooooooooo'* and built to a finish. *'GO DAWGS!'* They bumped chest again and began barking out *'woofs'* and the whole room joined in. It was quite a sight. Some people reached for their cell phones to record the show. They finished up with a bear hug and Catfish rubbed his big hands over the slick head of the fireplug.

"Dumptruck, I presume?" Alex said to me.

"You just never know what you might see when you decide to have breakfast at a whorehouse."

25

THE PANCAKES WERE, indeed, huge. So big they covered the plate and syrup rolled off onto the table. I knew I could never come close to finishing them but Alex was already halfway through her plate. Catfish was on his second round and Dumptruck carved on a large plate of steak and eggs with a big hunting knife.

"So, you two played at the same time?" Alex asked as she reached over and took part of my pancakes.

"This guy was the toughest damn fullback I ever played with," Catfish said.

"Had to be tough," Dumptruck said. "Running that veer like we did all I ever got to do was run head on into guys twice my size every dang play."

"Remember when Danny, Danny was our quarterback," he said to us and then turned back to Dumptruck. "Danny had to tell you to shut up and stop growling in the huddle so he could call the play?"

"You gotta play mean."

Catfish pointed to Dumptruck. "This man played in the pros. Four years in the pros."

"CFL not NFL and it was five years."

"Pardon me, five years. I do apologize."

Dumptruck stabbed at the steak with his knife.

"Then he boxed in Vegas."

"Tried to box in Vegas, ended up as a bouncer at strip joints."

"Till you stole the girl of some goomba."

"Elvis had to leave the building," he looked up and smiled between bites.

"Then on to Texas and became a rodeo clown," Catfish said as he stuck an entire biscuit in his mouth.

"That lasted about an hour. Them bulls are some damn mean suckers."

"Arkansas was next, right?"

"We don't talk about Arkansas."

"Right, I forgot."

"Then I discovered Florida. Taught myself to fly crop dusters down there. Loved that."

"Till you crashed."

"Got fired the third time I crashed."

"Then you became a sponge head."

"A what?" Alex interrupted the flow and plucked another of my pancakes off the plate.

"Tarpon Springs is known for sponges. Sea sponges. The Greeks used to harvest them long ago. It's a tourist thing now. I went to work on the sponge boat tours. Then I got my own boat."

"Tell them how you got your boat," Catfish said.

"Won it."

"Tell 'em how."

"Man bet me I wouldn't jump off the town's water tower head first into the bay. He lost."

"And you became a boat captain," Catfish grinned.

"I quickly named her *Hard Head*," Dumptruck said with his mouth full.

Make A Note: A man that will dive head first off a water tower to win a bet but won't say what happened in Arkansas, is a man best left to his secrets.

Alex finished off the last of her pancakes and mine. She had another question.

"So, how is it that they call you Dumptruck?" She asked.

I wasn't so sure that was a question I wanted answered.

"Was it from football?" She persisted.

"Yes and no," he said and looked over at Catfish.

"Spring practice our third year and we were busting out butts everyday. Come Friday night we were ready to let loose and party," Catfish started up.

"This frat house was having a big ass fancy pool party that night and we showed up."

"They had a sign on the porch," Catfish said. "*NO JOCKS ALLOWED.* Pissed us off."

"They didn't allow football players at a party?" Alex asked.

"It could have been about homecoming," Catfish answered.

"They had a float in the parade. Tissue paper and crap. Frat guys on the float were dressed like they were football players. Had uniforms like ours and everything."

"We didn't take too kindly to that."

"We set the dang thing on fire in the middle of the parade," Dumptruck grinned. "Went up like a weenie roast on the Fourth of July."

"Made the news."

"Made the yearbook."

"Got us in a heap of trouble," Catfish said. "Ran those damn stadium steps for weeks."

Dumptruck pointed his fork at us.

"So that night we decided then and there to finish it with those weak ass frat boys."

"Dumptruck here grew up around his daddy's construction business up in Eastanollee. Knew all about big machinery, graders and such."

"I was driving a front end loader when I was knee high to a bullfrog," he said.

"So, we drove over to where the college was building some new dorms. We broke in and my boy here hot wired the biggest damn dump truck on the site."

"Then we went over to the Ag Farm and loaded that sucker up full," Dumptruck said.

"Loaded it up with what?" Alex asked.

"University of Georgia certified recycled vegetation," Catfish answered.

"Recycled vegetation?" Alex asked. "Recycled how?"

"Through a cow," Catfish said with a big grin.

"Twenty five thousand pounds of steaming hot cow manure," Dumptruck said proudly.

"We went down fraternity row with that big truck and drove right across that frat house yard. Ran it right through a dozen or so tables, a transom with flowers, two huge stereo speakers, a row of beer kegs and two charcoal grills."

"I backed that bad boy right up to the edge of the swimming pool, hit the hydraulic ram lever and the load poured right out into the deep end of the water."

"Should have seen the steam rising when the manure hit the water," Catfish laughed.

"Girls were screaming and running. My boys were all hanging off the side swinging shovels and rakes at the drunken frat boys and I drove the hell out of there with the bed still up. Took out tree limbs and a bunch of power lines. Best night of my whole time at Georgia."

"A legend was born and ever since that night this man has been known as just Dumptruck."

"Hellava night."

"Hellava man," Catfish made a toast with his coffee cup.

I looked over at Alex. "And you just had to ask, didn't you?"

Catfish's phone buzzed on the table. He picked it up. He listened for a bit, then chuckled.

"We gotta get going," he said to all of us as he hung up.

"Where?" I said.

"Press conference at BTSN," he said. "And you don't want to be late."

"Why?"

"Because it appears you are item number one on the agenda."

"Me? Why?" I asked.

"Seems Billy Ray Kincaid is going to blame you for everything that went down last night."

"Are you serious?"

"Want me to go get another truck?" Dumptruck asked.

26

WE WENT BY the RV to check on Chance and let Alex
pick up her gear. Dumptruck spotted the breakfast bar and beer kegs being rolled out and opted out
of the press conference. The event was scheduled at the
TV compound but due to the large turnout of media it
had been moved into a lecture hall in the Student Center.
From a back hallway, we could see the crowd through a
window in the doors and tell that it was already underway.
The room had rows of tiered seats that rose to a walkway
high in the rear. The seats were already full of media and
other officials. Cameras lined up in a long row across the
back, inches between each one. In the middle of the pack
I spotted Shaky. He leaned down into his camera and let
out a big yawn. He most likely got about as much sleep as
I did last night. Newspaper photographers with cameras
held to their eye sat on the floor down front. A long table
was set up on an elevated stage and a BTSN banner hung
across the front. The network logo also spun in a loop on
a video screen in the rear.

On the stage with a microphone in front of each were Boo, Billy Ray and Cissy. Boo was doing the talking for now and seemed to be speaking about the network and ratings and such. Kincaid had a huge unlit cigar in his mouth and Cissy sat with her head down.

"Damnation," Catfish said. "There's more cameras here than when we hired the new football coach."

"He doesn't have the legs that Cissy has," Alex noted.

"And nobody is out to kill him," I said.

"Not if we beat Alabama today," Catfish replied.

Boo finished up and introduced Kincaid who took over and began with a joke about ESPN being there to cover him for a change. The officials down front laughed along with him. He finished the joke and rolled the big cigar around in his mouth and then took it out with a flourish. He was dressed down today. A white polo shirt buttoned at the top under a maroon blazer. Black silk slacks, penny loafers and dark red socks.

"Watch my other gear," Alex said to me. "I better get in there."

"You shooting this?"

"Some people earn what they are paid, even if they aren't paid as much as they should," she said and pushed through the door. Don't think I was going to hear the end of this matter for a while.

A few jokes later Billy Ray got down to business about last night.

"Today we are quite fortunate not to be here talking about a tragedy. Last night one of our BTSN family had to

endure a horrific assault at a downtown hotel. We are so proud of Cissy and her heroic and brave efforts to fend off the cowardly thugs who tried to do her harm."

"Brave and heroic?" I said to Catfish. "What is he talking about?"

"Think he is planting what I would call a seed of exaggeration."

"When confronted with danger she did not run, she did not cower. She fought back hard and did not give into danger. She stood her ground and fought back."

"I don't remember that part," I said.

"Maybe he's talking 'bout her squirting that crap in your eyes."

"While we are glad she is safe, we must address the failings of the security provided by the University of Georgia Police Department and Major Jay Clark. We have since found out that the person assigned to guard Cissy last night, one Jay Ellis, was not an employee of the police force and in fact doesn't even do this on a full time basis. They provided Cissy with a rank amateur. He was rude to our employee, failed to even check her room as required, was not at his post when the assault occurred and did not have his weapon with him when he eventually responded. There were also indications that he was drinking on the job. This is unacceptable and we plan to address it with our lawyers. In the future, you can rest assured that Cissy will be guarded on a 24-hour basis by my own agency, HOT LZ Security, a professional unit staffed by former military special operators and we will

no longer leave her safety in the hands of an unqualified security guard."

"Now I'm a security guard."

"A drunken security guard," Catfish noted.

"Without a uniform," I noted.

"He got your name wrong."

"That's a good thing."

"Yeah, but damn shame you finally get a chance to get mentioned on ESPN and they screw up your name."

Billy Ray turned the microphone over to Cissy and you could see the cameras come to attention and the people shift in their seats. She looked up and held a long pose right into the cameras. She had her long blonde hair pulled back in a ponytail and wore a pretty conservative top, for her. You could hear the clicks of the cameras down front as she sat silent. Then a small tear formed in her left eye and rolled down her cheek. The camera operators were locked into their viewfinders. A full minute passed before she spoke.

"I'm sorry. I thought I could come here today and talk about this but I can't. I just want to get back to work and cover this game. I will continue to do the job I love. I will not be scared into hiding…. I'm sorry…I'm so sorry…I can't talk anymore."

She wiped at the tears, pushed back her chair and left the stage. She headed toward the door where we stood. The door pushed me back as she charged through it. She stopped short when she saw me. The tears made a very quick twist to a scowl.

"Get out of my way, fool," she said and wiped her face dry.

"Thanks for saving my butt last night," I said.

She flipped me the middle finger and headed off down the hall.

Alex came through the door and watched Cissy rush away. She looked at me.

"Hey Jay," she said. "Cissy turn you down for the prom?"

"Did you get a close up of those tears?" Catfish asked.

"I did. That girl is good," she said. "Crazy like a fox, but really good."

Jay Clark came down the hall and joined us.

"They get your name wrong but mine they get right," he said.

"Sorry about that."

"I can handle it and him."

On that note Billy Ray burst through the door with a big laugh. He saw us all and his chest seemed to puff out even more. He turned and tilted his big head to the right.

"Well, if ain't Booby with Butch and The Sundance Kid," he said making fun of Catfish's real name.

None of us spoke. He squared up and turned his attention to me.

"You just might be one of the biggest dang screw ups I have ever met but I want to thank you."

"For what?" I asked.

"Did you see the cameras in there? Hell boy, the dadgum coach of frigging Notre Dame don't get that many to show up for a press conference. After Cissy hits the air today the ratings gonna shoot right through the damn roof and I'll be wallowing around in a big ol' pile of green money."

"You do realize somebody actually attacked her?" I said. "That doesn't worry you?"

"Not anymore," he said. "My boys are here now and they are locked and loaded. You can stand down."

"Your boys, as you call them," Clark spoke firmly. "Will not be allowed to carry weapons anywhere on this campus."

Billy Ray looked at him. Stuck the cigar in his mouth and made a crooked smile.

"That's a damn shame," he said. "Spent a fortune arming those boys."

Clark shifted his weight. Catfish stepped forward. "Billy Ray, are you really so damn greedy that you would let something happen to that girl just to make a buck?" Catfish asked him.

"I'm so greedy I'd sell the shoes off my Grandma's feet if somebody made me an offer," he grinned.

"Oh, you've done way worse than that," Catfish said. "I've seen it up close."

"Well, if you're waiting for me to give a good crap," he said as his smiled faded. "Then pack a lunch fat boy, because it's gonna be a long wait."

"A lot of people trusted you through the years."

"That's their own fault," Billy Ray said.

"They trusted you and you turned their lives upside down," Catfish countered.

"Damn right," he said. "Trust is the key word. They should have known better. You can't trust people. I don't trust nobody. Never have. Never trusted a damn lawyer, business partner, a woman for sure and sometimes I have lost trust in the Lord himself but I tell you what, the one thing I ain't never lost trust in is the power of money. Money don't talk back, don't try and sue you, never complains and never lets you down."

He let out another laugh and turned to walk away. He stopped for a beat and lit up the huge cigar. He took a few puffs and blew out a stream of smoke. He turned back toward us and pointed at Clark.

"Send a Brinks truck my way later today and make sure they got plenty of room," he laughed out loud.

He blew out a perfect smoke ring and looked at Catfish.

"Roll Tide," he said and winked.

We all stood and watched him walk down the hall and clang his way out the exit.

"I never understood exactly what Roll Tide means," Alex said to all of us.

"I still don't understand why they have an elephant as a mascot," I said.

"I've never understood anything about Alabama," Catfish concluded.

"Except that they always seem to have the best team money can buy," Major Clark said.

"Ain't that the truth," Catfish agreed.

I turned to Jay Clark. "I guess I am now officially relieved of my duties?"

"Afraid not," he said.

"No?"

"Don't care how you do it but figure out a way to keep an eye on her till she is good and gone."

"She might object."

"Sure, she will, but it's not my call. This comes from above."

"Your bosses?"

"Bigger than that. Matter of fact, the guy now in charge of this whole case wants to talk to you."

"Okay," I said. "Always good to speak to the top guy."

"I wouldn't be too sure about that," Clark said with a smile.

27

I DIDN'T RECOGNIZE HIM at first because of the outfit. It was odd and would have been way out of line anywhere except at a college football game. Then he spoke.

"I thought it couldn't be true," his voice sounded like sandpaper on wood. "But I was wrong."

"Hey, Captain," I said with a smile, "The GBI get a new dress code?"

"There is no such thing as Captain in the GBI," he growled.

"Then why have I been calling you Captain for the last few years?"

"Good question," he said. Major Clark looked at the two of us and smiled.

"You already know Special Agent Nick Allen, the northern Section Chief of the GBI," he said.

"So, when you make Section Chief you get to wear this outfit?" I asked.

Allen had on a sweater that was split right down the middle with two different designs. One side had red and black stripes and the other had maroon and white stripes. The left side said *UGA* and the right side just *'BAMA*. Across both sides it said *A House Divided*. I had never seen anything like it.

"This outfit, as you call it," he said. "Is because I went to Georgia, my wife went to Alabama and I have one kid here at UGA and another is over at Tuscaloosa."

"And why are you wearing it at work?"

"Because I wasn't at work. I was here like everybody else. Standing behind a grill cooking up burgers, drinking beer and getting ready to watch a football game."

"So, what happened?"

"You happened," he said and pulled at the sweater and ran a hand across his head.

"And you couldn't delegate?"

"Not when you have two kids in college and a Director who went to Clemson."

Major Clark interrupted to excuse himself. He shook hands with Allen and then turned to me and whispered, "Careful, he's got a snub nose .38 under that ugly thing," he smiled and walked out.

We were in some sort of conference room with a big polished table in the middle. Allen walked to the other end and raised the window blinds. Outside you could see the football stadium in the distance. It was early but people were moving about, the sidewalks and streets beginning to fill up. The buzz of game day was just starting up.

"There I was," Allen said as he looked out the window. "Cold beer in hand, stretched out in a lawn chair, belly full and watching the sports show with my boy and then the phone rings."

"Guessing that was late last night?"

"They tell me what was going on. They tell me a guy working private was involved in what went down. They tell me his name. I never heard of this fellow but he reminded me of somebody I knew and suddenly that big ol' steak I just grilled is not sitting so easy on my stomach."

"Rib eye or T-Bone?" I asked. He ignored me and continued.

"Then I get up this morning and get dressed in my *outfit* and I get another call. It's Major Clark. You want to guess what he told me?"

"Pick one team and stay with them?"

He didn't even pause.

"He tells me that the name in the report is wrong. The name should be Jake Eliam. Somehow, I knew it. He tells me you are working for him and was the fellow involved in the mess at the hotel."

"And now the case is yours?"

"And my weekend at the biggest game of the year is quickly shot to hell."

I didn't answer. He walked over to the table and picked up a folder. He held it up in the air.

"Can I ask you something?"

I shrugged.

"How come every time a case falls in my lap that is a dog. I'm talking about a big ol' mean dog that I know is gonna come right back and bite me in the ass. How come every time that happens somehow your name is attached to it?"

"I seemed to remember you looking pretty sharp on TV when you hauled Billy Joe Weede out of centerfield and off to jail, thanks to my help."

"You mean the time you nearly got yourself killed before Toot Thompson saved your ass?"

"You knew about Toot?"

"I'm the Section Chief. I know everything," he said.

"So, here we are again."

"Even when the name was wrong, somehow I knew it was you. I just knew it."

He pulled out a chair and motioned for me to do the same.

"Talk to me," he said and opened the case folder and reached for his coffee cup.

I went over everything with him. From the top to the bottom, as he made his own notes and underlined a few things in the report.

"That the best description you can come up with for the two guys in the room?"

"I was a little busy," I answered.

"Then you were a little blind."

"That, too."

"So, everything Kincaid said at this so called press conference was bull?"

"It was," I said. "You know him?"

"Know of him. Know about him. Fraud division been watching him for years."

"But no case?"

"He's as slick as butter on a corn cob."

"So, I've heard."

He closed the folder and rested his hands on the extra twenty pounds he carried at his waist.

"What now?" I asked.

"Now you go earn your money and make sure this lady leaves the state with no more issues. Next week's game is in Tennessee where I have no jurisdiction."

"That's it?" I asked. "What about last night?"

"Once she is gone, I take this file and stick it at the bottom of the pile of the two hundred files on my desk and I let it stew for a year or so until I forget about it."

"Unless something else happens," I noted.

He let out a deep sigh. "This lady is going to be on live TV most of the day. Inside a stadium with nearly a hundred thousand people and surrounded by her private army. What the hell could possibly happen?"

"Guess you're right," I said. "What will you be doing?"

"I'll be in Suite 3025 drinking warm beer in a paper cup."

He opened the file again. "One more question," he said. "It says here the paramedic gave you a large supply of Percocet. And it was noted that you were seen drinking beer with Catfish later, correct?"

"Correct."

"Should I be worried about you?"

"You should be worried," I said. "But not about that."

"Then just what should I be worried about?" He asked.

"What people are going to think when you wear that sweater out in public."

28

I RAN INTO SAM and Shaky as I left. Sam's eyes got big when she saw my face but Shaky gave me a fist bump and a laugh. She asked me If I was going to quit. I told her I wasn't. I didn't tell her it was not my first choice. I left them and joined Alex and Catfish out on the plaza. Catfish greeted me with a big grin.

"Did Allen rip you a new one?"

"He politely reminded me that I had royally screwed up his football weekend," I said.

"What's he gonna do about it?" Catfish asked.

"Sit in suite 3025 and drink warm beer."

"Unless you screw up again."

"Unless I screw up again."

"Then my advice to you would be not to screw up again."

"Glad you thought of that."

"Thinking is what I do best."

"Is that more than coffee in the coffee you're drinking?"

"Touch of the medicine."

"Rum?"

"Bourbon."

"Not like you to start up drinking this early in the day."

"Option I reserve only for when we play Ala-damn-bama."

Alex was facing the opposite direction and her eyes grew big. She pulled a camera up to her eye.

"Holy moly, check this out," she said and her camera clicked away.

We turned to look. A golf cart was approaching at a good speed. In the driver's seat was Dumptruck and beside him was Chance. Both wore big smiles. Dumptruck drove with one hand and held an open red plastic cup with the other. They rolled up to us and stopped hard.

"Hey there, big fellow," he said with a toast. "I got your dog here."

"I know who he is," I said. "What is he doing with you?"

"I rescued him."

"From what?"

"Some lady was trying to make him wear one of those silly damn little sweaters they put on poodles."

"And I guess he didn't warm to that idea?"

"He was about to detach a couple of her fingers from her ring hand when I intervened."

"Did he bite her?"

"No, but before I could wrangle him he did manage to pretty much destroy her red floppy hat that fell off during the incident."

"That's not too bad."

"The woman is really pissed. That's why I got him out of there."

"About a hat?"

"A hat with autographs of just about every Bulldog star from Fran Tarkenton to Herschel Walker."

"That's bad?" I asked.

"That's real bad," Catfish said.

"Worse than bad," Dumptruck added.

I looked at Chance. He did not show any sign of remorse. Dumptruck took a sip from his big cup and held it out to Chance who lapped it up with glee.

"Is that water?" Alex asked.

"Beer," Dumptruck said.

"You're letting a dog drink beer?" Her voice raised a notch.

"He asked."

Chance jumped out of the front seat of the cart, stretched out long and let out a yawn.

Make A Note: A dog that refuses to wear a poodle sweater and drinks beer at a football game is a damn good dog.

Dumptruck hit the gas and sped off in the cart. Chance made his way over to Alex where she bent down to rub his head.

"So now what do we do with him?" She asked.

"I wouldn't advise taking him back around that lady right now," Catfish noted.

"He can just stay here and hang out around the TV trucks," I said.

"No, he can't. We've got to work," she protested. "You can't just leave him here alone."

"He's already ate a hat and drank beer," I said. "What more trouble can he get into?"

"Take him down to the field and let him hang out with *UGA*," Catfish said.

"*UGA* is the mascot," Alex said with exasperation. "That dog is on a leash and surrounded by more security than the Secret Service."

She shot us a look. Catfish noticed and winked at me as he left.

"I can't believe you guys," she said as she dug into her gear bag. "I'll take care of this."

She dug deeper and pulled out a tiny little device the size of a quarter. It was green plastic and maybe a half-inch thick. She punched at it for a few seconds and then reached over to Chance and took his collar off. His floppy ear rose a bit and he tilted his head. She attached the small device to his collar and put it back on. He shook his head and grinned.

"What is that thing?" I asked her.

"It's a device designed for idiots who let their dogs run free and drink beer," she said.

"So, what does it do?"

"It is called CheetahSpy," she answered and took her purple second phone from her back pocket.

"What?"

"It is a duel position GPS tracking device that works with an action app on your phone."

"I have no idea what you just said but why do you have it and why did you put it on Chance?"

"Now I use it to track my gear and cameras on location. It's designed to track people."

"People?"

"People, like a kid or a cheating boyfriend," she said as she fiddled with her phone.

"Cheetah," I said. "So, you have used this before?"

She didn't answer me. She held the purple phone up and showed me the screen. It was a map and it showed the football stadium in the center. Two dots glowed on the screen. One was red and one blue.

"The blue dot is Chance," she said. "The other one is my phone. When he moves the dot will show where he goes and the same for my phone."

"It shows both?"

"It can show up to five devices at one time if you want and it works both ways."

"So, you can look at this and tell where Chance is?"

"Right, and the other dot would be our location."

"Why would he need to know where we were?"

"He wouldn't. Unless he runs out of beer."

29

THEY WERE CALLING for rain later today. It seemed every-body was prepared but me. Rain parkas and umbrellas were all around. The BTSN pre-game show was underway and the players for both teams were out on the field running through drills. A few drops of rain fell on and off from cloudy skies. Alex and I had joined Sam and Shaky on the bridge above the football stadium. Students and fans alike had gathered in a huge mob to hold up signs and scream out loud every time the camera on a big boom flew over them. The high-pitched noise of their screams made my ears ring. It didn't seem to bother the others but I guess they were used to it and Alex was wearing tiny little earplugs. It was obvious who the rookie was among this group.

Sam and Shaky were dressed alike in red BTSN rain slickers with a huge logo on the rear and blue logo polo shirts underneath. Shaky had a BTSN ball cap turned around backward on his head and wore a one-sided headset with a microphone attached. Sam had the same kind of headset and at least five or six more small boxes or devices hung off her belt. She had a big microphone in one hand with yet another logo and her fingers flew across one of those tablet things in her other hand. She spoke into the headset to somebody every now and then. Shaky was busy taking shots of the screaming kids and I even noticed that his camera wore a raincoat.

Alex looked professional as expected. Black jeans, white long sleeve t-shirt and her fifteen-pound black vest packed with gear. A rain parka was tied around her waist. I on the other hand looked like I had stopped by a yard sale to get dressed. Due to the long night, my bag was a mess so I had taken the clothes from the day before and ran them through a quick wash at the police barracks. They did not get dry and the pants were ripped and wrinkled, plus I discovered the sweatshirt had been torn. So, I wore the last piece I had, a dark blue pullover hoodie with *Rawlings Baseball* written across the front in white. It was more wrinkled than the pants but baggy enough to cover up the gun clipped to my belt. I was seriously considering using it on the kid next to me in face paint and red leotards when Alex leaned into my ear.

"Pretty wild scene isn't it," she shouted.

"What's with all the face paint?" I asked.

She shrugged her shoulders.

"I feel like I went to a college football game and an Alice Cooper concert broke out."

"Alice who?"

"Never mind," I shouted back as the kid in leotards bumped into me hard. I touched my gun.

Sam motioned for us to join her at the edge of the bridge railing. Shaky made his way over as well.

"We are about five minutes out from our live hit with Cissy," she told us all.

"Where is she?" Alex asked.

"On her way, according to the young intern they assigned to her," she said. "But the intern didn't sound too good. I think Cissy has been giving her a rough time."

"I'm shocked," I said.

Shaky let out a small rumble of a laugh and rolled his toothpick around near his gold teeth.

"I thought she was the star of this show?" Alex asked.

"Normally she is," Sam replied. "But today they wanted to build up the tension a bit more. She will front and back this hit and then they will wait until the game to turn her loose. Billy Ray and Boo's idea. More publicity for her return from danger they said."

Shaky shook his head.

"Front and back?" I asked.

"She just intros the tailgate piece we did last night and tags it out. Then she will change outfits and be back for the game."

Sam paused for a beat to listen to her headset and then cupped her hand around the mouthpiece and spoke into it.

"Three minutes out," She said to Shaky. "Keep an eye out for her,"she said to all of us.

"Is she normally this late?" Alex asked.

"She cuts it close all the time but it's up to the college intern to make sure she gets here. We use them every week. Broadcast students who work the game to gain experience. I did it when I was in school."

She turned to Shaky. "I'm going to put her up here on the sidewalk against the railing. Should be a good shot with the stadium in the background."

"I'm cool," Shaky said and adjusted the camera on his shoulder.

"Two minutes out," she updated.

Alex moved into a good position with her camera and I moved out of the way, behind and to the left of Shaky. I didn't think she was in danger up here unless somebody tried to paint her face. Down the way a bit we noticed a clamor of sorts. The crowd parted a little and you could sense movement.

"Here she comes," Sam said into her headset. "Less than a minute, I know, I know," she said into the microphone. "I got her."

Out front one of Kincaid's security guys pushed through the crowd. Cissy trailed behind him and a young girl with a terrified look on her face was next to her. I assumed she was the college intern. The security guy made his way forward and Sam held up her hand for him to see. Cissy emerged from behind and Sam began to work. She tossed the microphone to her in a flash, stuck things into her ear and half shoved her into position against the railing. Cissy cursed her.

"Live mic, live mic," Sam shouted. "In ten seconds. Stand by."

Cissy took a deep breath and her scowl turned to a smile. Sam pointed at her and she thanked somebody named Dan and then spoke for about five or ten seconds and held the smile. It was a beauty.

"In tape," Sam said.

The smile left. Cissy was wearing a pink top and green pants. The tiny edge of a green bra strap was just outside the left shoulder of the blouse.

"Was my bra strap showing?" She asked Sam.

"I have no idea," Sam said. "You got here ten seconds before air."

She turned to the intern. "Why didn't you say something?"

The young girl didn't answer. She looked like she couldn't speak.

"You're useless," Cissy said. "Bring me my mirror."

The intern had the big toolbox or the first aid kit as Shaky called it in her hands. She came forward and Cissy took out a mirror and turned her back on the intern. The girl looked to be near tears. Cissy worked on her face.

"Fifteen in package," Sam said out loud.

While Cissy held the mirror up she apparently spotted me over her shoulder. She spun around.

"What the hell?" She pointed toward me. "What the hell is he still doing here?"

"Ten seconds," Sam said. Shaky moved into place.

"Get him out of here," she said to the security guy. He had no idea who she was talking about.

"Five seconds, stand by," Sam yelled. "We'll deal with it in a minute."

Sam pointed and the smile returned. She told the camera how much fun she had meeting with the tailgaters and then she tossed it back to Dan. Then she charged me like a bull in heat.

"I thought I made it clear to Billy Ray that you were fired?"

"Guess it's a good thing I don't work for him then," I said.

"I've got a job to do today and I don't need fools hanging around me."

"Yeah, I just watched you do your job and fool is a word that does come to mind."

She was more than a foot shorter than me but I think she was about to punch me when the security guy stepped in. He wasn't a foot shorter. He met me eye to eye.

"I got this," he said to her. His voice was a deep baritone and he was close enough I could smell his cheap aftershave.

"Hey there," I said. "Nice outfit."

He didn't answer. He was dressed in black from head to toe. Black utility pants tucked into combat boots shined to a gloss. Just like the guy last night but without the metal tip on the toe. A tight black t-shirt that barely held back his puffed-up muscles and a black baseball cap pulled down near reflective sunglasses. His belt held mace, handcuffs, a small radio and a big head knocker. No gun as Major Clark had ordered.

"You must be the campus security guard Kincaid talked about."

I didn't answer.

"You don't look like a security guard," he said and inched in closer.

"You know," I said. "Now that I can see myself in your sunglasses. I agree. I don't look much like a security guard."

"Keep your distance smartass or we'll keep it for you."

"Can I ask a question first?"

He didn't respond but put his right hand on his head knocker.

"Is it true that using steroids can cause your penis to shrivel up and shrink?"

Sam stepped in between us.

"Let's go," she shoved at the big guy. "Get Cissy back to the compound now."

He stepped back. He looked at her and back at me. He lifted his cap and pulled it back down tight around his eyes. He winced a little when he pulled the cap tight.

"Go now," Sam said. He left with Cissy and the intern followed with the toolbox.

"Well, that was fun," I said.

Sam grinned and Shaky clapped a hand on my shoulder. Alex rolled her eyes.

"Thanks," I said to Sam.

"That guy looked like he was about to take his night-stick to you," she said.

"I do believe he was about to do just that."

"So, are you going to take his advice?" She asked.

"I doubt it."

Alex let out a short laugh. "Taking good advice is not one of his strong points."

"So, what now?" Sam asked.

"Any advice?" I asked.

30

THE LAST TIME I was on the sideline of a football game I was in a uniform. It was in high school and I was the quarterback. I was mediocre at best. Football was not my game because of one simple thing. I did not like getting hit.

Kickoff was just a few minutes away. The marching band blasted away on the field and all of the 90,000 plus fans were on their feet. The first thing you notice from the field is just how huge this place is. The nickname of Sanford Stadium is *Between the Hedges*. Catfish said it went back to the beginning of the field and remains today. A long row of privet hedges encircles both sidelines at the edge of the seats and covers up a chain link fence designed to hold back the crowd from storming the field. It hasn't really worked out very well in that regard.

The hedges now are lost in a towering three level stadium that rises sharply from the natural valley it sits in and looms over the field like a monster of concrete and red. The sight from the field is disconcerting. In baseball, when a player comes up to the Majors the first thing they have to acclimate to is the third level in a ball-park. It changes how you see the ball, how you read the ball and it takes some getting used to. These college players are just out of high school but I guess it doesn't bother them at all. When I was their same age I was playing my games in an old ballpark that had wooden bleachers, concrete dugouts, portable toilets and we dressed in our bus. Maybe I should have worked a little harder at football.

The teams were about to make their entrance on the field and both the band and cheerleaders headed toward the right end zone. The noise level grew and the sound of the crowd washed over you like a huge ocean wave. I found myself lost in the commotion as people scattered by and glanced off me. Alex shook me out of my daze.

"Look," she said close to my ear. "Here comes the Prom Queen."

Down the sideline we could see Cissy headed our way. A young man with long blonde hair was beside her. He wore long shorts, hiking boots, t-shirt and a dirty pair of work gloves hung from his belt. The red toolbox was in his left hand and with his right hand he held an umbrella over Cissy. It wasn't raining at the moment. The security guy was a step out front. Cissy moved past the crowd with speed and indifference as they all yelled out her name. She had changed into a new outfit for the game. Brown leather boots ran all the way up and over her knees. A tight pink skirt that landed just above mid-thigh and a light blue blouse that dipped into dangerous territory. A gold choker circled her neck. Nice look for a nightclub. Not sure about a football game.

Sam and Shaky appeared out of the crowd. Shaky looked like he was out for walk in the park. He had been doing this for a long time. This was just another day at the office for him and his office was a roaring football stadium. Sam motioned to me and I leaned down so she could speak above the noise.

"As soon as Georgia comes out the tunnel Cissy will interview the head coach on the field. After that we just see what happens in the game."

Cissy strolled up to Sam and held up her arms. Sam went to work running cables up and inside her clothes. The young man in the shorts put down the umbrella and toolbox and joined Shaky. He slid on the gloves, grabbed the cable from the camera and curled it into a circle with deft quick moves. He tapped Shaky on the shoulder and gave him a high sign. He was there to guide Shaky through the crowds. Sam spoke into the headset. She nodded and then turned to Shaky and gave him a nod. Sam picked up the red toolbox and handed it to me.

"Can you hold onto this?" She shouted.

"Really? Me?"

"Please."

"What happened to the intern?"

"She quit."

"Quit?"

"Left in tears."

"Cissy?"

"Cissy," she said. "Poor girl. She will be an education major by Monday."

"And you want me to carry this?"

"I do."

"I'm not too sure she is going to approve."

"Just think of the look on her face when she wants her makeup and you show up."

"I'm in," I said with a smile.

The band broke into the same song I had heard about a dozen times before over the weekend and I had to assume it was the fight song. Shaky led the way and everybody headed onto the field.

I wanted to see the interview but had no idea where it took place. I had a sideline credential but didn't have one of the armbands that allowed me on the field like the others. Sam had shown me what she called an air monitor over near the hedges where they had staged all their extra gear. I pushed my way through the mob on the sideline. On a stand was a television monitor covered in a blue nylon case and with a viewing tunnel of sorts made of cardboard. I looked down into it and could see the game broadcast. I spotted headphones on top and pulled them on. I could hear the announcers. I leaned into the monitor to check out the game and see if Cissy had made her appearance yet. I didn't have to wait long. The announcers tossed it down to the field to Cissy and the Bulldogs head coach. Shaky had the two framed up side-by-side and I had to assume Sam was right next to him ready to feed lines.

The smile glowed once again and Cissy introduced the coach. He looked like he would rather have been anywhere else in the world at that moment. I have never understood exactly what they expect the coach to say in these interviews but now everybody does them and not just in football. Her first question was a tough one.

"Are you guys ready for Alabama today?"

"Well, we better be," the coach said, his eyes off into the distance. "That's a good football team over there and we are going to have our hands full with them."

"How do you plan to move the ball against the Tide's top ranked defense?"

"We just have to be smart. Keep our heads about us and stick to our game plan."

"Thank you, coach, good luck todayyy."

He ran out of the frame. Shaky zoomed into a close up of Cissy.

"Georgia's plan today. Be smart. We will see how it works out. The kickoff is coming up next on the BTSN Game Of The Week."

The shot went to an aerial view from what I guessed was the blimp above the stadium and then the monitor went black. Alex thought I was being paid too much for my work. I removed the headphones and heard the crowd noise rise up. It was different, hoots and whistles.

I looked up at the oversized video board and the camera had a shot of Cissy as she walked off the field. She was blowing kisses to the crowd.

It made me think back to a hitting instructor I had in Class A ball. I was young and stubborn and refused to take his advice on how to hit a cutting two-seam fastball. Frustrated with me he took a huge wad of chew out of his cheek, tossed it at my feet and told me. *'If you hurt the trainer can fix you, if you sick the doctor can treat you, but dammit son, I ain't got no cure for stupid.'*

31

AFTER WATCHING THE first part of the game from the side-lines I had no more ideas that I had chosen the wrong sport to play. High school was one thing but this was something different. These kids were big. They were fast and the hits made my bones rattle just to watch. It made me wonder how Catfish had survived those years in the trenches and come away with only a limp. One skinny young player caught a pass right in front of me and turned to head up field only to be knocked back five yards by a much larger guy from Alabama. The skinny kid bounced up without a flinch. Ambulances would have been called if it had been me.

Cissy and the security guard were camped out near the air monitor. She was seated in a chair and locked into her phone. She still had not noticed I was around. I passed the time watching both the game and watching Shaky work the sidelines with his camera. He was as fear-less as the young receiver. Time after time players rolled out of bounds right at his camera and he did a smooth slide step to avoid them. On one play the receiver and defender came right at him in the corner of the end zone. The two went up into the air for the ball and flew out of bounds right where he was planted. He pivoted off his right foot, leaned back out of the way and then pivoted back to follow them out of bounds. He took a few steps toward them and was in the face of the Georgia player who came up with the ball for the touchdown. The big video board showed the shot a moment later and the crowd roared. He followed the kid down the sideline and then he and the cable wrangler were back in position. It was like watching a NASCAR driver head into a turn at 200 mph with a yawn.

The game was tied 14-14 with about three minutes left in the first half. Sam had told me Cissy would be doing an interview with the Alabama coach at the end of the half so I made my way back over to where she sat. I jumped when somebody pounded me on the shoulders from behind. Catfish.

"Speak to me, son," he shouted. "Tell me now that you believe that football is a better sport than baseball."

"If you like getting the crap knocked out of you," I said.

"Long as you're the one doing the knocking."

Dumptruck came up beside him. He was wearing a helmet made of leather or something that looked like a helmet. It was shaped like an old football helmet from the past and sported earflaps with holes that flopped on both sides. A red letter G was sewn into the front and it was too small for his big head. He was playing a tune on the headgear with his hands.

"You plan on getting in the game?" I asked him.

"I could still hit harder today than any of these so called 5-Star recruits," he shouted back.

"I thought you two were watching the game from up in one of the fancy suites?"

"Bunch of pussies," Dumptruck spat.

"We got tired of doing the alumni dance," Catfish said. "Escaped down here where the hitting is taking place."

"Plenty of that," I noted.

"What's that red box you toting?" He asked.

"First aid kit," I told him.

"Really?"

I cracked open the tool box and showed him the makeup, brushes, lipstick and mirrors.

"What is all that stuff?"

"I stand at the ready for Cissy."

"Glad to see you earning your keep."

Georgia was on a drive as the clock ticked down to halftime. They came up less than a yard short on third down near the 20-yard line. Dumptruck offered up his advice to the coach.

"Man up, and go for it, you yellow-bellied wussy," he shouted. "Stick it in their ear!"

The coach did not listen. He sent the field goal kicker out on the field.

"He's kicking it!" Dumptruck yelled. "You got time. What the hell are they thinking?"

Alabama waited until the ball was almost snapped and called a timeout. You see this all the time in football. They think it ices the kicker while he thinks about it. I never thought this was a good idea but this time it seemed to work. The kicker shanked it. It didn't even come close. A dying duck that missed left by a mile and fell short as well. The crowd groaned as the Alabama sideline celebrated. The kicker came back to the sideline and yanked his helmet off. He was a short chubby kid with huge black glasses.

"Our kicker is wearing frigging glasses," Dumptruck pointed at the kid. "A blind field goal kicker. Hell, I bet you he was seeing two goalposts with those dang coke bottle glasses."

"I hate kickers," Catfish added. "I hate 'em. Send his blind butt back to the soccer team."

Over the noise I heard my name being called. I turned to see Sam over with Cissy. She made a motion to the toolbox and grinned. Cissy needed her tools.

"Here's your stuff," Sam said to Cissy.

She looked up and saw me holding her toolbox.

"You have got to be kidding me?" She glared at Sam and cursed under her breath.

"I swear I didn't use your hairbrush or your lipstick," I said with a smile.

"What are you still doing here?"

"Every army needs somebody to carry the spears," I replied.

She grabbed the box from my hand and went to work. She worked on her cheeks. She worked on her lips. She worked on her hair. She worked on her eyes. She checked the work in the mirror. She closed the toolbox satisfied with the repairs. She shoved the red box back at me with a scowl.

"I've seen less paint on a 65 Mustang," I said to her.

"Shut the hell up," she told me and stood to adjust her outfit.

"Let's go," Sam said to her and smiled at me. "We need to get over to the other sideline."

They met up with Shaky and the guy with his cables and waited for the first half to end. I kept my distance but watched from the edge of the end zone. The coach began his sprint off the field and Sam met him in a trot. She led him by the arm and guided him over to Cissy. He did not look eager to talk. There was a delay for a beat and he looked like he was about to leave. Sam held onto his arm and then Cissy and her smile lit up and the interview began. I couldn't hear this one but I could see Sam once again feeding her a question in her ear. Shame they couldn't just let Sam do the on-air stuff as well. She was doing all the work. They wrapped up and the coach ran off. Shaky followed with the camera. Cissy tossed the microphone back to Sam and headed off the field trailed by the security guy. Sam joined me.

"Where is Cissy going?" I asked.

"To lunch," she said. "They have a big spread of food, wine and beer for the talent, clients and the bosses upstairs."

"Should I go with her?"

"You should, but I don't think you would get by Billy Ray and his guys."

"Are you going?"

"No, I go to the truck and build out the first half highlights."

"No beer?"

"Not even a cold hot dog," she said.

"You have a very strange job."

"I do indeed," she said. "So, what did you think of Cissy and the interviews?"

"You have a very strange job," I repeated.

32

THE SECOND HALF was played in a slow on and off rain. For late fall, it was warmer than it should be. The clouds in the distance grew darker and you could sense that by later tonight big storms would be rolling in. The dark mood seemed to have encircled both teams. Neither Georgia nor Alabama could generate much offense. The punters were kept busy as each team took turns with three and outs. In the first drive of the fourth quarter Alabama got tired of punting the ball and sent the kicker out to try a field goal of 58 yards. He nailed it. He didn't appear to be wearing glasses. Alabama led 17-14.

I didn't have to worry about Cissy right now because she apparently refused to work in the rain. She was somewhere underneath the stadium. Sam said it might be in her contract that she didn't have to work in bad weather. I wasn't sure if she was joking or not. I still had her toolbox and had grown tired of it but then again, they were paying me 500 bucks to lug it around.

With about four minutes to go, Georgia snapped the ball six feet over the head of their quarterback and it rolled all the way inside the 5-yard line. A bulldog player fell on it but two plays later Alabama sacked the quarter-back in the end zone for a safety and a 19-14 lead. Down the sideline where Catfish and Dumptruck stood on metal chairs I could see Dumptruck take his chair and smash it into several pieces. Catfish pulled him away before security could see what was going on. They joined me further down the sideline away from the bench.

"We're going to blow this damn game," Catfish rubbed a big hand across his head.

"Damn fancy pants offense ain't worth a crap," Dumptruck said as he pulled a silver flask from inside his belt and emptied the last bit in one swallow. "Can't even hike the ball anymore."

"What's in the flask?" I asked him.

"Not a damn thing now," he said and held it upside down. "I gotta get a bigger one to watch this dumbass team."

Sam found me to tell me that at the end of the game she would be on the field with Cissy to interview the winning coach most likely at mid-field after the handshake.

"Have you seen Alex?" I asked her.

"She's back in the tunnel with Cissy," Sam said. "Bored as hell and really mad."

"Mad?"

"Not like you can get any great promo shots with Cissy hiding from the rain and smoking a cigarette."

"Does Cissy need her toolbox?"

"I'm sure she would like it but she doesn't want to deal with you."

"You could take it to her," I said and held it out.

"I could," she said. "But I won't." She grinned and jogged off.

Make A Note: Beauty can be dangerous but a sense of humor can be deadly.

Georgia got the ball back but time was running out as the clock ticked away. They crossed mid-field at the two-minute mark and picked up another first down at the Alabama 35-yard line with 1:10 left in the game. Down by five they needed a touchdown to win. A pass across the middle bounced off an Alabama player and into the hands of a Georgia player for another first down just inside the 25. They called timeout to stop the clock with :38 seconds left. A busted run and two deep passes failed before Georgia took their last timeout with :07 seconds on the clock. They only had time for one more play on fourth down.

"Dammit to hell. Dammit to hell," Dumptruck paced in a circle. "I'm about to lose three thousand dollars on this game."

"You can afford to bet three grand on a football game?" I asked him.

"Hell no," he spat. "That's why I'm so pissed off."

The band broke into the same song once again. They had played it maybe a hundred times already. The crowd sang along with it and Dumptruck and Catfish joined in as loud as they could. The lyrics were the same repeated over and over and it ended with something about Georgia Tech, which confused me since they were playing Alabama. They punched the last line with a fist and then let out a double dog woof at the end.

"That's your fight song?" I asked.

"Great one ain't it?" Catfish shouted.

"Did they stay up all night writing those lyrics?"

He ignored me. The Georgia head coach had called his entire offense over into a tight circle. They all closed in around him. The other coaches leaned in to hear. The long TV timeout was about to end. The players broke the huddle and the head coach did a little jig and pumped his fist. Dumptruck noticed.

"I think he is gonna run your play," he said to Catfish.

"Ain't no way," Catfish waved him off.

"No man, I'm serious as a cocked shotgun. I think he just sent it in."

"He ain't got the guts to run it," Catfish said. "Or the kid to pull it off."

"The fat kid, number 71. He could do it," Dumptruck challenged him. "I'll bet you five hundred bucks."

"You ain't got five hundred bucks and you about to lose three grand."

I had no idea what they were talking about but it was too late to ask them. Both teams headed out for the last play and the crowd noise wiped out any chance of conversation. I turned to watch. The Georgia team broke the huddle and lined up. The Alabama coaches raced down the sideline and called a timeout. The crowd noise drained out like the air hissing out of a balloon.

"What is this play you guys are talking about?" I took the chance to shout at Catfish.

"Aw, that's just Dumptruck being a fool," Catfish said in my ear. "They ain't gonna try something crazy in this day and time."

"Something crazy?" I asked. "You mean a trick play or something?"

"We were at practice Thursday and I was just telling a story about this play we ran once and the young offensive coordinator got all hot and bothered about it."

"A trick play, you guys used in a game?"

"We used it against Ole Miss but not on the last play and sure as hell not with the game on the line."

"And they were thinking about using it?"

"Well, the coordinator sent his grad assistant to pull the old film but no way they would try it today. Too much money involved to try something stupid at this point in the game."

"Was it a stupid play?" I asked.

"Stupid, but just stupid enough to work."

Dumptruck interrupted us.

"Oh, hell yeah!" He shouted to Catfish. "Oh, hell yeah! I seen him. I seen him. The head coach had the fat kid by the facemask and yelling in his ear. Bet your sweet ass they gonna run it."

Dumptruck pounded Catfish in the right arm like he was hitting a punching bag. He let out a whoop and spun himself in a circle a few times.

"Is he getting drunk?" I said to Catfish.

"Getting drunk?" He grinned. "He was drunk before the refs showed up."

33

THE TV TIMEOUT seemed to last an eternity. I guess when two of the top teams in the country face off and it comes down to one last play you take all the time you need to sell some hamburgers. I looked across the field to try and spot the crew. It wasn't easy with a long line of cameras that ran from the bench to the end zone and more. It took a while but I spotted Shaky away from the other cameras and squeezed in among the Alabama coaches near the 50-yard line. Sam was on one knee beneath him and the cable wrangler right behind her. It took me a bit longer to find Cissy. She was a few yards behind the camera. The security guy loomed near her and an officer that appeared to be a Georgia State Patrolmen was holding his rain parka over her head. Alex was on the other side of the trooper and she did not look happy. I should have stayed by Cissy's side but I was quickly losing interest.

It was mid-afternoon but the lights had been on for the entire game. The rain wasn't really a rain at all but a mist that swirled in the lights and hung low near the top row of seats. Raindrops graced the helmets with tiny beads like the hood of a waxed car. A young ball boy kept a towel over the game ball. The teams headed back on the field as the long commercial break ended and the crowd came back to life. The sound spilled downward and made my ears ring and flutter.

"Think they're gonna throw it up for grabs to the left end zone," Catfish shouted behind me. "The big kid, number 88, that boy has got a vertical leap like a damn firehouse ladder."

"They gonna run your play, dammit," Dumptruck insisted. "Why don't you ever listen to me?"

"Last time I listened to you I spent two days and two nights in the Stephens County Jail."

"But I was right, wasn't I?"

I didn't have time to inquire about that episode and maybe I didn't want to know. The Georgia team broke the huddle and came to the line. The quarterback waved his arms to try and quiet the crowd a bit so he could hear. It didn't work. The noise seemed to grow. The Bulldogs sent three receivers out to the left side. The quarterback went under center so he could take the snap in the noise. His count was long and he stood up twice and pointed to the defense. The Alabama defenders moved about, one faked a blitz and backed off. The center snapped the ball.

The quarterback turned and made a nice play action fake to the tailback and kept the ball low on his hip. The tailback picked up a stunting linebacker. The quarterback turned, set up and looked left downfield. The tackle, number 71, the kid Dumptruck had mentioned, battled the defensive end and pushed him left and to the rear of the quarterback. The quarterback pump faked once and all eyes moved to the wide receivers headed to the left end zone. Number 71 made one last shove at the defensive end and let him go. The Alabama end surprised to be released from the block, dove back to reach for the quarterback and got a hand on his jersey. At the same time, the quarterback spun toward him and tossed a perfect over the shoulder hook shot lateral to the big number 71 who was now headed right in a slow trot. The ball landed softly in his huge gloved hands and he started to juggle it. It bounced once, twice, three times and then the kid finally managed to grab hold of it and grip it with his right hand. A stunned linebacker had spotted what was happening and started to close in on him.

"Oh, hell yeah!" Dumptruck screamed. "They running it! I told you! Throw that damn ball, fatso!"

"He's wide open!" Catfish yelled. "Get rid of it! Throw that tater you fat sonofabitch!"

The Georgia tight end, number 81, had slipped out and into the right flat and was indeed wide open. There wasn't a defender near him. The big kid stopped short and hurled the ball just as the linebacker crashed into him. It was an ugly pass. Could have been the worst in the history of college football. It wasn't so much a pass as it was a shot put. It tumbled end over end and then sideways in the wind as it fluttered toward the sideline. The tight end chased it like a bird dog on point and snagged it out of the air at the 10-yard line. He turned up toward the end zone. The Alabama safety had given up on the other side and was now headed back toward the tight end at full speed. Near the goal line the two collided and number 81 went airborne. His body looked like the blades of a helicopter as he twirled twice in the air. Somehow, he held onto the football when he landed and more importantly he landed in the end zone. The official threw up both arms. TOUCHDOWN. Georgia had pulled it out on the final play to win the game.

"Slap me silly and call me Lucille!" Catfish shouted as he grabbed me from behind and lifted me off my feet. "Bless my big old Bulldog butt!"

Dumptruck ran straight at us yelling as he came. I sidestepped him and he jumped right into the arms of Catfish and wrapped his legs around him.

"Mudcat Moon!" He screamed. "Mudcat Moon! Open up the pearly gates, I can die and go to heaven. We done beat 'Bama."

He spun down from Catfish and did a little dance. We were all being pushed and shoved in the chaos of the sideline as the players ran toward the end zone. I bounced off one huge player and the toolbox went flying out of my hand. Bottles of makeup, brushes, lipstick and some unmentionables went everywhere. Another player stomped on the toolbox with his cleats and crushed it into pieces. I was glad to see it go. Dumptruck grabbed Catfish and put him in a headlock.

"Now you gonna listen to me, you big damn redneck?" He yelled at him. "Mudcat Moon. I told your big old fat ass that's what they were about to do."

He let Catfish go and grabbed me around the neck and planted a kiss on my cheek. I shoved him away and he took off running onto the field at a full gallop. The earflaps on his helmet bounced as he ran. The crowd had poured over the hedges. Security had no way of slowing them down and they didn't seem to be trying. There was no way I was going to be able to make it out to meet Shaky and Sam even if I knew where they were. The thought of Cissy trapped in the middle of all this made me smile.

Catfish took both his big hands and rubbed them over my head and then gave me a big bear hug.

"Dammit, I love football," he shouted. "And I love it a lot more when we beat Ala-Damn-Bama."

A much older man wearing a red blazer and red pants grabbed Catfish by the shoulder and pointed at him with a long bony finger.

"Mudcat Moon," the man said and grinned. He only had a couple of teeth left in his mouth.

"It ain't dead yet, coach," Catfish told him. "Just been in hibernation."

"Who's that?"

"Two Teeth Presley," he said. "Coached here for about a thousand years."

"So, what is everybody talking about?" I asked him. "What does this mudcat moon mean?"

"It's the name of the play," Catfish said.

"The play they just ran to win?"

"My play."

"Your play?"

"I was the fat guy who threw the ball the time we ran it," he answered. "It was the same damn play."

"And how does everybody know the name of it?"

"They had it in the paper back then," he said. "They use to put photos frame by frame of big plays in the newspaper."

"And they called it that?"

"I made up the play so I got to name it. Mudcat Moon-77-Bootleg Red," he said proudly.

"And you threw a touchdown pass?"

"First and last time."

"Well I hope your pass was better than the one that fat kid just threw," I said.

"What you talking 'bout, son," Catfish grinned. "That pass just now was the most beautiful pass I have ever seen in my whole damn lifetime."

34

WADED INTO THE mob on the field to try and find the crew. I wasn't having much luck. Each step I took forward some fool bounced off me and knocked me back two steps. The mass seemed to move toward the right end zone and the student section but it lurched in all directions. The noise was an odd mix of screams and barking accented by the band that played the fight song on a non-stop loop. I pushed my way toward the center of the field where I thought I might see Alex and the crew, but it was like trying to step through molasses.

I decided to go against the flow and retreat to the sideline. I crawled up on a water table on the sideline and scanned the field. I thought I saw Shaky for just a second but then I wasn't sure. I couldn't see any sign of Sam, Alex or Cissy for that matter. I gave up.

I was stunned at how long it took me to leave the stadium. I am sure there was a better way but I just followed the crowds and it took me almost an hour to exit and find my way back to the plaza that led to the area near the TV set. A middle-aged man wearing a Georgia pullover and visor stepped right in front of me.

"You for Dawgs or 'Bama?" His breath was thick as his accent.

"What?"

"Dawgs or 'Bama?" He repeated.

I considered his question and based on his outfit I took the easy choice.

"Dawgs," I said.

"You damn right," he said and tipped a full cup of beer over my head. "Sic 'em Dawgs!"

I jumped back to avoid some of it and was about to draw back and knock the hell out of him. He let out a big laugh, grabbed me around the neck and leaned in close.

"Don't it feel sooooo damn good to beat Alabama?"

I pushed him away and headed down some stairs. I never saw anything like this in all my years of baseball. The guy seemed like a reasonable adult. I would guess that by Monday morning he would be back in some insurance office in a nice suit doing paperwork but today he was flat out drunk, happy as hell and perfectly fine with going up to a total stranger and pouring a beer over his head. Catfish was right about how much people cared about winning a football game.

Twenty minutes later I made it through the crowds and back to where the TV trucks were parked. I went in the building, found a restroom and cleaned myself up. I didn't know where Catfish was right now and I had yet to find any of the crew, Alex or even Major Clark. What I did know was that I was good and ready to go home and hopefully in time to watch some baseball. My first trip to a college football game was certainly interesting but I was ready to get the hell out of town.

I heard my name called and turned to see Sam headed up the hill toward the truck. She motioned me over as she spoke into a radio and then shook her head.

"I'm really sorry," I said as I approached her. "I tried to find you guys but I couldn't."

"Hang on," she held up a finger and spoke again into the little radio. "Nothing? No sign of them at your location either?"

The voice on the other end of the radio crackled out a 'negative.' Sam looked worried.

"Everything okay?" I asked her.

"No," she said. "I can't find them."

"Find who?"

"Cissy," Sam answered. "She was supposed to meet me back here to record tracks for a post game package more than an hour ago."

"Wasn't she with you at the end of the game?"

"She did the interview with the coach on the field and I left with Shaky to do locker room sound."

"And where did she go?"

"She left with that security guy and they were headed back here. Now, I can't find them."

"Knowing Cissy," I said. "Her and the security goon are off somewhere knocking knees."

"I've checked everywhere. Called everybody and nobody has seen them in the last hour."

"I'm sure they will turn up soon," I said.

"It's not just Cissy I'm worried about."

"Then what?"

"It's Alex."

"What about her."

"She left with them."

"So."

"So, you don't get it," she said. "I can't find her. Alex is missing, too."

35

"THANK GOD AND Greyhound, she's gone," Catfish said when I told him Cissy was missing.

"How much have you had to drink?" I asked him.

"Why? You got something against it? Drinking is what you do when you beat Alabama. Hell, I might not stop drinking until we play them boys again."

"Did you hear me when I said Alex was with her and she's missing too."

He waved me off.

"Crazy as things are, she most likely is just roaming around taking pictures."

I doubted that. Alex was like me. She was sick of Cissy and ready to get out of here.

"Why you even care 'bout Cissy?" Catfish asked me. "As of right now your job is done and the check is in the mail."

"I don't care about her. Just worried about Alex."

"Alex is fine, quit worrying."

The door to the center opened and Sam came out with Major Clark. His head was turned to the left as he spoke into a small radio clipped to the left shoulder of his uniform. Sam still looked concerned.

"Any luck?" I asked as they joined us.

"No," Sam said.

"When did you last see them?" Clark asked me.

"I saw them across the field near the end of the game," I told him. "But I couldn't get to them after the game because of the crowds."

He nodded.

"What about the security guy?" I asked.

"Can't find him," Clark said. "My men have accounted for all of Kincaid's guys except him and one more."

"They know anything?"

"If they do they aren't talking to us."

Catfish seemed to sober up as he noticed the serious look on Clark's face.

"You really think there is something going on?"

"I don't know," Clark shrugged. "I just got a bad feeling. I also got a hundred thousand drunks on my hands, so I need help."

"Who is your help?" Catfish asked.

He didn't have to answer. The answer walked up. GBI Special Agent Nick Allen. He still had on the silly two-team sweater but it was now covered by a black windbreaker with GBI written across the back in big letters. A younger man in dress slacks, white polo and the same windbreaker was with him. Allen stopped and looked up at me.

"I knew it," he said. "I was sitting up there enjoying the game but it just kept tugging at me. Kept having this feeling."

I didn't say anything.

"You know that feeling?" He said to me. "That feeling that keeps nagging at you?"

"I'm not sure. What feeling would that be?"

"The feeling that somehow you were going to screw up my day."

"That was the feeling you had?"

"I didn't know how. I didn't know when. I just knew that when your name popped up that somehow, someway you were going to screw up my day."

I waited while he stewed a moment.

"And now here it is," he said and waved his hands wide. "About to enjoy a nice night with the family but here I am back down here looking for a lady. A famous, well known lady. A lady everybody in the whole damn United States of America could spot in a crowd and you have done gone and lost her."

He paused and then dove right back in.

"Is that it?" Allen asked. "I got all this about right? Plus, you also lost another lady and some security guy."

"Yeah, that all sounds about right," I said.

"Good," he said. "Because you seem to have a habit of leaving out crucial facts whenever I end up having to step into a mess of yours."

"Not sure this is my mess," I said.

"You were being paid to keep an eye on her, right?"

"I was."

"And you lost her didn't you?"

"I did."

"Then it's your mess," he said. "And now you drop your mess in my lap."

The door to the production truck opened and Shaky came down the steps. The laid back look on his face was gone. He looked serious.

"Something going on in the exec trailer you guys need to know about," he said to all of us.

"What's up?" Sam spoke up.

"Boo is in the trailer with Billy Ray and locked onto his laptop looking at something serious."

"What?" Clark asked.

"Ain't sure," he shook his head. "But I don't think they watching game highlights."

"How can you know where they are?" Clark followed up.

"We got tiny cameras in every trailer that feeds to the big truck," he said.

"No sound?" Clark asked.

"Can't patch the audio while the post game show is on live," Sam told him.

"You think this has something to do with Cissy?" Clark said to Shaky.

"Have no idea," Shaky answered.

"It is odd for them to be around this long after the game is over," Sam said.

"Why is that?" I asked.

"Because by now," Shaky said. "Those two fools are usually in the back of a limo smoking big cigars and drinking good whiskey while we work."

"That so?" Clark said.

He turned to look at Nick Allen. Allen turned to the young agent with him.

"Go bring me those two fools," he said. "And don't forget the laptop."

36

THE YOUNG AGENT had Boo by the arm as he walked him over. A uniformed cop from the UGA force trailed Kincaid as he had a phone stuck to his ear. The young agent took the laptop and handed it to Allen.

"You have no right to take my laptop," he said.

"What's your name, kid," Allen asked him.

"I'm Boo Dickman, Executive Senior Producer of Programing and Production for BTSN Network Sports."

"Didn't ask for your resume, just your name," Allen said. "So Boo, what's on this laptop that you and your boss gave up good whiskey for?"

"You have no right to ask for my laptop," Boo puffed up a bit. "I know my rights."

"You are correct. You do have rights. Except for one little problem."

"What's that?"

"A guy named Boo wouldn't do very well in prison."

Billy Ray stepped in between Boo and Allen and poked a finger at him. "Everybody stop what you are doing right now," he said. "Cease and desist."

"That your lawyer on the phone?" Allen asked.

"Damn right," Billy Ray said.

Allen grabbed the phone out of his hands.

"Cease and desist this, counselor," he said and clicked the phone off.

"That was my attorney," Billy Ray declared. "I need to talk to my lawyer."

"Yeah you do," Allen said. "Hope he's a good one."

"Listen, you do know who I am?" Kincaid raised his voice.

"I do. Do you know who I am?"

He didn't answer.

"I'm GBI Special Agent Nick Allen and you are Billy Ray Kincaid. To us, you are what we sometimes call a person of interest," Allen said and handed him his phone back. "We have files as thick as a triple stack of pancakes on you and your bad deals. Most of them are gathering dust on my desk but I would be more than glad to dust a few of them off and take another look."

"What the hell do you want?"

"Just your permission to look at this laptop."

"I'm handling it," he said.

"Handling what?" Allen asked.

There was a standoff for a good minute. Everybody waited to see who would say something next. Then Billy Ray broke the silence.

"They have Cissy," he said.

"Who has Cissy?" Allen's voice was firm.

"Kidnappers," he said. "Same folks that have been messing with her. The same guys that he let get away last night."

He pointed to me.

"They sent us a cell phone video, to my e-mail," Boo blurted out. Kincaid shot him a glare.

"We're handling this," Billy Ray said forcefully. "Cissy is my employee and I ain't having any cops involved."

"But Alex Trippi is missing too," Jay Clark spoke up. "So as of now we are involved."

Allen handed the laptop to his agent and told him to fire it up. Kincaid made a move toward the agent. Allen stuck a big hand hard in his chest.

"Sit tight, big shot," he said.

The agent opened up the laptop and punched a few buttons. He clicked around the keyboard, found the e-mail and then turned the laptop around so we all could see it and hit the play button for the video.

The video began with a shaky dark shot. The phone camera tilted and swung a bit to show a brief glance of a car window and then it moved around to a shot of Cissy in the back seat of a vehicle. She stared straight ahead into the camera. I couldn't tell if she was scared to death or mad as hell. Maybe both. A deep male voice spoke into the phone's microphone.

We have little Miss Cissy and her friend. She is unharmed and she will remain that way if we get what we want and you do exactly as we say. Now listen Kincaid, here is what you do. You get fifty thousands dollars in cash. Make it in smaller bills. Put it all in a bag and take that bag to Lake Herrick. Take it out on the bridge and put it down and clear out. If the money is all there, we will release Cissy and send her across the bridge where she will wait for you. If we see a single cop or a camera we will kill the photographer lady. Then it will cost you a hundred thousand to get Cissy back. Now, talk nicely to the camera pretty lady like you do on TV.

The phone moved in closer to Cissy and she leaned into the screen.

'Billy Ray, you take care of this dammit. I mean it. I didn't sign up for this kind of crap. When I get back we are going to talk about a new contract....'

The voice put his hand in front of the phone's camera and cut her off.

She don't seem too happy with you Billy Ray. So get off your rich fat ass and get the cash together. You got to midnight to deliver. One minute late and the other lady dies.

A hand grabbed the cell phone and pulled it left. Alex appeared in the frame.

'I'm fine guys. Do what he says. Just keep an eye on Chance for me. Please keep an eye on Chance.'

The voice yanked the phone back toward Cissy.

Shut the hell up. Midnight Kincaid. Fifty grand. No games, no cops, no cameras.

The video bobbled a bit then went to black. Allen turned to his young agent.

"Get EAT and TACT 5 on the move," he said. "Tell SWAT it will be dark and get the level 4 Command Vehicle on site now. Make it Code 3."

"Hold on here," Kincaid said. "I already got my security team on this."

"Your security team couldn't find a fart in the wind," Allen said. "Tell them to stand down or get locked up."

"No way in hell," he said. "This is the biggest story of the year. This is bigger than football."

"Listen to me and listen carefully," Allen moved in close to him. "This is my show. If the media gets even a whiff of this we are up the proverbial creek without a paddle."

"Well it's too late for that. Boo already sent this video out to all the media outlets."

"You did what?" I interrupted and made a move toward Billy Ray. Allen put a strong hand on my chest to stop me. You could see the veins pop out a bit in his neck.

"You did hear the guy on the video say he would kill Alex if he saw a camera, didn't you?"

"This thing is going to make Cissy the biggest star on TV and I'm not going to miss getting the whole thing on video. That's the beauty of this whole mess. Got to have the media on it. Hell, I'll even give you the extra fifty grand myself. I can make that much back in one day from the coverage of this."

"And get an innocent young lady killed?" Allen pressed.

"I don't give a rat's ass about her. Cissy will be bigger than a pop star after this."

I pushed pass Allen and reached for Kincaid. Allen didn't stop me. I shoved him hard up against the brick wall of the building and pressed my forearm against his throat. His red face turned a bright orange.

"Let go of me, you crazy sonofabitch," he squeaked.

I pressed down harder on his windpipe.

"Get him off me," his voice wheezed out in a choked whisper.

Jay Clark stepped in and pulled me back with ease. He was a strong man. Billy Ray coughed, spat and then lunged at me. Shaky grabbed him from behind and wrapped him up with one move. We stood a foot apart and glared at each other. Clark eased his grip on me.

"He assaulted me," he croaked and coughed. "I want to press charges against that idiot."

"I didn't see anything," Allen said. "You see anything, Major?"

"Nope," Clark said. "Not a thing."

"Dammit to hell," he wheezed. "You Georgia boys cheated us out of the game with an illegal play and now you want to cheat me out of a big publicity payday."

"Not a damn thing wrong with that play," Catfish pushed his way forward. "I'm the one who drew that play up."

"A fat ass illegal play made up by a fat ass."

"Check the scoreboard, dickhead," Catfish moved closer.

"A chicken shit way to win a game," Billy Ray croaked. "Run it again and we'll kick your ass."

Catfish charged toward him. Clark let go of me and did a basketball style pick to block Catfish. Shaky wrapped up Billy Ray tight and he fought to get free.

"Let go of me, you fool," he said to Shaky.

"Be my guest," Shaky grinned and let him go. "This is an ass whipping I would pay to see."

Allen had reached his boiling point. His face was red with anger. His ears were even red.

"Shut the hell up the all of you," his voice hard and loud. "Just shut up."

"Get moving," he said to his young agent. "And take this fool Boo with you. Lock him up."

Boo looked shocked. His face turned white.

"You can't do that," Billy Ray said. "What's the charge?"

"I'm thinking on it," Allen answered. "For now, let's just call it criminal stupidity for sending out this video."

"I'm calling my lawyer back."

"Good idea," Allen said. "Better get Boo a lawyer too."

Billy Ray started to say something else but Allen wasn't finished and cut him off.

"You're about two seconds away from wearing my cuffs," he told him. "Get your ass out of my sight. If you or any of the other media idiots you called screw this up and get somebody hurt I will personally set your butt down in a jail cell for the next twenty years."

Billy Ray stared back at Allen but turned to walk away. He dialed his phone and stuck it to his ear. He turned back and pointed right at me.

"This ain't over," his voice still hoarse. "You take me on, you better come with a full bucket and I got a good damn idea that bucket of yours ain't even half full."

37

MAJOR CLARK WENT inside for a few minutes and emerged with two other officers. One of them, a young woman, had a small laptop open in her hands. We stood close by and tried to listen in.

"Where is this Lake Herrick?" Allen asked Clark.

"Less than a mile from here off East Campus Road."

"Good cover for a drop?"

"Not really," Clark said. "It does back up to the Oconee Forest but it's next to the intramural fields, apartments nearby and right off highway 78."

"What about this bridge?"

"Wooden walking bridge that crosses the lake. Not a good place for a quick exit."

"That doesn't make any sense," Allen said. "Why would they pick that spot?"

"I can think of a dozen better ones," Clark said.

"And just where are Kincaid's missing security idiots?"

"Another good question," Clark replied.

The young woman with Clark stepped close and pointed to the laptop.

"Bad news," Clark said to Allen. "Media trucks are already showing up at the lake. The video is out and making the rounds I guess."

"Crap," Allen said. "Get your men out there quick. Move them out and set up a perimeter and make it wide."

"Got it," Clark said and he and his team departed.

I took the chance to step in and thank Allen for having my back.

"If it wasn't for you and your screw ups I would be drinking cold beer and cutting up a steak thicker than a damn spare tire."

He turned to Catfish and turned on him as well.

"And you," he said. "I don't want to hear no more about that damn silly play. Take your buddy here and keep him out of my way. We'll call you if we need you and I can pretty much sure as hell guarantee you that I won't be needing you."

Catfish saluted him and took me by the arm and led me away. We walked over to a low brick wall and took a seat. I was still hot. Catfish had cooled down a bit quicker and after a minute he asked the question we should have already asked.

"What do you think Alex was talking about when she mentioned Chance?"

His question stopped my slow burn and cleared my head a bit.

"Where is Chance?" I asked.

"Where you left him, I guess."

"I'll be right back," I said and jumped up and headed off in a trot.

We had left Chance upstairs on the second level of the big set under the crew lunch tents. I bounced up the stairs and looked around. No sign of him at first but soon I spotted him sound asleep under a table among all the noise and chaos. At least a half dozen paper plates were scattered about him. Most likely he had been eating leftovers since the first quarter. He woke up with a long yawn and followed me at a slow pace back down to the trucks.

The door to one of the production areas opened and Sam came out in a hurry. She was loaded down with a backpack, a tablet, a radio, notepad and a handful of large black batteries. I yelled out her name and she turned and stopped, glanced at her watch. She was in a hurry.

"Where you headed?" I asked her.

"To that lake," she answered. "Not sure what we can do, but we got to go."

"I'm really sorry I screwed up and couldn't get to you guys," I told her.

"Cissy wouldn't allow it anyhow," she noted. "I really like Alex and that's my concern now."

"Mine, too."

"Thanks for kicking Billy Ray's ass back there," she said. "I enjoyed that."

"Don't think it was one of my smarter moves but it did feel good for the moment."

She let out a small grin and looked down the hill. At the bottom, Shaky was packing gear in a SUV.

"I gotta go," she said.

"You're better than all the rest, you know that, don't you," I said to her.

"Not sure about that, especially right now."

"If there is one thing I have learned to spot is a number one draft choice," I told her. "And Sammy Sosa DeNelli, you are a number one draft choice."

She kissed me on the cheek and took off down the hill toward the SUV. I looked down and caught the eye of Shaky. He gave me a wave. He took both of his index fingers and tapped on both his ears and gave me a thumbs up. I had no idea what he meant but I gave him a thumbs up back.

Chance and I headed back up to meet Catfish. By the time I got back Agent Allen and all his people were gone.

"You found him," Catfish said.

"And I know what Alex was talking about."

"When she said keep an eye on Chance?"

"Right. She was talking about this thing she put on his collar."

I pointed at the little green device.

"A GPS tracker," Catfish said.

"She called it by name. Spy something."

"CheetahSpy," Catfish said. "Two way location tracking phone app. Thing is a big hit. Everybody knows about it."

"Really?"

"Everybody but you."

Make A Note: Set aside some time later to learn what an app is.

"She said it could tell where Chance is and show her location on the phone too."

"That's right but you gotta figure they took their cell phones," Catfish said.

"But Alex had two phones."

"Two phones?"

"She connected this thing to her purple phone. It was a small personal one, not the big one she had in her vest."

"So, she still might have that phone on her."

"I think that is what she was trying to tell us on the video. Keep an eye on Chance," I said.

"Does Allen or Clark know about this second phone or the tracking device?"

"No, they would have no way of knowing."

"For now, we keep it that way," Catfish said.

38

"**C**AN YOU ACTUALLY track that thing to her phone?" I asked Catfish.

"Can a snake find a rat under a rock?"

"What?"

"Do you doubt my technology skills?"

"Never have."

"Then be quiet and let me do my thing."

We were back at his RV and Catfish had taken the tiny device off Chance and had it out on the table. He had a laptop open and his big fingers punched at the tiny keyboard. He would pause, mumble a bit, and then start up again. He knew computers like the back of his big hand but I had my doubts this time as he fiddled with the tiny tracker device.

"I'm in," he said.

"In what?"

"I figured out her password and got the CheetahSpy app going on my laptop."

"How did you do that?"

"Because you doubted I could," he said.

He spent the next five minutes or so with his head buried deep in the screen. He would punch at the computer then pick up the device and punch it. The pages on the screen flicked by so fast I had no idea what he was doing. Twice I saw maps pop up and then go away. I heard something beep a few times. Catfish would cuss out loud and pound the machine again. He slowed down a little and on the screen I could see a map of sorts and the little colored dots Alex had shown me earlier. He pulled up another page, typed in a few words and then went back to the map. He stopped and stared at the screen.

"Sonofabitch," he said. "The pickle factory."

"The pickle factory?"

"They're at the pickle factory."

"Who is at the pickle factory?"

"If I'm reading this thing right," Catfish said. "Alex and her phone are in Picketts Corner at the Dixie Dew Pickle Factory."

"I know you been drinking but now you're talking pickles. What the hell are you trying to tell me?"

"Picketts Corner is a small town north of here up in the mountains," he said. "And just outside of town is an old abandoned bunch of buildings. The Dixie Dew Pickle Factory."

"A closed pickle factory?"

"Closed down a few years back."

"And that thing is showing you that Alex's phone is at that old pickle factory?"

"It does," Catfish said. "And guess who used to own the Dixie Dew Pickle Factory?"

"Billy Ray Kincaid?"

"Billy Ray," he said. "That crooked sonofabitch."

Catfish filled me in. The pickle factory was one of the many places Kincaid had purchased in small towns around the south. Like always he would come to town with big plans and big promises to provide jobs and keep the tiny community alive. But like always he drained the place dry and left with the profits stuffed in his pocket. Nearly three hundred people had worked at the place for over seventy-five years and it was the only place left for a decent paying job in Picketts Corner. In less than two years, he had cut the workforce down to about one hundred people and a year later he sold it off to foreign investors and fired the rest. Now the traditional southern Dixie Dew Pickles were made somewhere in Bangladesh.

"So, you think this means Billy Ray is involved some-how?" I asked.

"Don't know," Catfish said. "But it does stink like a dead polecat."

"Could be his security guys. There is at least one still missing."

"Maybe," he said. "But I doubt it. Most them boys dumb as dirt."

"Why would he try and pull off something like this?"

"Did you see the cameras in that room this morning?"

"Publicity?"

"You heard him while ago. Publicity means money. Big money."

"The other things?" I wondered aloud. "The break in at Ole Miss. The two guys I tangled with last night. The car in the alley that tried to run over me. You think all of these things were staged?"

"That is one damn good question."

"You got an answer?"

"Nope. We got bumpkus," he said. "All we got is a little dot on this here Cheetah app."

"We need to call Agent Allen," I said.

"And tell him what?" Catfish said. "We took a tiny thing off your dog and we think we found Alex or maybe just her phone at a broken down pickle factory up in the mountains?"

"When you put it like that maybe calling Allen isn't the best thing to do right now."

"You think? He's damn near primed to snatch a knot in your tail already."

"But what about the money drop at the lake."

"GBI and UGA got that covered," he said. "Hell, far as we know this thing might be wrong. Or maybe they just took 'em up there for now before heading back down here."

"We don't have a lot to go on, do we?"

"We ain't got a pot to pee in."

"Any ideas rolling around in that big bourbon filled head of yours?" I asked.

"Go find out things," Catfish answered.

"You mean we go up to the pickle factory?"

"Not we."

"You mean me?"

"We can't go to the GBI without knowing what we're talking about."

"And you want me to go up there and find out things?"

"You asked and that's the idea falling out of this big head."

"And what are you going to be doing while I do that?"

"Sit here, drink more bourbon and watch this damn little dot," he said. "I'll let you know if it moves."

"But I don't know anything about this place," I said. "I don't even know where this town is."

"Then you need somebody who does."

"That would help."

"Got anybody in mind?"

"I can think of one person."

"Buddy Lee Bowman?"

"That was my first thought."

"Good thinking," Catfish said. "Lives one county over."

"But I rode down with Alex," I said. "I don't even have a vehicle to get up there."

"I can think of one guy to help with that."

"Same guy that was hanging off the goalpost a little bit ago?"

"That's the one."

"I was afraid you were going to say that."

39

"**D**UMPTRUCK DRIVING ME up there is a really bad idea," I told Catfish.

"You got any other suggestions for a ride?"

"I don't."

"He's perfect for the job," Catfish said. "Got a 4-wheeler, knows the town, knows the back roads to get there fast and that fool can be really clever in tight situations."

"That fool was hanging upside down off the goalpost two hours ago, drunk as a skunk."

"That is exactly why he is the perfect choice to help us."

"I think we need to talk this over," I said to him.

"Talk fast," he said. "He'll be here in ten minutes."

"I guess we're done talking."

Catfish had moved all the computer stuff over to the main table in the RV and sat up what amounted to his own command center. He had the laptop, his phone, a tiny TV tuned to the news, a few other devices I didn't recognize, four big cigars, an ashtray and two bottles of Old Scout Single Barrel bourbon.

"Give me your phone," he said.

I fished in my pocket and handed him my small battered flip phone.

"This thing work?"

"Last time I used it," I answered.

"When was that," he asked. "1996?"

He opened it up, poked at the tiny keys and scrolled through things I didn't even know existed. He picked up a thin little device about two inches long with a plastic loop attached and handed it to me.

"Try this and make sure it works," he said.

I took it from him and stared at it.

"Put the loop around your ear," he instructed.

I did what he said. It felt like a bad growth hanging off my ear.

"Now punch the tiny button on the side of it," he told me.

"Do what?"

"Touch the little button on the top end near your ear."

I fiddled around with my finger and then found the tiny inset. I touched it. His phone rang. He looked at the number and picked it up.

"Got me?"

"Oddly enough, I do."

He hung up.

"What is this thing?"

"Bluetooth headset. Hands free. Keep that on your head and touch that one thing and it will ring my phone."

"What if I need to call somebody else besides you?"
"Then you're on your own," he said. "They call that dialing. You study on that a bit and figure it out."

We heard a big rumble outside the RV. The sound of a big V-8 engine without a muffler. It popped once and halted. A door slammed with a clunk and then the door to the RV flew open. Dumptruck plowed inside.

"Raining like a cow peeing on a flat rock," he said and headed straight for the bourbon bottle on the counter.

"That's my good stuff," Catfish protested.

"We just beat 'Bama," he raised the bottle. "A toast to the return of Mudcat Moon."

"That's an odd name for a football play," I said. "Where did it come from?"

"Tell him the story," Dumptruck said.

"You guys need to get going," he said. "Ain't got time for a long story."

"Tell the short version," Dumptruck said.

There is no such thing as a short version for Catfish. They don't sell the Cliff Notes for his stories.

"Long story short," he started. "It goes back to when the NCAA didn't rule practices and every summer we would go up to Cherokee, North Carolina for a full week of two-a-days to kick off the year."

"Three-a-days if we screwed up," Dumptruck said. "Which we did a lot."

"At the end of the week they would let us make up one play on our own for fun and if it worked they would add it to the playbook. Since I was the captain I got to think it up that year."

"And you came up with the play from today?" I asked him.

"Always wanted to throw a pass, so I drew up a play where I got to throw the ball."

"Except he couldn't throw the ball worth a damn," Dumptruck added.

"We kept trying and trying and it was getting dark. Sun going down, big moon coming up, every time we ran it, we messed it up worse."

"My grandma could throw a hard biscuit farther than he could throw the football."

"Who's telling this story?"

"Excuse me," Dumptruck said. "Carry on Johnny U."

"Coach gave us a five-minute break and told us we had one more chance to make it work or we were done. I ran over into the woods to relieve myself under the trees."

"Take a leak," Dumptruck clarified for me.

"Got it," I said.

"I'm 'bout halfway done and I look up and leaning on the tree next to me is this old man with long white hair in a ponytail. His face weathered like an old baseball mitt. I don't know where he came from. Just showed up outta nowhere."

"Old Indian guy," Dumptruck said.

"Native American," Catfish corrected.

"Yeah, a real Cherokee dude."

"I didn't know what to do, him just standing there while I went, so I looked up at the moon. It was coming up through the trees and it was huge and blood red."

"Bulldog red," Dumptruck noted.

"So, I just said to the old man, nice looking moon ain't it?"

"Tell him what he told you."

"I'm doing that," Catfish cut him off. "He didn't even look at me. He just spoke low and smooth in this scary voice, *'That is a mudcat moon. Bad moon. Only evil can happen under a mudcat moon.'* I looked down to button up and when I looked up he had disappeared. Just like that. He was gone. Just gone."

"Just gone," Dumptruck said. "Ain't that spooky as all get out?"

"I hauled butt back to the field and we had one more chance to run the play."

"And it worked?" I asked.

"Everything clicked. We ran it twice. Both times we scored. We were dancing around like school kids at recess."

"And coach blew the horn and told us we could put it in the playbook," Dumptruck said.

"And then old two teeth asked me what I wanted to call the play," Catfish said. "I looked up at that big red moon as it crept up over the top of the trees and I told him to name it *Mudcat Moon.*"

"And you used it later that year in a game," I said.

"First and last time. Mudcat Moon-77-Bootleg Red. Dead and buried until today."

"And now we done beat Ala-damn-bama with it," Dumptruck grinned and finished off his drink.

"You sure you didn't just make up the stuff about the old man just to have a story to tell?" I asked.

"I love a tall tale," he said. "But I ain't near enough a good storyteller to make up something like that."

"Shake a leg, big man," Dumptruck yelled at me. "Getting dark, rain getting harder and the roads are gonna be slicker than my tires."

Catfish joined me at the door and smiled as I took in Dumptruck's vehicle. Chance stuck his head out to look but felt the rain and went back in. It was an old Ford Bronco, with oversize tires and no top. It had a canvas tarp of sorts as a roof. The front panel was bright blue but the rest of this side was either brown or maybe it was just rust. It was hard to tell.

Catfish handed me my cheap pullover nylon raincoat and I slipped it on.

"I'm beginning to think this whole thing is a real bad idea," I said.

"We don't have a good one," he replied.

"You sure we are doing the right thing by going up there?"

"I ain't sure 'bout nothing right now."

"I'm sure he shouldn't be driving," I said and pointed at Dumptruck behind the wheel. He lifted a bottle from between his legs and took a big swig from it.

"He drives better drunk than sober," Catfish said.

Catfish kept the jokes coming but I could tell this situation had him worried. We had been in scrapes before but it usually was just him or me. This time it involved Alex. A crack of thunder rumbled hard and rolled over us.

"Alex is a tough cookie," I said to him.

"A damn site tougher than most," he replied.

"But Billy Ray and his guys are crazy as hell."

"Not as crazy as we are," he glanced at Dumptruck.

"So, we go do what we do," I said.

"We do, indeed."

Dumptruck honked the horn and yelled again. I gave him a signal that I was coming. Another low rumble of thunder stretched out for maybe thirty seconds and faded away. The rain picked up harder. Catfish went back inside and returned with a hat. He handed it to me. It wasn't a very good hat. It was a baseball cap but it had no shape and was made of cheap material. It was red on top with a white brim. Written across the front was the phrase *God Made--Jesus Saved--Georgia Raised*. I put it on and snugged the ugly thing down to block the rain.

"Fat guys throwing touchdown passes, Cherokee Indians disappearing into the night, thunderstorms booming in October and TV stars getting kidnapped," I said to him. "What the hell is going on here?"

"That's what you're going to find out, ain't it? Now hunker down and get going."

40

DUMPTRUCK DROVE THE old Bronco like a tank. Twice he went nearly a full block on the sidewalk as we made our way off campus and out of the post game traffic. A half hour later we barreled along a tar and gravel road in the middle of nowhere. The sky was dark and I had not seen a light or a house in a good twenty miles. The pine trees flew by in the flicker of only one working headlight. The windshield wiper worked on his side but not mine. The tarp roof flapped in the wind and my right arm was soaked from the lack of a window. Every now and then he would take another pull off the bottle between his legs and two tires would leave the road and veer back on.

I tried to reach Buddy Lee several times but got no answer. That was odd for him. There would be times when I needed some wood billets on short notice and he would always pick up on the first ring. Without his help, we would be lost. I told myself I would try one more time before I punched the little thing in my ear and call Catfish to bag the trip. He picked up on the fifth ring.

"Speak to me, boy," Buddy Lee Bowman said.

"Thank goodness," I said. "I was beginning to think I couldn't reach you."

"I was in a bar," he said. "Watching football and drinking beer."

"Lot of that going around today," I said.

"Speak up," he told me. "You sound like you calling from a freight train."

I told him where I was or where I thought we were. I wasn't quite sure.

"So what kind of trouble you in this time?" He asked.

"Who said I was in trouble?"

"You don't call five times on a Saturday night to order up ash billets."

"No, I don't."

"Fill me in," he said.

So, I did. I backed up to the day before and ended up fast as I could with where things stood today. I don't think I had his full attention until I told him about Alex. He helped me out once with a situation with one of her former boyfriends, and I think he took a liking to her. That was not unusual for guys who meet Alex.

"For that little lady," he said. "Count me in."

"For this we might need more help," I said. "What about your cousin, Gator?"

"Gator is gone."

"Gone. Gone where?"

"Joined the Army."

"The Army. Whose Army?"

"Our Army."

"Why doesn't that comfort me?"

"Especially since they training him to fire a 252 Mortar," he said.

"You got anybody else in mind that can help out?" I asked him.

"Near Picketts Corner there is only one guy that comes to mind."

"Who is that?"

"Fellow I served with in the Marines. Name is Lester Tibby but everybody calls him Boobytrap."

"Booby trap? Why?"

"He was in a demolition unit in the service. Likes to blow things up."

"He around?"

"Just got out of jail," he said.

"Jail? What did he do?"

"Blew up the car of his former boss," Buddy Lee said. "Most of his house, too."

"That will, indeed, get you sent to jail," I said.

"His poor mama spent thirty years working at that pickle factory before she lost her job. Now she drives forty miles each way six days a week to clean a resort motel for half of what she was making."

"So, you think he might be around tonight?"

"Oh, I know right where he is."

"How's that?"

"He's under house arrest."

"Ankle bracelet?"

"24-hour monitoring."

"That's not good."

"Call you back in five," he said and jumped off.

While we were on the phone, Dumptruck had crossed over a larger highway and turned past a brightly lit convenience store and onto another dark road. His shortcuts didn't seem short but I had no idea where we were headed or where I was, so I didn't protest. Four minutes later the phone rang.

"He's good to go," Buddy Lee said as I picked up.

"You sure?"

"You driving?"

"No," I told him. "Friend of Catfish is driving. He knows the area. Fellow named Dumptruck."

I heard him chuckle a bit.

"Tell Dumptruck to take State 23 past the factory. Take a right on Devils Pond Road. You'll hit a dead end about a mile down, right on top of a big hill above the pickle place. We'll meet you there in an hour."

"Devils Pond Road," I repeated. "That doesn't sound good."

"Could be a sign," he noted.

"What about the ankle bracelet?" I asked him.

"You don't mess with Boobytrap's mama," he said and hung up.

41

WE HAD OUTRUN the storm for now and Dumptruck had picked up speed as the rain let up. The roads were still wet and I could feel the Bronco slide sideways just a bit each time he turned hard into a curve. He gripped the oversized steering wheel with both hands and pushed on into the darkness.

"So, who is this fellow, Buddy Lee?" He asked me when he got the truck straight.

"He's a friend and a lumber man that supplies me with billets," I answered.

"With what?"

"Ash billets that I use to make baseball bats."

"You make baseball bats?"

"Custom bats for Minor League ballplayers," I told him. "It's my other job."

"Sounds like a boring job."

"Not to me."

"But ain't exciting like this, is it?"

"This, whatever it is, doesn't excite me very much."

"You're lying like a dog."

I didn't respond. It doesn't do much good to get into a back and forth with a drunk. Especially a drunk who holds your life in his hands as he turns into one dark curve after another.

"Tell the truth," he continued. "If you don't like it, then why you doing it?"

"This whole thing was Catfish's idea," I said. "Every time I find myself tangled up in something like this it seems to be his idea."

"He put a gun to your head?"

"No," I said. "I usually agree because I need the money."

"I guess making them ball bats don't make big money?"

"Not big at all."

He headed hard into a deep curve and pulled with both hands on the wheel. Two tires bounced off the edge of the pavement then fishtailed back on. I reached up and gripped the roll bar tight.

"How many years you play pro ball?" He asked.

I thought he had changed the subject.

"Seventeen years playing and five coaching."

"You miss it?"

I shrugged.

"Come on now, talk to me big man," he said.

"Every single day," I confessed.

"Damn straight," he agreed.

He took the bottle from between his legs and took another drink. It was nearly empty. He offered up the last bit to me but I declined. He finished it off with one swallow and tossed the bottle into the ditch.

"That's the reason we're out here," he said.

"What is?"

"We're different you know?"

"You and me?" I asked. "Different how?"

"Ballplayers," he said. "Professionals. Once you've played ball for money, it changes you."

"How's that?"

"It's like some kind of addiction. Maybe a bit like a long ago lost love you left behind that you can't shake," he said. "Gets down inside you and settles in your gut like some old tapeworm."

I didn't answer him. I didn't know how to answer him but I understood him.

"Once you have faced that kind of pressure," he continued. "The kind of pressure that comes with knowing that if you screw it up today, you might not be around tomorrow. It never leaves you."

I stayed silent.

"It don't matter what sport it is," he kept on. "Football, baseball, hell, even a sissy ass sport like golf, once you start up playing for your dinner the pressure is real."

"I hear what you saying."

"In college, I was just playing for fun. But when I got into the pros I knew it was damn serious."

"I was eighteen years old when I first got paid to play," I said.

"There ain't no feeling like it nowhere else," he said. "Riding bulls, gambling, fighting, diving underwater. I done them all. Nothing like playing ball for a living and getting paid for it."

"But it is a hard way to make a living," I said.

"Every day was like trying to take food away from a damn grizzly bear."

I nodded in agreement. A blast of water from a road puddle washed over the windshield.

"You know, if you could bottle that feeling we talking about," he said. "You could make a million bucks. Stronger than any damn drug I know about."

"Easy to get hooked."

"And then one day they just go and take it all away from you. No matter what you do you can't find that feeling anywhere."

"I admit that I have spent some time searching for it," I told him.

"Like an old dog looking for a bone," he said.

We both were silent for a mile or so. We crossed a bridge over a lake that you could barely make out in the dark and headed up a long hill bordered by tall pines. He downshifted and pushed his foot into the pedal. The old Bronco growled and surged up the mountain.

"So, quit lying to me about Catfish being the reason you do this kind of stuff."

"Who says I've been lying to you?"

"You been listening to anything I just said?"

"I've been trying to keep up."

"I'm talking about that feeling we been chasing."

"I heard that part."

"Then you got to understand the real reason why the two of us are out here on this damn dark night with our butts flapping in the wind."

"And what reason would that be?"

"We just two old dogs looking for a bone."

42

THERE WAS NO pond on Devils Pond Road. It was barely a road, a rutted path with high weeds in the middle. I wasn't sure about the Devil but he could be near considering the thunder that rumbled above us. The road hit a dead end in a circle of tall wet millet surrounded by trees. Dumptruck cut the engine and the one headlight and we sat there in the dark silence. The abrupt change sent a cool shiver up my back.

"What now?" He asked.

I was about to answer when a light flashed on and off twice to our left. I nearly fell out of the truck.

"Over here," I heard Buddy Lee's voice in the dark.

I looked hard but couldn't spot him. The flashlight flicked on and he held it under his chin. I saw his face. He smiled.

"That him?" Dumptruck asked.

"That's him," I said with some relief.

A moment later a pair of headlights buzzed and the light raked across the tall grass. Buddy Lee Bowman cast a huge shadow as he crossed over in a stream of yellow light. The thunderstorm had caught up with us as the wind picked up and light rain began to fall. He shined his flashlight in my eyes.

"Nice hat," he said.

"Nice outfit," I said back to him.

He had on denim overalls, half buttoned on the side and a t-shirt without sleeves. His big arms were bare and the rain made his faded Marine tattoo glisten a bit. The overalls were tucked into a pair of tall hunting boots. His dark baseball cap was turned around backward. His belly was big and strained at the bib of the overalls but it never slowed him down. He was huge, stronger than three men and could toss a large tree like it was a fence post.

"Drinking clothes," he said. "Didn't have time to change."

I introduced him to Dumptruck and Buddy Lee told him he liked his truck. This made Dumptruck smile. Always nice to see people make new friends.

"So, is this other guy you told me about coming?" I asked Buddy Lee.

He grinned and shined his flashlight over toward the trees. Twenty feet deep back in the pines sat an old dark van. It faced outward and was squeezed tight between two trees. The side doors were open and a tarp spread out to make a tent of sorts. In the dark you could just barely make out a figure moving around.

"That's him in the woods?"

"That is Boobytrap."

"What's he doing?" Dumptruck asked.

"Getting things ready," he answered.

"Getting what things ready?" I asked.

"Not too sure. It's better if you don't ask him a lot of questions," he said.

"I gotta meet a guy that calls himself Boobytrap," Dumptruck said.

"This from a man who calls himself Dumptruck?"

"I worked hard to earn this name," he said with a grin.

"So did Boobytrap."

Buddy Lee shined his light over to the van again and held it. He stuck two fingers in his mouth and let out a sharp whistle. He made a hand signal of some sort and clicked off the light. A minute later, Boobytrap came out of the dark and emerged into the glow of the headlights. He was maybe six feet tall and skinny. That is all I could tell about him. The rest was hidden. He had on black fatigue bottoms, a black hoodie with the hood down low over his head and a pair of goggles that might have been green camouflage. His hands were covered with slick tight black gloves.

"These here are the guys I told you about," Buddy Lee said to him.

He may have nodded. I'm not sure. He didn't speak.

"Why they call you Boobytrap?" Dumptruck spoke up.

I shot a look at Dumptruck. Boobytrap didn't answer. The rain came down harder and the wind made the top of the trees sway in the dark. The silence was awkward.

"Appreciate you coming," I broke the silence. "I know this is not your deal."

He nodded just a touch. I didn't expect him to speak but he did.

"I got this itch that needs scratching," he said.

His words slipped out like the hiss of a snake, slick and quick. The voice seemed even odder if you considered the setting and the rain. I assumed he was talking about Billy Ray but I wasn't going to follow up with him about that or his Mom. Just looking at him spooked me. I wasn't sure what to say but felt the need to thank him for coming.

"I'm glad you're here," I said.

"I ain't here," he hissed. "You never saw me."

Dumptruck cut his eyes at me and I think he was about to say something but Buddy Lee cut him off.

"We got to scout things out," he said. "Go ahead and get your stuff fixed up."

"It was cool meeting you, man," Dumptruck said as Boobytrap turned away.

"I ain't never met you and I ain't never been here," he said as he snaked his way back into the dark.

We watched him disappear into the woods and saw him duck under the tarp and flick on a small light.

"Well," I paused. "I've never met anybody like him."

"That there is one odd dude," Dumptruck observed.

"That he is," Buddy Lee grinned. "But very talented."

"But talented at what is the question?" I noted.

"You ain't gonna see his kind of talent at a piano recital," Buddy Lee said.

"What is he doing over there in the van?"

"Getting fuses and stuff rigged I guess."

"Fuses?"

"I told you he likes to blow things up."

"I don't want him to kill anybody," the alarm showed in my voice.

Buddy Lee waved me off. "Don't worry 'bout it," he said. "I made it real clear to him that everything had to be non-lethal."

"What exactly does non-lethal mean?"

"It means he blows up things not people."

"Things?"

"I didn't ask him for a damn itemized receipt," Buddy Lee said. "I just asked him to do what he does best."

"That's what worries me," I said.

"You want his help or not?"

A big spark and crackle emerged from over near the van. A puff of smoke drifted up into the trees. We heard a yelp.

"I'm starting to think it wasn't a good idea to bring him here," I said.

"You heard him," Buddy Lee said. "He ain't here."

"The invisible man," Dumptruck smiled as he said it.

We heard another small pop come from the van and another whoop. A second later another flash and more smoke rolled out from under the doors. A light flashed around and made streaks through the mist. What sounded like a low moan came next. Then a short sizzle and sparks shot out the tarp and up into the wet tree limbs.

"What is all that?" Dumptruck asked.

"Delicate and tricky work dealing with old explosives," Buddy Lee answered.

"Old explosives?"

"Been in jail," he said. "Reckon some of his material is a bit rusty."

"How long was he in jail?"

"Maybe two years and now the Feds got him locked down at home."

"How did he get out of the ankle bracelet?"

"You gonna stand around and ask questions all night about his resume or we gonna light this fuse?"

Another pop and puff of smoke rose from inside the van. We heard him yell.

"No, I'm fresh out of questions," I said. I was afraid of the answers.

43

THE RAIN CAME in sheets as we made our way down what may have been a path at one time but now was a small ditch filled with water. All we could see in front of us was the flicker of a flashlight as Buddy Lee led the way. He moved fast and we splashed behind him, trying to keep up. He stopped and gave us a hand signal to follow him to the left and up a tiny ridge. We reached the top and peered down. Below us you could make out the outline of a large building. A hulking water tower loomed to the right and a soft glow of light peeked out from somewhere on the opposite side of the structure. Buddy Lee had a canvas duffel with him and he sat the big bag down at our feet with a clunk.

"That's the Dixie Dew Pickle Factory, gentlemen," he said to us both. "Or what's left of it."

"It looks huge," I said.

"That's just the old warehouse building straight down," he said. "There's about five or six more buildings on the other side of the property. Some already run down, some in good shape still."

"I don't see anything or anybody."

"Can't from this angle. Anybody around would be holed up on the other side near the highway. That's why we came in this way."

"Well, let's go check it out," Dumptruck said and stood up.

"Put your pecker back in your pants," Buddy Lee told him. "I got to do some recon first."

He unzipped the duffel back at his feet and pulled out two small walkie-talkie radios. He fiddled with the buttons on both, clamped one to his chest and handed the other one to me.

"Got three of these things," he said. "Boobytrap has one, this one is for you two."

I took it and looked at the buttons.

"You press the trigger to talk, stick it to your ear to listen and speak easy."

"Easy?"

"Talk soft in case somebody nearby is listening."

That wasn't a comforting thought.

"If you can't speak," he continued. "Just key the trigger. See the red button when you do it?"

He pointed at the tiny red button that lit up when he pushed the trigger.

"One click is affirmative. Two clicks for negative. Three clicks will tell me you in trouble."

"Three clicks for trouble," I repeated. "This from an ex-Marine."

"Ain't no such thing as an ex-Marine," he said and threw the duffel bag over his large shoulders.

"Where we going now?" Dumptruck asked.

"You two ain't going nowhere. Just sit tight right here while I take a look," he said.

"Why just you?" I asked.

"Ain't the first time I've done this," he said without explaining.

"So we just wait for you?"

"I'll click three times if I need an ex-ballplayer to come a running."

He paused for a beat and dropped the bag back to the ground. He reached in and pulled out another flashlight and handed it to me.

"Take this," he said. "Give me twenty minutes or so to find my way around and I'll give you a shout."

"Okay."

"By the way," he said. "I've seen your shop with the old gear from the last century and you ain't exactly the hipster type, so what's that little phone doohickey doing in your ear?"

"A direct line to Catfish," I replied and touched the little device. "He set this up."

"That boy is always thinking, ain't he?" He grinned. "He standing by tonight?"

"Waiting and watching with two bottles of bourbon and some cigars."

"And he's got a bead on just where the little lady might be?"

"That's what he tells me."

"Call him."

"Now?"

"Let's see if he's still seeing what he is seeing."

I reached up and found the little indention and pushed on it. My ear exploded with a ring and Catfish picked up before it stopped.

"Talk to me, son," he said. "You up on pickle mountain yet?"

"We're here above the place. In the woods up the hill," I told him.

"Raining up there?"

"You want to talk about the weather?"

"The dot is still right smack dab where it was when you left," he jumped to the point. "Ain't moved."

"So, you think Alex is here?"

"I would bet your ass," he answered.

That was exactly what was on the line I thought. Not to mention some time in jail if we screwed this thing up. Agent Allen might see to that. Maybe I could share a cell with Boobytrap. Get to know him better.

"Any word from Allen or the others?" I asked.

"Not a peep," he said. "I think he's glad you gone and out of the way. TV is still going on about the video and they all over the place out at that lake."

"Which makes me real nervous about following some dot we found from a dog collar."

"Don't go doubting my dot," he said. "You get yourself some help besides Dumptruck?"

I said I had. I told him I found Buddy Lee and how he had rounded up Boobytrap.

"So, he found a guy to help that just got out of jail?" He asked.

"That is correct."

"And this fella named Boobytrap was in jail for blowing things up?"

"Blowing up a lot of thing we hear."

"A damn good day is turning into a damn good night," he chuckled. "Call me when things go boom."

He hung up.

"He still seeing that dot?" Buddy Lee asked.

"He does."

"Then it's time I take a look."

Dumptruck turned to his left and pointed down through the trees.

"I just saw that guy Boobytrap rolling some wires down the hill," he said.

"Yep," Buddy Lee said. "Setting up traps."

"Traps?"

"Did you see what all that fool was toting when he left his van?" Dumptruck asked.

"I tried not to look," I said.

"He had a whole little trailer of stuff he was pulling down the hill. Wonder what it all was?"

Buddy Lee slung the duffel bag up across his shoulders again and turned to leave.

"That stuff," he said. "Is our insurance policy."

He slipped down the hill. The fog and rain covered him up as he disappeared into the dark.

44

WITH THE FLASHLIGHT off, the night seemed to grow darker. We lay flat on the ground. The trees moved in the wind. The only sound was the steady drumbeat of raindrops on my cheap parka. It did not keep the water out and I could feel the rain trickle down my back. Dumptruck rose up on his knees to shake his fishing hat off and pulled it back on.

A strong gust of wind shoved the limbs of the pine tree above us into each other and it sounded like somebody clicked two drumsticks together. The shadow came from my right and emerged without a sound. I felt my heart jump and let out a breath that might have been a small yelp. Buddy Lee slid up beside the two of us.

"Holy crap," Dumptruck said in a whistle. "You scared the hell out of me. I didn't hear you coming."

"You weren't supposed to," he answered.

He was carrying a pair of bolt cutters, a spray can and some heavy leather welding gloves.

"I had to backtrack to my truck to get some stuff," he said.

"Anything down there?" I asked.

"Yeah, trouble."

"Any sight of Alex?"

"Ain't sure. That's what these things are for," he motioned to the bolt cutters.

"What do you mean by trouble?"

"Bunch of guys like you described. Wearing black and with big guns."

"Kincaid's security guys," I said.

"At least five I could spot," he said. "Two in a big black truck. Two out front of a warehouse door and one on some steps to the second level."

"Inside?"

"Couldn't see. Lights are on and I found the back way to the top level but it's gonna take some doing to get up there."

"Let's get after it, then," Dumptruck said.

"I like a man ready to test the unknown," Buddy Lee said. "Let's rock n' roll."

I didn't fall into that category but I followed both down the hill on a muddy trail. The three of us had to slide down a deep slope to get to the rear of the factory grounds. He told us to stay close and keep away from the fence that wrapped around the place. We made our way past two other buildings. The first was intact but all the windows were gone and the second one had fallen into itself in a pile of old bricks. Buddy Lee led us around the last building and to the edge of the water tower. The old tower leaned to the left a good ten feet. We looked up at it through the rain. Buddy Lee put the bolt cutters around his neck, the bag over his back, stuffed the other stuff in his overalls, grabbed the bottom rung of the old metal ladder and headed up.

"Follow me," he said.

"That thing is leaning like it might fall over," I said.

"Shoot, it ain't more than a hundred feet tall," Dumptruck said and scattered up after Buddy Lee.

This observation coming from a man who once jumped off one twice as tall to win a boat.

"Right behind you," I said with a great lack of confidence.

We made it to the top of the water tower one by one. It was covered with rust but you could still make out a logo and words that said *Dixie Dew Pickles, The Sweet Taste Of The South*. You could feel it sway with the wind. I was anxious to get off the tower until I saw where he was headed next. Extended from the water tower was a rusted steel catwalk that led all the way back to the main building. It was missing bottom sections and the hand railings were only two feet tall. Buddy Lee didn't hesitate. He moved across it with ease. Dumptruck followed with a wobble and I brought up the rear. I resisted the temptation to drop to my knees and crawl but staggered along far behind them.

They waited on a roof at the end of the catwalk for me to catch up with them.

"Easy as stealing third base, right?" Buddy Lee smiled at me in the dark.

I didn't answer. He turned and made his way across the roof to where a tall six-foot fence with rolled barbed wire across the top blocked a pair of stairs that led down to the second level of the main building. It was the rear of the warehouse he had scouted. Two large factory windows bracketed a massive industrial fan. The fan rumbled and roared, the big blades pushed the rain around in circles. The window on the right was just above the bottom of the stairs and had those huge panels that opened to let air in. Soft light glowed from inside. I was amazed that Buddy Lee had been able to scout all of this out and find a way to access it. The only thing standing in the way was a metal gate in the fence with a large padlock.

"So that's what the bolt cutters are for?" I asked.

"Partly," he answered.

"Let me have those," Dumptruck said. "I'll cut that lock off."

"I wouldn't do that," Buddy Lee said.

"Why not?"

"Unless you want to light yourself up like a roman candle."

"That is an electric fence?" I asked.

"Wired to fry."

"So, what do we do?"

He picked up the bolt cutters.

"Are you crazy?" I said. "We're all standing in water."

"Pay attention," he said.

He pulled out the spray can from his overalls and handed the gloves and bolt cutters to me. It was a can of foam insulation. I had no idea what he had in mind.

"Now listen," he said. "I ain't gonna mess with the lock. We gonna cut a hole in the gate big enough to squeeze through. I'll spray the links and when I spray one then you cut it."

"Do what?"

"The foam spray nullifies the high voltage for just a little bit and we can cut a hole in the fence."

"That will really work?"

"If you don't screw up it will," he said. "Just follow my moves and when I nod you cut."

Make A Note: The more you roll along in life, the more you learn that there is a very fine line between being brave and just plain damn crazy.

I have faced pressure plenty of times. I have been shot at. I have been shot at and missed. I have been shot at and hit. I have been hit in the groin with a 90-mph fastball. I have done a lot of things I regret and some I knew at the time to be careless. I have never done anything like this. I stood in a huge puddle of water and aimed the bolt cutters at a link of a high voltage fence. Buddy Lee would spray, nod and I would cut. Each snap of the bolt cutters sounded like a bomb going off in my head. He would shake the can and repeat. I focused hard and tried to keep my hands steady as rain rolled down into my eyes. One by one we made a three-foot square in the fence. When we got to the last link he emptied out the can and told me to pull it back and out of the way. I dropped the square piece of fence gently to the roof. I let out a long breath.

"How the hell did you know that would work?" Dumptruck asked him.

"Unwritten military training," he said. "Courtesy of your United States Marines."

We each bent down and made our way through the small opening careful not to touch the rest of the fence. Buddy Lee eased his big duffel bag through and we made our way down the stairs. The window at the bottom was about ten feet off the ground. Dumptruck pointed to his right and lugged over a wooden pallet. He leaned it up against the wall.

"You're the tallest," he said. "Can you reach the edge of the first window with this?"

"I think so," I said.

"Crawl up there and take a look," Buddy Lee said. "But go easy in case somebody is watching."

"Watching?"

He shrugged.

"They can't hear anything with that big fan running," he said into my ear. "But ain't no telling if they got anybody inside or not."

I wiped the rain out of my eyes and started up the pallet using the wall to brace myself. I eased up over the edge of the first window. Inside was a long empty warehouse with green scoop lights that hung from a tall ceiling lined with beams. It was split in the middle with a loft that made a second floor on this side. The open area below the loft was dark and I couldn't make out much or see anyone. I inched myself right and grabbed the edge of the window to pull myself up to the last rung of the pallet. With the few extra inches, I could see clearly down into the lofted side. The old plank floor was covered with dirt and old cardboard shipping boxes were scattered about. Down the right side of the loft was a row of metal storage cages each about ten feet square with a sliding door. All of the cages were open, empty and dark except one. The cage near the end was chained shut with a lock and lit only by a bare bulb. In the corner of the cage I spotted them. I crab walked down the wall and jumped off the pallet.

"See anything?" Buddy Lee asked.

"Yeah," I said. "A dot from a dog collar."

45

"**W**E CAN'T GET in through the window," Buddy Lee said. "There's a door down at the bottom of the stairs that leads to the roof. That's where we go in."

We moved to the edge to check out the staircase.

"The stairs are gone," I said.

"That's not good," Dumptruck noted. "Must be thirty feet straight down."

Buddy Lee shook his head at us and reached into his duffel bag. He pulled out a nylon bag and removed one of those fold up tree ladders for hunters. He rigged the hooks to what was left of the top rung of stairs and let it roll out. It came within maybe five feet of the bottom.

"Well, would you look at that," Dumptruck said with amusement.

"Three easy payments of $19.95," Buddy Lee said.

Dumptruck was over the edge and hit the bottom quick. I followed him and Buddy Lee lowered his bag with a nylon rope and followed it down. He took the bag over to a set of double doors at the rear of the warehouse.

The doors were secured with a very large padlock. Buddy Lee pulled out a small leather pouch filled with tools that resembled something you might see in a dental office. He pulled out a long one and went to work on the lock.

"Point your flashlight right here," he told me as he poked at the lock with the odd tool.

"You done this before?" I asked.

"I have, indeed."

"The Marines teach you this, too?" Dumptruck asked.

"Nope. Learned this from my Uncle Billy."

"Locksmith?"

"Thief," he said and kept working the lock.

Dumptruck looked at me and grinned.

"Got it," he said and the lock popped open.

He told me to cut the light. He opened the door a few inches and stuck his head in. He leaned back and told me to grab the duffel and follow him inside. Dumptruck went first and I followed with the heavy bag. We stopped inside the door. We were on the bottom level of the lofted warehouse. In front of us was an old forklift parked and left behind. Large aluminum vats ran along the left side all connected by wires and tubes. Pickle vats I guess. The building smelled of dirt and vinegar. The only light on the lower level came from two light bulbs with industrial covers on the left wall. Boxes of empty mason jars were stacked behind the forklift and up against a set of metal stairs that led up to the loft. The stairs were in bad shape. The outside railing looked loose and about every other metal step was missing. Buddy Lee motioned for us to head up behind him. I went last with the heavy bag over my shoulder. When I placed my full weight on the last step it popped and gave way. I fell forward and hit the floor with a thud. The items in the duffel bag made a loud noise. I reached back and grabbed the metal step just as it was about to fall and rolled back onto the loft floor.

At the front of the warehouse a door popped open and a bright flashlight panned the walls. Dumptruck and Buddy Lee had ducked down behind a stack of pallets. He reached out and grabbed my belt and pulled me back toward them. My head and shoulders stuck out in the open. I pressed flat against the floor. The flashlight moved around the bottom and then up the stairs and around the pallets. I heard a voice say something in the distance. Then another voice maybe from outside the door. The flashlight made another pass and then it disappeared and we heard the door shut. I got up to my knees.

"Who's there?" A voice came from the other side of the pallets. Alex.

I stood up and moved toward the storage cage. Alex sat on the floor against the wall. She jumped to her feet when she saw us.

She moved to the front of the locked cage. "I don't believe it. Unreal."

Buddy Lee already had the bolt cutters out and aimed at the lock.

"You remember Buddy Lee, don't you?" I said to her.

"How could I forget my hero," she said to him.

He removed his cap, ran a big hand across his crew cut and I think he may have even blushed.

"How you doing, darling," he said to her. "Have you outta here in a few shakes."

"So, you got my clue in the video?" She said to me.

"I did. Very smart idea. Keep an eye on Chance. The little thing on his collar."

"They took my vest, my camera gear and my phone but they didn't know I had the second phone."

"Whoever thought having two phones would be a good idea?"

She pulled the purple phone out of her pocket and held it up.

"And what happened to the video?"

"Billy Ray and Boo released it to the media."

"That's crazy. Why?"

"Publicity and money. Said it would make Cissy a big star."

"What about me?"

"Don't think they thought much about you," I said. "You just kind of got in the way of the plans."

"So what happened with the money at that Lake?"

"The TV crews and the cops are all there now waiting to see what happens."

"And we are here in a pickle factory."

"That's where the little dot on your Cheetah App told us we would find you."

"So, you were able to take the collar off Chance and track my location to here?"

"That is exactly right."

"Wait a minute," she said. "A coffee maker confuses you. How did you know what to do with the app on Chance's collar?"

"I'm a highly paid and trained investigator with a surprisingly wide range of skills."

"Catfish," she said.

I tapped the phone thing in my ear.

"He's on the other end of this thing. You should see what all he hooked up to find you."

"Surprised he was able to do it since he started drinking early this morning."

"He's still drinking," I said. "But he can still talk the talk."

"And even drunk he knows more about computers than you do."

"Drunk or sober," I admitted. "And smart enough to send me up here instead of himself."

"The app tells me my gear is here as well. Most likely still in the truck outside."

"Do you think they were going to take you guys back down there at midnight?"

"No idea," she said. "All I know is that Cissy and her guys set this whole deal up."

"That's what Catfish was thinking."

She pointed over at Cissy against the far wall. You could see the mean in her eyes. You could also see her left eye was bruised and turning black. Her hands were tied behind her. Her feet were bound with a cord of some sort and her mouth gagged by a dirty rag around her neck.

"But if she was involved," I asked. "Then why would her guys tie her up and give her a black eye?"

"They didn't," she said. "I did."

"You?"

"It's been a really long day."

I smiled and looked over at Buddy Lee who had just cut the lock off.

"Plus," she said. "Unlike you, no way I'm going to get paid now since they have my cameras."

"We will deal with that later," I said. "Right now, we got to get out of here and call Catfish. Let him call Clark and send the Calvary."

Dumptruck moved forward and picked up the big duffel bag. Buddy Lee slid the cage open and handed the bolt cutters back to him.

"If you two are finished reunionizing," Dumptruck said. "We got to go. Plus, I drank way too much whiskey on the way up and I gotta pee like a Mississippi bullfrog."

"Hang on one second," Alex said.

She walked back over to Cissy. Cissy glared up at her and muttered something under the rag. It didn't sound nice. Alex kicked her hard in the upper thigh and the force rolled her over. Cissy's big boots pointed toward the ceiling.

"Cool as a jarhead tool," Buddy Lee said as Alex left the cage.

We made our way to the staircase and headed down. Buddy Lee led the way, Alex next to him. Dumptruck had the bag over his shoulder and I was close behind. Going down, Dumptruck braced his hand on the railing as he moved over a missing step. The rusty railing gave out. I leaned to grab him but missed. He tumbled head over heels toward the boxes below. The railing clanged off the forklift. Dumptruck and the big bag landed flat on the stack of boxes filled with pickle jars. The sound of crashing glass bounced off every wall in the old warehouse.

It seemed like it only took a second before gunfire erupted. Streams of light flashed around us. Gunshots from automatic weapons raked the wall and brick chips rained down on us. Voices shouted and more gunshots. The rounds pinged off the forklift with a sharp echo. I grabbed Dumptruck off the boxes and pulled him to the floor. Alex and Buddy Lee hit the ground beside us. A bright flashlight from above found us and locked in.

"Cease fire," The voice connected to the flashlight yelled. The shooting stopped. My ears rang from the incredible noise. Buddy Lee cursed and banged his fist on the ground.

"Stay where you are and lace your hands over your head," the voice shouted.

We couldn't see with the light in our eyes so we each did as we were told. Dumptruck was on the ground flat on his back but he laced his hands over his head anyway.

"Don't move," another voice shouted from near the forklift.

We didn't move.

"Well," Dumptruck said. "I don't have to pee anymore."

46

"**W**ELL, LOOK WHO is back."

My left eye opened. My right eye joined it reluctantly. I was flat on the floor on my back. The factory scoop light above me slowly came into focus. My head pounded. I touched the area near my right temple and felt it wet. Blood. The last thing I could remember was being hit in the head with the butt of a black rifle. I had no idea how long I had been out.

"Sleepy time is over," a voice said from my left.

All I could see was his boots. I rolled up onto my elbow and moved into a seated position. The move made me dizzy and a small wave of nausea washed over me. I coughed and touched the side of my head again. It was wet with blood right at the hairline. I wiped the blood on my pants.

"Remember me, smartass?"

I focused in on the large man standing above me. It was the security guy with Cissy at the football game. Still dressed in full black but now he had some sort of automatic weapon in his right hand. He pulled his black cap back and pointed to the clear bandage I thought I saw earlier today.

"Now we're even," he said.

"So that was you last night doing that kicking crap?"

He pulled the cap back down tight over his close-cropped hair. My gun was in his belt.

"We can't go on meeting like this," I said.

"Shame we couldn't finish you off then," he said.

"Why didn't you?"

"Orders," he replied and seemed disappointed with the reason.

"Who gave you the order?" I asked.

He didn't respond. He motioned to one of his other guys with the rifle.

"Grab his ass and put him with the others," he directed.

This guy was bigger. Maybe the Anaconda. He yanked me up and grabbed both my hands. He took a pair of black cable ties and locked my hands in front of me. He shoved me over to where the others stood in front of the forklift. Everybody was lined up with the same cable ties and other than me, they all looked unharmed. On a workbench to our right was all our gear. The radios, my little ear thing, the duffel bag, keys, the purple phone and a small pistol that I guess Buddy Lee had stuffed in his overalls. A third member of the team pointed a long pistol at us. Hogtied and ready for the barbecue.

The guard from the game walked over to the table and picked up the purple phone. He held it up and pointed the screen toward us.

"Clever," he said and turned the screen and looked at it. "A tracking device. Can't believe we missed this."

He ran a gloved hand over the screen.

"This little thing is used to catch cheaters," he eyed Alex. "You got a guy watching somewhere?"

She glared at him.

"No? You sure?"

He dropped the phone to the floor and stomped it hard with his boot. It broke into pieces.

"Guess now he'll know you cheating on him," he grinned.

I wondered if Catfish was watching when the little dot disappeared from the screen.

We heard a sharp crack of a rifle in the distance. Then another round. Our guy grabbed a radio off his belt in a flash.

"What the hell was that?" He said as he clicked the talk button.

"DK spotted movement in the woods near the LZ," the radio crackled.

"Tell that idiot to quit firing at deer and make sure the landing is cleared," he clicked back.

"Copy that," the answer came.

I looked over at Buddy Lee. He let a small smile slip out. The deer was most likely Boobytrap.

"Who are you clearing a landing zone for?" I asked him. "Thought the Army kicked you out?"

He took a few steps toward me. "Did I ask you a question?"

I didn't respond.

"Let me tell you something about my time in the Army. Over in Iraq they got this big badass spider. They call it a camel spider. Damn thing is bigger than your hand. If you leave it alone it just moves along looking for food," he stepped in inches away from my face. "But if you mess with that bad boy, poke at it, try and disturb his mission in any way, then you better be ready for a fight. That spider will pucker up your butt in a heartbeat."

"Can you repeat all that again," I said. "My head is a little bit foggy for some reason."

He paused and leaned back. He grinned and touched the side of my head with his rifle. He looked at the blood on his gun barrel and wiped it off on his black pants. In the distance, we could hear the sound of an approaching helicopter. The distinct sound of a Bell Ranger. The sound got closer and the guard looked up to listen for a beat and then back down at me.

"Pizza delivery?" I asked.

"Pucker up," he grinned and moved toward the door.

47

THE DOOR TO the warehouse flew open and Bill Ray Kincaid strolled in with his chest puffed out. He was dressed in the same crimson blazer from earlier today but had covered his head with a dark baseball cap with a white A.

He strolled over to us with armed guards on each side of him and stopped. He smiled and shook his head. He took a stub of a cigar from his lips and rubbed it out with his foot. He reached into his coat pocket, pulled out a new one and took his time firing it up. He sucked on it a few times and then let a long stream of smoke pour upwards before he spoke.

"Ain't this a sight," he said. "Ain't this a damn sorry sight?"

None of us spoke.

"All the tiny bait fish on the hook and the big Catfish nowhere in sight."

Another guard came in and Cissy was with him. She had tried to clean up a bit but still looked like hell. Her top was dirty, she moved with a limp and the bruise on her eye had turned even darker. She walked right up to Alex and kicked at her. Alex reached out with her hands tied, grabbed Cissy's leg and flipped her right on her rear. She hit the floor. Her short skirt slid up to expose bright blue underwear and the guards took a good look.

"Get her up," Billy Ray said with disgust. "It's amazing I can make anything work surrounded by idiots like her and Boo."

He paced in front of us. The smoke from his big cigar drifted up, hung in the stale air and mixed in with the smell of vinegar and lost years.

"You and the girl I expected. Dumptruck is just a stupid old drunk bulldog," he pointed the cigar at him. "Adding in a fat farmer is a nice touch. Where did you get him?"

He was enjoying putting on a show and I didn't think it was a good idea to interrupt him. He turned his back and shook his head again. He turned around and let out a huge belly laugh that bounced off the pickle vats.

"Damnest thing," he said. "I worked for months on this. Planned it all out. Thought it all up. Coaching up that fool kid Boo. Had to pay Cissy here more money than I can count, talking up the media, my Army boys here asking for raises. Lot of damn hard work. I had everything in place, ready to roll. Then Catfish comes along and all of sudden I got to adjust on the fly."

He paused and flicked some ashes on the floor.

"Catfish and me go way back," he said. "Never liked him. Matter of fact, I hate his fat ass. But now I owe that fool a case of good bourbon and fine cigars."

"What the hell are you going on about," Dumptruck was the first to speak.

"I am a man of opportunity," Bill Ray reached and hitched up his pants. "I see opportunity. I create opportu-nity and then I seize opportunity. And this is one frigging beautiful opportunity."

He looked over at Cissy who was wiping her eyes. He scowled.

"Leave that alone, sugar," he said to her. "I'm gonna need that black eye and crap running down your face when you're shedding tears in front of the cameras."

She glared back at him but stopped what she was doing.

"I thought I had come up with a good plan to make Cissy a big damn star and make me a lot of cash at the same time and save the network."

"That was your plan?" I asked.

"It was and it was a good one. But this?" He waved both hands wide with the cigar in one. "This is just so damn beautiful. I could stay up thinking all night long and not think up something this good. You idiots just gave me a story that is gonna make me a pile of money big enough to get naked, dive in and wallow around like a pig in mud," he said with a laugh.

"What story is that?" I asked.

"The story about how some fools tried to stalk, attack and then kidnap my star sideline reporter. The story about how they found out about my old pickle factory and lured me up here in my whirlybird to make a payoff with a lot of cash. The story about how I came here with that money but then things went sideways and my boys here had to step in and take some unfortunate but necessary action."

"You doing all this just to save the network," I said.

"Don't forget the profits," he answered. "And mostly future opportunities."

"So, this is all about money?"

"Money first, but then opportunity, fame and power," he said. "You've heard the old saying, 'A fool and his money are soon elected.' Been thinking about running for Governor of Alabama. How's that sound to you?"

"Sounds bad for the state of Alabama," I said.

"You think I'm joking? I pull this here thing off, the election will be like taking candy from a baby."

"And you really think you are good enough to pull this off with Nick Allen on your case?"

"I told you to bring a full bucket if you gonna take me on, didn't I?"

"And you really think anybody is going to believe your story?"

"I do. That is the least of my concern. The TV folks don't give a crap about facts. Media loves a good story.

Especially one about a pretty young gal in trouble who gets rescued by some hero soldier boys."

"And what about Catfish, Agent Allen and the GBI?"

"I ain't worried a good diddly damn 'bout what they might think."

"Why is that?"

"Because when old Billy Ray gets up in front of all them cameras and microphones and I get to weaving my tale and talking up them media folks," he said with a puff of the big cigar. "Even ol' J. Edgar Hoover gonna wake up from his grave and testify to God himself that I'm telling the truth, the whole truth and nothing but the truth."

He laughed hard. "So help me, God," he said and strolled toward the door and then turned back to face us.

"Ya'll hear this ol' boy when he's talking," he grinned wide. "Listen when I tell you how much I love it, I really do. I do indeed love it when opportunity comes rolling along and just jumps right up and bites you in the ass."

48

THEY LEFT US with just one guard. He had a firearm, a stun gun and a short stock rifle in his hand. He moved over next to the workbench and pulled up a stool.

"Sorry I screwed the pooch, guys," Dumptruck said.

"No talking," the guard barked.

It was still raining and it pinged off the metal roof. The guard stood up and lit a cigarette. Dumptruck took a step toward him.

"Where you going?" The guard placed a hand on his pistol.

"Come on, dude," Dumptruck grinned. "Give me a smoke. I can't stand smelling one and not smoking."

"No way."

"What the hell difference does it make?" He said. "They even let the badasses on death row have a smoke before they go."

Dumptruck held his tied hands out in a plea. I looked over at Buddy Lee. He looked back with a small roll of his shoulders.

"Come on man. I need one last smoke."

The guard motioned for Dumptruck to come toward him. He tapped a cigarette about two inches out of the pack and held it out. Dumptruck bent over and took it with his teeth. The guard pulled out his lighter and held it to the cigarette. It bounced up and down in his mouth. Smoke curled up around his big craggy face.

"Oh damn, that's better than a good woman," he said.

The guard smiled. Dumptruck dropped his head and rammed the young guard like a bull in a ring. His head hit right in his chest and they both slammed up against the old workbench. The guard reached for his pistol but it fell to the floor. He spun away from Dumptruck and grabbed his stun gun. Buddy Lee and I moved forward. The guard stuck the stun gun in Dumptruck's gut. The charge fired and Dumptruck's whole body shook. With both hands tied he reached out and wrapped his big hands around the guard's wrist. They both started to shake and convulse. Buddy Lee jumped back. We stood and watched them both fall to the ground from the strong electric shock of the stun gun. The two of them were out cold.

"What the hell just happened?" I said.

"That fool grabbed on to the boy's arm," Buddy Lee said. "A stun gun will kick your ass good but it will also transfer that power right back to the shooter if you grab hold of them like that."

"You think Dumptruck knew that?"

"If he did," Buddy Lee said. "He's crazier than any-body I ever met."

"Crazy is his middle name."

Alex went to Dumptruck and began to tend to him. She rolled him over and slapped him on the side of the face. Buddy Lee already had his big foot on the guard's neck in case he woke up. He told me to get his big knife out of the bag. I dug in with both hands tied and found it. I gave it to him. He flicked it open with one motion and cut my hands free. I cut his and then Alex and she cut Dumptruck free. Buddy Lee had the guard hogtied in less than thirty seconds, grabbed an old gas rag from the forklift and stuffed it in his mouth. He motioned to me for help and we took the kid by both feet and pulled him out of sight. We took his guns, his radio and then got all our gear back. I stuck the little phone thing back in my ear.

"Ohawwwohaw," Dumptruck moaned as he started to come around.

Buddy Lee handed Alex some water in a canteen. She poured it over his head.

"Before I die and turn to dust," Dumptruck said in sing-song. "I hope I can drive the wheels off a Greyhound bus."

"Slap him again," Buddy Lee said.

"We got to get out of this warehouse," I said to Buddy Lee.

"First, we gotta know what's shaking," he said. "Get Catfish on the hook."

I reached for the thing in my ear again and punched it. It rang. Catfish jumped on the line.

"The last time a dead man called me I hung up on him."

"Last I checked I'm not dead but the night is young," I said into the crackling phone.

"That's not what's on the TV news," Catfish said.

"The news says I'm dead?"

"Watching it now."

"Any details you care to share?" I asked.

"Yep," he said. "Says you were killed when Billy Ray's security goons rescued Cissy."

"Rescued Cissy from me?"

"You and your associates they say."

"I have associates?"

"Apparently."

"And we're all dead?"

"According to Channel 10."

"Breaking news," I answered.

"Tragic. They still got your name wrong."

"So, I suppose now would be a good time to fill you in on what's really going on up here?"

"I was standing by for your call."

"You were?"

"Billy Ray has been lying out his fat rear end since he was knee high to a billy goat."

"And now he's lying about this. You ready for the real story."

"Talk fast. You running out of time."

"How can I be running out of time if I'm already dead?"

"Cause Billy Ray has called the GBI and every damn news truck in two states."

"How much time?"

"Hour at the most."

"We need to get a move on but can I ask you a question, first?"

"Make it quick," Catfish replied.

"Did you just say this wasn't your first call from a dead man?" I asked.

"I was drinking one night and I think I got a call from my dead high school football coach."

"You're not sure?"

"Could've been a dream or it might have been the whiskey."

"Well you did start up with the bourbon two hours before kickoff today. You still drinking?"

"Why stop now," Catfish said. "I'm talking to a dead man."

49

"I EXPECTED THAT," BUDDY Lee said when I updated him on what Catfish told me.

"Was that Boobytrap you were talking with on the radio?" I asked him.

"His trigger finger is getting itchy."

"What does that mean?"

"Again, with the questions," he said.

We moved over to the forklift where Alex had Dumptruck leaned up against one of the big tires. He was shaking both his hands and moving his head in a slow circle.

"Did you do that on purpose?" I asked him.

"No," he choked out in a raspy voice. "I just decided to electrocute myself for the pure hell of it."

"So, you actually did that on purpose?"

"I'm the one who got us caught, so I had to do something."

"But what if he had used his gun instead?"

He looked puzzled. His shoulders shuddered and he blew snot out of his nose.

"Guess I didn't think that all the way through," he said with a crooked grin.

Alex pulled him to his feet. He braced himself for a moment and then stood up straight.

"Boy howdy, I'll tell you what," he said. "50,000 volts will sure as hell sober you up in a hurry."

I smiled at Alex. She rolled her eyes.

"I need a drink," Dumptruck said.

Buddy Lee told us to gather around and listen up. Boobytrap had given him a rundown of where the guards were located outside and he laid it out for us.

"Two under the canopy in front of the big door. Two at the rear of the SUV. Kincaid and Cissy are in the back seat out of the rain talking on the phone and a pilot is up the hill at the chopper."

"When do we do whatever it is we're going to do?" Alex asked.

"Now or never," Buddy Lee said. "Dumptruck, do you think you can get this forklift cranked and then ram that door with it?"

"Can a dog lick his own butt?"

We took that to be a yes.

"I think we are outnumbered and outgunned," I said. "You sure we shouldn't just make a run for it out the rear like we planned."

"And have that fool blame all this on us?" He said. "That ain't what I signed up for, you?"

"No, it's not," I answered.

"Then we got one chance at this, and only one," he told us. "Nothing we do is gonna work unless it comes off as a surprise. We got to shock and shake them up with our one move."

"Just like today," Dumptruck spoke up.

"What about today?" Alex asked.

"The trick play that won the game," Dumptruck said. "Catfish's play. Mudcat Moon."

"What do you mean?" Alex asked.

"Catfish came up with it years ago," Dumptruck said. "We ran that same play when we were at Georgia. He made it up."

"I watched that," Buddy Lee said. "Damn good play. Caught 'Bama flat on their feet."

"That's why it works," he said. "Nobody thinks the fat guy is gonna throw a pass."

"There it is," Buddy Lee said. "We got to hit them with our own trick play."

"That's about all we got left," I said. "One play."

"Then we better make it a damn good one," he said.

"Hot damn," Dumptruck said. "Mudcat Moon. Twice in one day."

Like a schoolyard football team Buddy Lee got down on one knee and drew out the play for us on the dusty floor of the warehouse. He drew out where the SUV was parked, where the guards were, where he thought the chopper had landed and where each of us should go and what we should do when we made our move. He talked fast and with confidence. I had known him a while, ever since I started buying wood from him to make baseball bats. He worked hard, laughed hard and enjoyed a cold beer or three at the end of the day. I had never seen him this serious. As a Marine, I am sure he saw combat at some point but he never talked about it. He might make a joke every now and then but I had never heard a single war story or any bravado from his time in the service. It was a bit disconcerting to see him slip into that mode now. On the floor of an old pickle factory he had transformed from a good ol' boy in a pair of overalls to a Marine veteran on one knee drawing out a mission in the dirt with his finger.

We clung to his every word. He was the only one of us that had even entertained doing anything like this. Dumptruck had tried some odd things in his years. Alex was fearless in life. I had been able to survive in baseball for most of my adult life. But not one of us had ever faced what we were about to face. Of course, none of us ever had a guy like Buddy Lee to lead the way and none of us had ever had a fellow named Boobytrap out in the woods with who knows what at the ready.

"When Dumptruck gets the forklift ready," Buddy Lee said. "I'm gonna give Boobytrap the signal."

"Then what?" I asked.

"Then he will rain down a world of confusion and intrusion."

Alex had not met Boobytrap.

"Who is this guy and what is he going to do?" She asked.

"When you were a kid," Buddy Lee asked her. "Your daddy ever take you to see the fireworks?"

"Yeah, every holiday," she told him. "We would go downtown St. Louis where they would shoot off fireworks from a barge on the river at the big arch."

"Well, little darling," he grinned. "You 'bout to see what it would be like to be right smack dab in the middle of that barge floating down the Mississippi River."

50

DUMPTRUCK SAT BEHIND the wheel of the forklift and held up a long red wire and a yellow wire. He showed them to Buddy Lee. We lined up just behind the old machine. Buddy Lee nodded and said something we couldn't hear into his radio.

"On my cue," he told Dumptruck.

The explosions came in a rapid burst and the windows of the warehouse rattled from the force. Loud blasts boomed from all directions and we could see flashes of light. Screams and shouts followed.

"Go. Go. Get after it," Buddy Lee shouted out to Dumptruck.

He spun the wires together and the forklift burped, belched smoke and fired to life. He threw one of the long gearshifts forward and the thing lurched and headed for the door. We had to run to keep up. The steel prongs rammed hard into the garage style door and the screech of metal and machine sounded like the yell of an angry hawk. The door tore off the roller and crashed forward as sparks flew and chains rattled. We could hear the two guards outside the door scream as they tried to escape the flying metal. They failed as the forklift blasted forward, over the metal remains and out into the night.

Boobytrap was indeed raining down confusion. Loud explosive charges were going off all around us. Buddy Lee had said they would all be non-lethal but even I wasn't sure and Billy Ray and his guys were certainly not sure. The explosions were loud, sharp and each one came with a huge roll of colored smoke. A blast and red smoke followed by green, then white. They came from deep in the woods, high in tree limbs, from behind the guards, in the tall weeds and down near the road. There was no way to figure out what was happening.

Next, came what I would only call an air assault when blue and green explosives rained down from above with a pop and thud like it came from a mortar tube. A bright white light, then another flashed like a strobe from two different directions up in the trees. Billy Ray opened the back door of the SUV and as he did a large red flash went off ten feet from the truck with the loudest boom yet. He dove back inside and shut the door. Cissy let out a long scream muffled only when the door slammed behind them.

"Incoming," a guard at the rear of the SUV screamed and ran toward the forklift. Buddy Lee stepped out and faced him. The guard opened fire with his Russian rifle. Buddy Lee took one shot and hit him right in the kneecap.

He spun to the ground and let out a long moan. The lead security guy that had nailed me on the head rolled to the ground and tried to make his way around the opposite side on his knees. Buddy Lee aimed again and fired. His shot hit the gun hand and the guard's pistol went flying as he went face first into the ground. Another explosion went off behind him. He screamed and covered his head.

"He's all yours," he yelled to me and pointed at the guy on the ground.

I didn't need a written invitation. I ran toward him as he rose to his knees. He shook his hand as he looked up at me.

"That hurt?" I said to him.

I took the butt of the Russian rifle and hit him hard as I could on the chin. His eyes rolled back to white and he fell over flat on his back. I put my foot on his chest and leaned in.

"Now," I said. "We're even."

"Use the cable ties on them all," Buddy Lee directed us.

Alex and Dumptruck pulled the metal door off the two trapped underneath. Dumptruck pointed the Russian pistol at them. There was no need. They were both unconscious. We used the cable ties to secure their hands and feet. Buddy Lee pulled the two other guys behind the forklift and wrangled them. There was a short lull in the blast and I thought maybe Boobytrap was finished. I was wrong. He was not even close to a finish.

"They're going to get away," Alex pointed toward the SUV as Kincaid and Cissy moved from the back seat to the front. Billy Ray behind the wheel. "All my camera gear is in that truck."

"Hang tight," Buddy Lee said and pointed at the hood of the truck. "Just watch."

A tin coffee can was in the center of the hood. A fuse led away from the can and into the tall grass. At the edge of the grass we spotted Boobytrap as he lit the fuse and slid away into the dark. Billy Ray hit the ignition and the truck roared to life. The fuse ran fast and hard and the coffee can exploded in a blast of sparks and fire. It sizzled and smoked and melted deep into the hood of the truck. The sparks and blaze shot up into the dark night, bright and gold.

"What the hell?" Dumptruck shouted.

"Thermite," Buddy Lee yelled back. "A pound of that stuff in a coffee can will burn right through the engine block and put on a pretty good show at the same time. Pretty sight ain't it?"

The engine choked to a stop. Kincaid bailed out of the truck as the hood still glowed and headed up the hill. Cissy came out the other side screaming like a kid on a roller coaster ride.

"He's heading for the helicopter," I shouted.

"If I know Boobytrap, that bird ain't gonna fly," Buddy Lee shouted back.

"Why not?"

"In the service, he was always getting thrown in the brig. At least three times for messing with choppers."

"But if it does, Billy Ray might get away."

"Then go get that fat boy," he said. "But don't get too close if that chopper tries to take off."

Cissy was heading toward the highway. The short tight skirt made her run like a barnyard chicken.

"Dumptruck, go get that lady," Buddy Lee instructed.

"I got this," Alex said and took off.

With her long legs and smooth stride, it took Alex only a few seconds to catch up with Cissy and her short skirt. She shoved her from behind and Cissy went down with a scream in a puddle of muddy water. Alex pulled Cissy to her feet by her hair and kneed her hard in the gut. She fell back into the puddle with a scream.

"That girl is one tough sweet potato," Buddy Lee said with a grin.

"You gonna stand there and gawk or you going after that boy?" Dumptruck asked me.

I turned and took off up the hill toward the clearing where the chopper had landed. The explosions had started up for another round. A blast high, a blast low, colored smoke drifted and hung in the trees and flickered when a light flashed. Then came a new twist. Speakers crackled in the trees and the sound of loud music roared through the rain, fog and smoke. Jimi Hendrix wailed from the mountainside as the strains of *Purple Haze* echoed through the night. I heard myself laugh out loud as I ran up the slick path after Billy Ray. This was one crazy show Boobytrap was putting on. If elephants and clowns showed up the circus could set up a tent.

Kincaid screamed and waved his arms as he approached the chopper. The pilot already had the engine fired up and the blades turned in a slow circle when Billy Ray scrambled in the back door. The helicopter was white with crimson stripes and the Alabama logo on the nose. The tail was painted with the words Roll Tide. I heeded Buddy Lee's warning and stopped short. I wasn't sure why I stopped because I didn't see anything wrong. There was nothing I could do now as the pilot kicked it into high gear, the blades picked up full speed with a blast of wind and the chopper lifted slowly from the ground.

I felt a rush of anger at the thought that Billy Ray was about to get away. The chopper rose off the ground, jolted and dipped nose down. The engine roared so loud I covered my ears and ducked my head. Dirt and limbs flew all around me.

Two bright lights twenty feet in front of the chopper flashed on and off, bright enough to blind the pilot. I looked up to see the pilot fighting the stick and fighting the lights. It bounced again and then nosed down. I saw it on the second dip. A huge log chain was wrapped around both rudders and looped around a couple of strong oak trees. The pilot could not have known. He gunned it and the nose went up and then slammed hard back into the ground. It tilted right and the blades tore into the muddy earth. I saw Billy Ray leap from the rear door and roll to the ground. The Bell Ranger rolled over and groaned to a stop as parts flew. The engine whined and popped. Mud and dirt kicked up and rained down all around. The sound of the blades snapping burst into the night.

I dropped to the ground and covered my head. Debris flew over me. The electrical smell of wires burning filled the wet air. I raised my head as the pilot bailed out in the flashing lights. I watched him run deep into the woods and fade into the rain and dark. I wondered just where he thought he was going in these thick woods. About fifty feet above me I spotted Billy Ray. He was in a half trot headed down the slick muddy path. He stumbled and struggled to stay on his feet. His shirt hung out of his mud covered slacks. His hat was gone and the look on his face reeked of fear. His eyes were large and he grunted like a hog on the run from a butcher.

I was in place and I had the rifle. I decided to sit tight and wait for him to come to me. I heard a noise behind me and turned to look. Dumptruck was headed up the path at full speed, his knees churned high. His head was down and I'm not quite sure with all the noise and music but I think I heard him bark as he flew by me. I jumped up and followed with the gun. Billy Ray saw him and skidded as he tried to stop his downhill motion. Dumptruck lowered his head and with his shoulder bull rushed into Billy Ray's gut, wrapped him up with his arms and they went hard to the ground. It was a picture perfect tackle. Billy Ray let out a strange noise or grunt and choked out a curse.

"Sooonnnnnaoofabitch," he groaned.

"Boom!" Dumptruck jumped up and pointed at him. "Mudcat Moon, you butthole!"

"Nice tackle," I said as I caught up to him.

"I do love knocking the snot out of some Alabama fool," he pumped both fists in the air.

Above us on the hill we heard a sizzle and a few electrical pops. We looked up just as the Bell Ranger exploded in a huge fireball. The flames ran up the trees, across the wet ground, lit up the dark sky and blended into a muddy mix with the sounds of Jimi Hendrix.

Dumptruck lifted his head toward the sky and yelled into the rain, "Roll Damn Tide!"

51

THE EXPLOSIONS, LIGHTS and music had stopped and the only sound was the rain and the low crackle and hiss of fire. The rain had put out most of the blaze around the chopper and only a few hot spots glowed near the wreckage. Dumptruck had Billy Ray in tow as we made our way back down the hill to the pickle factory. Billy Ray mouthed off to Dumptruck even after his tackle so he had muzzled him with his belt. He looped it across his mouth and pulled it tight. He had one hand on his arm and one on the belt. Each time Billy Ray tried to speak, Dumptruck pulled the belt tighter.

A dim glow from the open door of the warehouse gave off enough light to help us see. Cissy was tied to one of the metal roof rods of the forklift with a nylon rope. Cable ties held her hands and feet and she had three or four rounds of duct tape across her mouth. Her mascara was smeared and resembled the oversized eye black ballplayers smear on these days. I expected her to be mad but when I got close I could see she was in tears. Real tears this time. I shined the flashlight in her face. She now had two black eyes and a trickle of blood ran from her nose. Alex was nearby under the cover of the stairs that led upstairs. She was sorting her camera gear in two bags.

"Two black eyes?" I asked her.

"Fashion coordinated," she said without looking up. "Matches the nose job."

"Where were you when I was thirty years old?" Dump-truck said to Alex.

She looked up and smiled at him.

"Where's Buddy Lee?" I asked.

"Not sure," she said. "When you radioed that you had Billy Ray and was safe, he took the other goons and took off up the hill."

"He took the guards?"

"I didn't see where he went," she said. "I was getting my gear from the truck."

My ear rang and I jumped. I had forgotten about the little phone thing. I reached up and tried to hit the button. It rang two more times and buzzed. I slapped at it like a bug and moved in a circle. It rang twice more.

"What are you doing?" Alex stood up.

"Damn thing in my ear is ringing and I can't figure out how to answer it."

She came over and adjusted it a bit and touched it. It stopped ringing.

"Not like it's the space shuttle," she said. "It's a cell phone."

For a moment, I didn't hear anything. I thought maybe Catfish had given up. I tapped at it again.

"You there?" I heard Catfish's voice.

"I got you now," I said as Alex shook her head at me.

"Well butter my butt and call me a biscuit," he said into my ear. "Hell son, I was beginning to think what they're saying on the news was right."

"They still saying we're all dead?"

"I can't figure out what they're saying," Catfish said. "Getting information from the TV news is like trying to eat a steak with a spoon."

"Are they headed this way?"

"Like a damn herd of chickens," he said. "From every direction."

"Close by?"

"It seems the local boys have rounded them up just below you at the interstate."

"And the GBI?"

"I would guess even closer," he said. "Everybody good on your end?"

"We're good."

"Then talk to me," he said.

So, I filled him in. Told him about the forklift, the truck, the explosions, Billy Ray, Cissy and the music. I had to back up and explain the part about the music twice.

"And this jailbird Bobbytrap pulled this off all by his lonesome?"

"Buddy Lee said he was different," I answered.

"Sometimes it's good to have friends on the wrong side of the law," he said.

"Sometimes it's good to have a drunken fool named Dumptruck on your team."

"I told you, that boy has a way of growing on you, don't he?"

I told Catfish about the stun gun and how Dumptruck had taken out Billy Ray with a great tackle. I had to wait a full minute for him to stop laughing after I told him about Dumptruck yelling out *Mudcat Moon* when he knocked him to the ground.

"Best play I ever thought up," he said.

"Only play you ever thought up."

"But it was a damn good one."

"And you're sure you are telling the truth about the old Cherokee man and the moon?"

"To be honest," he said. "The truth can sometimes get lost in the weeds."

Make a Note: A smart man will sometimes let a lie grow into a story. An even smarter man will let a lie grow into a legend.

"This helicopter wouldn't be the one all painted up in Alabama colors, would it?" He asked me.

"That would be the one."

"And I thought this day couldn't get any better. Where is that idiot Billy Ray now?"

"Dumptruck has got him roped to the forklift with a belt stuck in his mouth."

"It just got better."

"But I got some talking to do when Agent Allen shows up," I told him.

"Glad you doing the talking and not me."

"Got any advice?"

"Keep your fences horse high, pig tight and bull strong," he said and hung up.

I had absolutely no idea what to do with that bit of advice.

52

"**G**IVE ME A hand here will you," Dumptruck motioned to me.

He had a roll of wet duct tape wrapped around Kincaid's mouth and was trying to seal it off. I pulled it out by the edge and Dumptruck tore it off with his teeth. I pressed the tape hard down on his mouth.

"That should shut his trap," he said as he put his belt back on.

Billy Ray tried to speak and a grunt came out. Dumptruck hand slapped him on the forehead.

"Well look at this," Buddy Lee said as he came up behind us.

I jumped when I heard his voice. This place and the whole night had made me jumpy as a racehorse.

"The pickles do taste sweeter when a plan comes together," he said and slapped me on the back.

"Where have you been?" I asked.

"Had to help Boobytrap clean up."

"Where is Billy Ray's army?"

"Left them boys up in the woods. Boobytrap is taking care of them."

"Taking care of them?"

"He tied them all to a big oak tree."

I relaxed a bit. I guess I was afraid he would do worse.

"Where is that fool Boobytrap?" Dumptruck asked.

"Gone."

"He left already?" I said. "We need to thank him and we need to think about paying him somehow."

"Oh, he got paid."

"He did? How?"

"Remember when Billy Ray said he brought some money to make it look like a payoff?" Buddy Lee said. "He had it with him in that chopper."

"And?"

"And Boobytrap secured those funds for safekeeping," he said.

"For safekeeping?"

"Would have been a shame to have all that cash go up in flames."

"How much was Billy Ray carrying?" I asked.

"Not sure?" Buddy Lee said. "Whatta 'bout it Billy Ray? How much cash you bring with you?"

Kincaid tried to speak and shook his head. His eyes bugged out and his body shook.

"Guess it was a pretty fair amount," Buddy Lee smiled.

"And that crazy fool took it all?" Dumptruck asked.

"Like any business, he's got expenses to cover."

"It does take some cash to blow up a mountainside," I said.

"And some severance pay for his mama," Buddy Lee grinned.

Alex had got her gear back together and took her camera out. The bright flash blinked as she took shots of Cissy and Billy Ray.

"Catfish says the GBI is close and the media too," I told Buddy Lee.

"Did you guys search both of them?"

"I searched her," Alex said. "Nothing but lipstick and two joints of weed."

"I'll take the weed," Dumptruck said and held out his hand.

Buddy Lee stepped forward and began to frisk Billy Ray. He did it with smooth practiced motions. Something else he learned in the Marines I guess. He handed a few cigars to Dumptruck and pocketed his lighter and a nice gold money clip. The clip still had a few big bills in it. He reached into an outside coat pocket and pulled out a small device. It was about two inches long and as thin as a pinky finger. A tiny cover of silver metal on one end and then rounded out a bit in the middle. He held it up and shined a small flashlight on it.

"What is that little thing?" Dumptruck asked.

I leaned in close for a look in the light. "I know what it is."

"You do?" Buddy Lee said.

"It's a tiny little voice activated recording device," I said. "Records up to 48 hours at a time."

"Wait a minute," Alex interrupted. "You don't know what the buttons on a microwave are for. So how do you know what a large gigabyte mini recorder is?"

"Because it is just like the one Shaky had yesterday," I said. "He told me he kept it on him to record what was said at BTSN so nobody could mess with his job."

I took it from Buddy Lee and shined my own light on it. On the back of it I could see the same little BTSN decal from yesterday. I thought about it for a moment. Shaky had intervened when I mixed it up with Billy Ray back at the trucks earlier tonight. He must have slipped it in his coat pocket when he held him back from me. Now I knew what he meant when he pointed to his ears as he and Sam left.

"Shaky put this thing in Billy Ray's pocket," I told the others.

Alex reached for it and headed to her bag. She pulled out her laptop and took a seat on a concrete block. She plugged the device into the side of the computer and we all gathered around her to listen. She put on a pair of small headphones and messed around with the buttons for maybe a minute or so. She paused and turned the laptop toward us.

"Listen to this," she said and turned up the sound.

You could see a green wavy line on her screen and two red lines bounced with the sound. The audio wasn't that clear but clear enough to understand. It was Billy Ray as he talked to us in the warehouse. We listened again to him talk, laugh and say how he was going to kill us all and blame the whole thing on us.

"Whoever this Shaky is," Buddy Lee said to me. "I think you owe him an ice cold beer."

"I think I owe him a case or two of beer," I said.

Alex popped the device out and handed it back to Buddy Lee. He handed it to me.

"Why you giving this to me?" I asked him.

"So, you can share it with the cops when they get here."

"You leaving?"

"Color me gone," he said.

"Same for me," Dumptruck added. "They might know about Arkansas."

I looked at Alex. She pointed at Cissy. "I'm not going anywhere until I see them haul her tiny butt off to jail."

"I need to do one more thing before you leave," I said to Buddy Lee.

I walked over to the edge of the staircase and picked up an old rusted metal bucket now filled with rainwater. I carried it over to where Billy Ray was tied up and held it up in front of him.

"You told me if I was coming after you I better bring a full bucket, right?" I said to him.

Alex pointed her camera at us. The water sloshed out the top of the bucket.

"This bucket looks pretty damn full to me," I said and dumped it over his head and shoved the bucket down to his chin. The muddy water poured over him and he sputtered and groaned from beneath the bucket. I banged the metal bottom hard with my fist.

"As Catfish might say," and I lowered my voice in my best imitation. "I think this here chicken done been plucked."

"You slick talking devil," Dumptruck said. "I told you, didn't I? You didn't believe me but it's the gospel truth. You and me, we just alike. We just two old dogs looking for a bone."

Buddy Lee took the Russian guns and tossed them into the rear of the SUV. He grabbed his bag and motioned for Dumptruck to follow him and they headed up the hill. He stopped and turned back.

"How you fixed for wood right now for your bats?"

"Wood?" I was puzzled at his question. "I'm stocked up good with billets to last the rest of the winter."

"Good deal," he said. "Then lose my phone number for a while."

53

SIRENS IN THE distance died off but we could hear vehicles. The rumble of larger trucks and a quick flash of a tail-light down the hill near the highway. No voices, but a clink or the sound of a door. I had a feeling what was about to come. I told Alex we needed to stand out in the dim light of the doorway and lace our hands over our head. She didn't like the idea but agreed while tossing in a hard glare my way.

The SWAT style team appeared with speed and no notice. They moved toward the warehouse with weapons out front. They were outfitted in heavy gear, helmets and tiny microphones at their mouth. Two stopped where Cissy and Billy Ray were roped to the forklift. I heard one of them repeat into his tiny headset. 'Yes sir, male subject has a bucket over his head.' I wondered who was listening to the other end of that transmission.

I couldn't dwell on it long. Two young SWAT guys appeared and shined a light in our face and told us to drop to our knees. We complied. The younger one took our arms and handcuffed us. At least he left our hands in front. Not like we were going to run away with these guys around. The men spread out and covered the area with impressive speed. Every minute or so you would hear one yell out 'clear' and then they would move on. A group of them headed up the hill where smoke still drifted from the helicopter. A few headed into the woods and the others moved through the factory warehouse.

Coming up from the highway we spotted Agent Nick Allen. Another agent was by his side. The second agent was dressed in SWAT gear without the helmet and had a rifle in his left hand. Allen wore the same bad sweater from the game but a long black rain parka now covered it. He wore a dark hat with GBI in white across the front. He walked right up to Billy Ray, paused and shook his head. The other officer started to say something but Allen waved him off. He looked over to where we knelt. He let out a big sigh and his shoulders dropped. We didn't hear a ring but he reached into his pants pocket and answered his phone. He listened for a bit and talked as his other hand moved about in a circle. He then listened for a long time without saying a word. He still had the phone to his ear as he made his way over to where we knelt. He motioned for us to stand.

"Yes sir. Yes sir," he said into the phone. "Yes sir. Got it. Understood." He clicked off and shoved the phone back into his pocket.

"What was all that about?" I asked.

"That?" He looked at me. "That was my butt sizzling in grease on a waffle grill. Thanks to you."

"Me?"

He held a hand up to stop me. It turned into a pointed finger and then he dropped it.

"Three hours ago, I was in the command trailer sitting pretty," he said as he paced in front of us. "Had a perimeter set, snipers, go team, air nearby, ransom at hand, roads blocked, three months of overtime approved and spent. I pulled off all that in just under two hours. Brass was impressed."

"Always nice to impress the brass," I said.

He held up his hand again. "Then I get told that the TV folks are pulling out. Word is they been told something else is going on somewhere else. I don't know what or why. My phone starts barking. The brass is asking me what's going on and I don't have an answer for them. I am sitting there in my nice high tech command center with my participles dangling."

I thought about saying something but he didn't give me a chance. He stopped me again. He looked over toward Billy Ray and pointed.

"Then I get a call from that fool over there with his head in a bucket. He's still got your name wrong but I know it's you he's talking about and he tells me some cockeyed story about how this fellow kidnapped little miss Cissy over there and his boys had to take all of you out."

"You didn't believe him did you?"

"Hell no. But I got the brass jumping up my behind because they're all sitting at home watching TV and they telling me I have to pack up and head up the mountain to the damn Dixie Dew Pickle Factory in the middle of absolutely nowhere," he said. "A pickle factory they tell me. A frigging pickle factory."

He reached into his pocket and pulled his phone out again. He held it up and then shoved it back into his pocket without answering.

"So, I'm on my way up here and I'm getting reports from the office, from folks driving by and the media telling me all kinds of odd stuff. They say they hear explosions, big blast, and lights flashing, smoke and even music coming from up here. Coming from a pickle factory. Can you believe that crap?"

"Does sound hard to believe," I said.

"And then I get here and find a million dollar helicopter all burnt up, place all torn up, holes in the ground with burn spots, tree limbs down everywhere and that expensive vehicle over there smoking has a coffee can filled with thermite on the hood that has done burned right through the engine block. Can you explain any of that?"

"Me?" I told him. "Do I look like the kind of guy who would even know what thermite is?"

"No, you don't," he said. "So I ask you, should I be looking for some other folks out here tonight other than you two?"

"If they are I'm sure these SWAT guys of yours will round them right up," I said.

He paced a bit, took his cap off, scratched his head and pulled it back on.

"And that chopper up the hill. Can you shed any light on what happened to it?"

"I can not."

"No?"

"Afraid not," I said.

He let out a long breath and kicked at the mud.

"So, how about them two tied to the forklift? You explain any of that? And don't leave out the part about the bucket."

"Them I can explain," I said. "But it's better if you let Billy Ray do the talking."

"What's that supposed to mean?"

"Reach into my right front pants pocket."

"Why?"

"Because your guy has me handcuffed."

He reached over and pulled the tiny recording device out of my pocket. He fished a tiny flashlight out of his parka and turned it on. He rolled it in his fingers.

"What is this thing?" He asked.

"Something that might save us both some talking time," I answered.

"Where did you get it?"

"Found it in Billy Ray's coat pocket."

"Have anything to do with why he is wearing a bucket on his head?"

"No," I said. "That was just following up on a promise I made."

"So what am I supposed to do with this?"

"Got a computer in that command center?"

"Got five and a geek to make them all work."

"Then go plug it in and take a listen."

"What am I listening for?"

"Answers," I told him.

54

"DO YOU REALIZE that we are just a few hours from being up for 24 straight?" Alex said.

"I do."

"How much longer before we can get out of here?"

"Last time I was handcuffed it took a while," I said.

"The last time?"

A good hour had passed since Allen took the device and I was glad to spot him coming back up the hill. The SWAT officer from earlier along with a woman dressed in a black GBI windbreaker and khakis surrounded him. A lanky older man was a step behind and wore the same outfit. Bringing up the rear was Major Jay Clark of the UGA Police Department. I didn't know he was here. Clark had added a yellow rain slicker and a blue cowboy hat but looked as buttoned up and polished as he did at six this morning. They stopped and huddled in front of Billy Ray and Cissy. No one looked our way. Allen pulled out his phone and poked at it. He listened for a moment and then hung up without a word.

"Do it," he said to the lanky officer.

The man motioned for two nearby uniformed officers and they went to work. One removed the bucket and the other the ropes. They cut them loose and the lanky one reached for the tape around Billy Ray's mouth.

"Leave that where it is for now," Allen said without looking up. The man patted the tape back down.

The officers frisked both while the lanky guy read them their rights. I let out a deep breath and looked over at Alex. She had a small smile on her face. With very little ceremony they walked them down the hill. Billy Ray looked really pissed off and Cissy switched from tears to sobs. Alex let out a small giggle.

Allen turned his attention to the young woman and they both had their ears angled down into her phone and each would occasionally respond to the caller. Major Clark was the first to make a move to where we stood. I nodded a hello as he approached. His eyes went to Alex.

"How are you doing?" He asked her.

"I'm fine. In fact, I'm good now," she said.

"You hurt or need any other medical attention?"

We knew what he meant. She shook her head.

"I spoke with Catfish," he said. "He filled me in and Allen has updated me."

"So, can you update us?" I asked.

"Sorry, not my jurisdiction," he said. "Just wanted to let you know we appreciate your efforts and to tell you that I'll process your fee and get it to you next week."

"Hold on," Alex raised her voice. "He still gets full payment, I get kidnapped by some idiots and now I don't get paid by the network?"

"What was your fee?" He asked me.

"Five hundred a day," I answered.

"And yours?"

"Three hundred," she said.

He reached into his pressed shirt pocket and pulled out a business card. He stuck it in her front pocket.

"First thing Monday call that number and ask for Dottie," he told her. "Tell her I said to process an invoice for fifteen hundred flat, for two days of crime photo work. Sound good?"

"What?" I said.

"Sounds good," she said and shot me a look.

"And ask Dottie to give you the number for Benny Kooper. Koop was our kicker when I played. Never liked kickers much but they're smart and now he is a hotshot lawyer. Loves suing stupid rich people for a lot of money when they screw up."

He glanced at me and tipped his big cowboy hat at Alex with a big grin. He excused himself and headed back down the hill.

"Fifteen hundred dollars," I said. "And a lawyer."

"And just think what the tabloids will pay for the photos I took tonight," she said with a sly grin.

Agent Allen finished with the female in the windbreaker and she departed with a handshake. He and the SWAT officer approached us.

"Cut them loose," he said.

A young officer took our handcuffs off and slid away without a word.

"How much longer before we can go?" Alex asked him.

"Got some more questions first," Allen said.

The SWAT officer with him spoke up. "I'll need to take them to TAC-4 for interviews, written statements and processing before they are released for the night."

Allen looked at him. "Why don't you go check on the helicopter and make sure the NTSB is notified."

The officer did not look happy but he turned and left with his orders.

"He wants my job," Allen said. "He can have it. Just not tonight."

"So, I gather that you listened to the recording?" I said.

"We did," he said and pulled out a small notebook. "And I got some questions."

"Question away."

"How come a man about to rack up some serious felonies and even murder charges would be dumb enough to carry around a recording device in his pocket?"

"I did wonder about that myself," I said.

"It's odd," he continued. "About as odd as the fact that he mentioned two other folks."

"He did?"

"A idiot named Dumptruck, who I recognize but don't know why he was here. He also mentioned a farmer. Any idea why he would mention Dumptruck and some farmer?"

"It was real hard to keep everything straight. Plus, I got hit up side the head," I pointed at my wound.

"Un-huh," he flipped the pages in his little notebook. "That could create memory issues every now and then."

"It could," I said.

"How about this, then," he paused. "My guys just found five of that idiot Kincaid's security team way up the hill in the woods. They were tied to a tree."

"Tied to a tree, really?" I said. "Odd."

"One of them had about half his kneecap shot off, another guy with his hand bleeding and his chin smashed up. Memory coming back to you about any of that?"

"No, can't say that it is."

"Okay then. Here's an easy question. You know a guy named Buddy Lee Bowman?"

"That I can answer," I said. "I buy wood billets from him."

"Good, we making some progress," he said. "Local deputy on a road DUI check just called me to tell me he stopped him not far from here."

"Wonder what he was doing out this way?"

"He said Mr. Bowman was soaking wet and dressed in overalls. Sort of like a farmer. Told the deputy that he had been out hunting in the rain."

"Boy does love his hunting."

"Yeah we all love to go hunting in the middle of a rainstorm after midnight."

He turned a few more pages in his little notebook and held it closer to his face. He squinted a bit.

"And then I got another call from the US Marshall's office," he said. "Know what they wanted to tell me about?"

"Something else odd?"

"Exactly. Told me they got a breach signal from an ankle bracelet up near here. It was supposed to be strapped to the leg of a guy named Lester J. Tibby. He goes by the alias Boobytrap," he read off his pad. "Just got out of federal prison on charges of blowing up stuff. A lot of stuff."

"Sounds like a dangerous man. Hope they were able to locate him."

"They did. But by the time they got up here from Atlanta they found him on his sofa watching TV. The ankle bracelet right there on the floor next to him."

"Now that is really odd."

"Know what he said when they asked him why he cut it off?"

"No idea."

"Said he had an itch that needed scratching."

He shut the notebook up and stuck it inside his raingear. He stood silent for a minute and looked up into the rain. He glanced around at all the activity as his men worked the scene.

"You sure know a lot about what happened up here tonight," I said.

"I'm the special agent in charge," he said. "I know everything."

"That's a heavy load to carry," I replied.

"Gets a lot heavier when you show up."

I didn't answer. He took out his wallet and plucked a card from it. He handed it to me.

"Next time you get your butt caught in a meat grinder," he said. "Call that number."

I looked at the card. It wasn't his card. It had another name, title and it said Federal Bureau of Investigation. FBI.

"Friend of yours?"

"Used to work for me," he said. "Now he's the FBI SAC for the whole Southeast Region."

"Good guy?"

"No, he's the most miserable S.O.B. I know. Fired him five years ago."

"Then why should I call him?"

"Because," he said. "I'm two graduations from doing nothing but sitting on a dock at Lake Rabun."

"And if I call him?"

"Then I can keep my butt off the waffle griddle and maintain my plans to drink and fish all day long."

I looked at the card again. I wasn't sure if he was serious or not but I think he was, so I stuffed in my pocket.

"So, what now?" I asked with a little hesitation.

"Maybe when you write up your official statements some of your recall might be better," he said to both of us.

"Are we going to have to go to wherever that other guy was talking about and be interviewed?" Alex asked him.

He shook his head. "It's too damn late and you're too tired."

"I passed tired three exits back," Alex said.

"Get some rest," he said. "First thing next week you call my office and get your butts in and make sure we get all this written down, signed, sealed and buttoned up tighter than a tick. Got it?"

We didn't say anything.

"And listen good, both of you," he pointed a finger at us. "Make damn sure your stories add up. I hate it when I have to deal with things not adding up. Things don't add up and bosses start asking questions. Bosses start asking questions and I get real aggravated. I don't like getting aggravated. Causes me stomach problems. You two understand what I'm telling you?"

We didn't answer him but we both nodded in agreement.

Allen turned his back on us and walked over near the forklift where he took a clipboard from a young officer and began to flip through some paperwork.

Alex looked at me. "Did he just give us time to make up our own story for this mess?"

"I do believe that is exactly what he just did."

"Can he do that?"

"I guess he can."

"But how can he know that everyone else will go along with it?"

"Because, he is the special agent in charge, he knows everything."

"Amazing," she said. "Now can we get out of here."

"We could," I said. "If we had a way to get out of here."

"You don't have a car?"

"I came with Dumptruck."

"So how do we get home?"

I shrugged and called out to Agent Allen.

"Any idea how we can get a ride back into Atlanta tonight?"

He turned back to us. "Sure," he said. "There's a bus station over in Clayton."

"A bus station?"

"Fifteen miles Northeast," he pointed. "If you start walking now you should be there by the time the first bus leaves in the morning."

55

WE WANDERED DOWN to where all the law enforcement vehicles were parked. We had no intention of walking to a bus station but we still had no idea how to find a ride. We stood among all the flashing lights. A kid approached us. He might have been about sixteen years old or less. He wore a long raincoat that dropped to his ankles and a large baseball cap that pushed down on his ears and made them poke out. I might have laughed but he was wearing a badge on his raincoat.

"That man next to the ambulance said you might be a Mr. Jake Eliam," the kid said. "Is that right, sir?"

"It is."

"Sir, there is a car waiting for you down at the road block."

"A car?"

"Yes sir."

"Does it have a police logo on the side of it?" I asked.

"No sir."

"And the car is waiting for me, you sure?"

"Yes sir," he said and looked at a wet piece of paper in his hand. "And somebody else, I can't read the name here."

"What's your name?" I asked him.

"Sheriff Doogin is my daddy. I'm his youngest son, Dickey."

"Dickey Doogin?"

"Yes sir."

I looked at Alex. "Lead on Dickey Doogin."

We followed the kid down the road to the spot where the local cops had set up a row of flares and blocked off access to the scene. Rows of cop cars from different departments strung along the ditch on both sides and we walked the middle of the road. Off to the right was a small gravel parking lot next to the remnants of a flea market. The kid pointed to the car. It wasn't a car. I not sure what the hell it was but it wasn't a car. It once could have been a Ford SUV but it was now stretched out to maybe fifty feet. A solid black stretch limo that was longer than half a basketball court.

"This thing?" I asked Dickey Doogin.

"Yes sir."

A driver in a white shirt and black tie jumped out and raced around to our side.

"Holy crap," Alex said. "Let's go."

"I'm not getting in that, whatever it is," I said as the driver reached for one of the huge doors.

"Why not?"

"Who do we know that would be riding around in some awful damn thing like this?"

"Who cares," Alex said and moved forward as the driver pulled the door open.

She disappeared inside and I carefully stuck my head just inside the door. My eyes slowly adjusted to row after row of colored lights that ran along the roofline. Gold lights embedded in the roof cast a spotlight downward. There he was. Catfish.

He sat back in a full-size recliner and twirled it back and forth with his bare feet. In front of him was a huge bucket of ice. The tops of cold beer peeked out the surface. He had a long neck bottle in one hand and a tall narrow crystal glass in the other. He balanced a bucket of fried chicken in his lap. Chance was curled up asleep on one of the long seats behind him. Three clean chicken legs scattered next to him.

"You gonna stand there and gawk, or we gonna shuck this corn?" He said.

I got in and the driver closed the door. We had a ride home.

I had the top off a cold beer before the driver could turn around. It took him ten minutes to get the tugboat of a limo out of the parking lot and back on the small road. Alex dove head first into the chicken bucket. We slid down the hill and through the roadblock. Out the window to our left we could see the media staging area. The woman agent we saw with Allen earlier stood on the tailgate of a pick-up and held court with the press. A pile of microphones taped to a stand in front of her.

"Look at all that," Alex said between bites of chicken.

"I haven't seen that many cameras since the OJ trial," I said.

"I saw that guy from Monday Night Football walk by a while ago," Catfish said. "Can you believe that, Monday Night Football up here at a pickle factory."

"This thing has got a TV," he continued. "We can watch what she is telling them."

"We saw it live," I said. "Don't need a replay."

By the time we made our way from the side roads back to the interstate I had caught Catfish up on all that had happened with Agent Allen and where things stood for the time being.

"So far as we know everybody is accounted for except Dumptruck," I said.

"That boy's fine," Catfish said. "He can drive these roads home with his lights off."

"He took off as soon as he heard the cops coming," I said.

"Why do you think I came up here in this dang contraption to get you?"

"You knew he would cut out?"

"Figured. Arkansas and all."

"What is this whole thing with him and Arkansas?" I asked.

He changed the subject. "You want the last piece of chicken or is it mine?"

I took the last piece of chicken. I washed it down with my third beer and ten minutes later I was out cold and slept the rest of the way to Atlanta.

The limo hit a pothole at the dead end of Bug Slinger Road in ChickenBone. Alex poked me.

"Where are we?" I asked with my eyes half open.

"New York," she said. "That's the Empire State Building out the window." She pointed at my place.

I tried to lift myself out of the big recliner. I had trouble getting out of the deep seat. It hurt to move and I stumbled a bit as I left the vehicle. Alex had no such trouble.

"What happened to Catfish?" I yawned.

"We dropped him off," she said. "He kissed you goodnight."

"Did what?"

"Never mind," she said. "I'm taking the last beer."

"First time I've ever been in a limo," I said to her as I gathered myself.

"You slept the whole way."

"First time I ever slept in a limo."

"Most likely your last time in a limo," she said. "Tip the driver."

The driver rolled down the window as I got out my wallet. I had used the ATM at the UGA police station that morning. I had a twenty, two tens, and a five. Forty five dollars. I gave it all to him and smiled. He frowned and rolled up the window. She was right. It would be my last time in a limo.

She gathered up her gear and headed to her place. I stood outside at the edge of the railroad tracks and let Chance run loose for a bit. Dawn would be here soon but it felt darker than usual as the clouds hung low and fog settled in over the tracks. The sleep I got in the limo had somehow given me a second wind. Maybe another surge of adrenaline. I felt wired and restless.

"Feels good to be back home, doesn't it," I jumped a bit when Alex came up behind me.

I watched Chance sniff his way down one of the side tracks.

"It does," I said. "Did you forget something?"

"No, just saw you guys standing down here."

We stood silent and waited as Chance crossed back over near us.

"I just wanted to say," she paused. "You know."

"Yeah, I know."

She stood silent again for a minute before she spoke.

"All in all, things worked out pretty good."

"All but one," I said.

"What's that?"

"I didn't get to see a single pitch of the World Series game last night."

She relaxed a bit. "So, you don't know what happened?"

"No."

"I do."

"How?"

"While you two slept, I turned on the TV in the limo and caught the highlights."

"I hate highlights," I said. "Watching highlights after the game is over is like wrapping a gift after somebody gives it to you."

"Come with me," she headed up the stairs to my place.

"I told you I don't care about the highlights," I said as I followed. Chance beat us both to the top.

"Just open the door," she said.

She went inside and I flipped on the lights. She headed straight to my TV and picked up the remote.

"See this," she said. "This little thing can control a brand new amazing type of technology that makes it possible to actually record a program on TV at a certain time and then play it back later."

"Now you're just being a smartass," I told her. "I had a VHS recorder for years."

"And I use to think Beverly Hills 90210 was the best show ever," she said. "But things change."

"What would that be?"

"Watch closely." She pointed the remote at the TV set and clicked through a few screens. "I can push this little button here called the PLAY button and by the miracle of technology watch what happens."

The screen flickered and the music for the Major League Baseball games kicked in. A blimp drifted above the stadium and the announcers jumped in. '*Tonight, we invite you to join us live for Game 6 of the World Series as the favored San Francisco Giants try and hold off the underdog Detroit Tigers. First pitch is only minutes away.*'

She muted the sound. "It's a miracle."

"That's what you were doing when we left," I said. "You recorded the game for me?"

"I did."

"That's amazing."

"Thank you."

"Now get out," I said.

"What?"

"Get out," I repeated. "You will screw up and tell me what happened in the game."

"I would never tell you what a great game it was," she said as I pushed her toward the door.

"Get out."

"It was such a close game."

"Get out."

"Great pitching, defense," she said. "And you will not believe how it ends."

"Get out," I said and shoved her out onto the landing of my stairs.

We paused there for a moment. The fog was thick and low. The lonesome sound of a train horn broke through the dark and the light from the front engine bounced off us.

"Thank you and the guys for coming to get me," she said. "That is what I really wanted to tell you."

"You're welcome," I told her. "Impressive moves on your part all night long."

"Thanks."

"And recording the game for me was a nice thing to do."

"You're welcome."

"Now get out," I said and slammed the door shut. I heard her laugh from the other side.

Make A Note: Honesty deepens friendship.

EPILOGUE

January hit town with the first snowfall in eight years. It was refreshing and different. Chance had a blast as he rolled around in the six inches that fell. It was followed by a few days of wind and cold. I was in my shop with both heaters cranked up and at work on a stock order for the Asheville Tourist. It had been a steady, if not consistent winter of work. I had taken on just two things for Catfish. Both were simple, took just a few days each and not a shot was fired.

I shared a few beers with Buddy Lee when he delivered my last wood order but we didn't talk much about what happened up at the pickle factory. Before he left I did tell him the whole thing would make for a great story one day. He reminded me that in the end, stories are all that we have. Buddy Lee is a wise lumber man.

Shaky came to town in December for the SEC Football Championship broadcast. ESPN had taken over the games again when BTSN crashed and burned. I tracked him down and took him out for a steak dinner. We went to one of those places that usually only serve actors and NBA players while they visited. It cost me a months' pay but was well worth it. I invited the young producer Sam to join us but she was too busy since she now had earned a promotion leading the entire pre-game show for the network. Shaky told me they were thinking about putting her in front of the camera as well. First round draft choice.

The media was still churning out stories about Billy Ray and Cissy. Kincaid was still a good talker and he was damn good at the jailhouse interviews. His trial was still months away and nobody knew how things would turn out. Cissy had a nervous breakdown the first night in jail and headed off to rehab. Last I read, she had gotten out and was soon to show up on one of those dancing shows on television. She was also talking with another network about a reality show. The mean, they do die hard.

I would see Agent Allen quoted in the newspaper every now and then but we had not spoken since the week after the game. We wrote everything up and left it with him. I think he shoved it under the pile already on his desk. Last month I did come home one night to find the goofy baseball cap I wore that night. I had lost it somewhere in the confusion. It was at my door in a plastic GBI evidence bag and had a note that simply said, *'This ugly thing is not considered worthy of state evidence.'* It was attached to a six-pack of good beer.

Alex not only got her bigger paycheck from Major Clark but that lawyer Koop jumped at the chance to take a bite out of the network and Billy Ray. He got her a settlement within a month. I have no idea how much it was but she now had a new red Jeep Wrangler parked outside. The tabloids also sent her a big check for a really nice photo of Billy Ray with a bucket on his head. I thought I should have gotten a cut of that one.

The old phone mounted on the wall rang and I put down a bat and went over to pick it up.

"Get cleaned up," Alex said. "I'm taking you to lunch."

"Why?" I asked.

"I just sold another picture of Cissy."

"The gift that keeps on giving."

"She is an American treasure."

"Where are you taking me?"

"Nicest place in town," she said. "Be ready in ten."

Twenty minutes later we were in the back booth of the *3 Pigs BBQ*. The nicest place in town. Catfish had joined us and we were about to partake of three Wednesday Specials of pulled pork, corn on the cob, hush puppies, cornbread and sweet ice tea. Blueberry pie was also included. The conversation was free.

"Read something yesterday in the paper that I liked," Alex said between bites.

"About Cissy?" I asked.

"No, Billy Ray Kincaid," she said and stole a piece of cornbread from my plate.

"What about him?" Catfish said.

"Courts just seized a towel factory he owned over in a small town in Alabama. He had to sell two of his boats and an airplane just to settle the debt and some guys out of Kentucky got the place in bankruptcy for a steal."

"What are they going to do with it?" I asked.

"They made a deal with the town," she said. "They are keeping it. Remodeling the plant and adding at least seventy five more jobs for now, maybe more later."

"Roll Tide," Catfish said and stabbed at the pulled pork with his fork.

"Go Dogs," I added.

"Speaking of Bulldogs," Alex said. "Have you heard anything lately from Dumptruck?"

"I have," Catfish said. "Called me last week to brag about his latest wager."

"Wager?" I asked. "What kind of wager this time?"

"That fool bet a guy down in Tarpon Springs that he could hold his breath underwater for fifteen minutes."

"He couldn't do that," Alex said. "I think the world record is about twenty minutes or so."

"That was the wager," Catfish said.

"What did they bet?" I asked.

"The bet was two way," Catfish said. "If the guy won, Dumptruck would owe him a thousand bucks."

"And if he won?" Alex asked.

"Dumptruck got five hundred bucks and the guy's girlfriend."

"They bet on a woman," her voice went up a notch.

"He said she was a hellava gal."

"So, what happened?" I wondered.

"Dumptruck had it all rigged. He buried a dang air tank under water somehow with a tube. Stayed down for eighteen minutes."

"So, he won both the money and the woman?" Alex wondered.

"According to Dumptruck she was pulling for him to win," Catfish said with a big laugh.

Catfish got up and returned with the blueberry pie for us all. He had two pieces for himself.

"One more question," I said.

"He didn't stay with the woman," he said. "But he kept the cash."

"That's not my question."

"Then what?"

"Once and for all, I want to know what the deal was with him and Arkansas. What happened out there that he refuses to talk about every time it comes up?"

Catfish put his fork down. "I've known Dumptruck since I was a freshman at Georgia and been good friends ever since then."

"So, tell us what happened," Alex said.

"We've been through a lot together," Catfish said. "Kept a lot of secrets just between the two of us."

"And Arkansas?" I prompted him. "Can you tell us about Arkansas?"

"You know how you told me he went on and on about how you two were just like a couple of old dogs out looking for a bone up at the pickle factory?"

"And as it turned out I think he was most likely right about that. But what does that have to do with Arkansas?"

"Well every now and then, a dog will go out looking for a bone and find himself a real good one. So good that he will bury that thing deeper than all the others."

"And your point?" I said to him.

"My point is simple. The dog done buried it too deep."

"So?" Alex asked. "What does that mean?"

"What it means," Catfish leaned in on his arms. "Sometimes it's just better to leave that old bone buried so deep that you can't ever dig it up."

"I still have no idea what this has to do with Arkansas," Alex said.

"I do," I said. "You don't know what happened with Dumptruck and Arkansas do you?"

"Not a clue," Catfish said. "Not a dadgum clue."

ABOUT THE AUTHOR

Cliff Yeargin has spent his life as a 'Storyteller'. The majority of that in a long career in Broadcast Journalism as a Writer/Producer/ Photographer and Editor. Currently he works as an Editor & Producer for CNN and lives in a downtown Atlanta neighborhood that is not called ChickenBone. There is no  neighborhood known as ChickenBone...but there should be.

He is the author of two other books in the Jake Eliam ChickenBone Mystery Series.

RABBIT SHINE and HOOCHY KOOCHY

■   ■   ■

Follow the full series at *cliffyeargin.com*

11699528R00214

Made in the USA
Lexington, KY
14 October 2018